Goodbye,
Mersey View

Lyn Andrews

Goodbye, Mersey View

HEADLINE

First published in 2022 by
HEADLINE PUBLISHING GROUP

1

Cataloguing in Publication Data is available from the British Library

ISBN 978 1 4722 8125 8

Typeset in Janson by Avon DataSet Ltd, Alcester, Warwickshire

Printed and bound in Great Britain by Clays Ltd, Elcograf S.p.A.

HEADLINE PUBLISHING GROUP
An Hachette UK Company
Carmelite House
50 Victoria Embankment
London EC4Y 0DZ

www.headline.co.uk
www.hachette.co.uk

To the memory of my very dear aunt Cecelia Ormesher
(nee Finnigan) who passed away on 30th May 2022 aged 96.
We miss you so much, Aunty Cee. You were such
a wonderful, kind, generous lady, and are irreplaceable.
I think of you every day. God bless and keep you.

Your loving niece, Lyn (Lynda) Andrews, Ballaugh, 2022

Chapter One

*Liverpool,
1940*

'Was it like this last time, Mam? I mean when the Great War started, were you all waiting every day for all the terrible things to happen?' Monica Eustace looked enquiringly at her mother as she poured herself a cup of tea and sat down at the kitchen table.

Nelly Savage sighed heavily and sat down opposite her elder daughter, Monica. She was twenty, far too young, Nelly thought, to be a married woman. Her daughter was a very attractive girl though, with a fine complexion, blue eyes, thick, wavy light-blonde hair and a good figure – it was little wonder she'd been snapped up. And she had to admit the girl had made a good match, although in her opinion that wasn't the same as a good marriage. Richard Eustace, or 'Rick' as he was called, was the only son of parents who owned three hairdressing salons he would one day inherit. It was through the salons that

1

they'd met, and Monica had now just finished her training as a hairdresser in her father-in-law's Liverpool salon – a fully fledged 'stylist', as they liked to be called. They had too many fancy ideas in those salons, in Nelly's opinion, even being called by French Christian names instead of what they'd been called at birth, something Nelly viewed as pure, unnecessary affectation.

She took a sip of her tea as she looked across at Monica, and smiled briefly as she recalled her beautiful wedding in St George's around the corner, and how her daughter had declared that she was ecstatically happy with Rick. But like all the other young men he'd been called up when war was declared and was now stationed with his regiment somewhere in the south of England.

'I don't like to dwell on the Great War, luv, you know that. I just thank God your da came through it safely when so many didn't. "The war to end all wars", they called it. And now, well, here we are again, with the damn Germans overrunning Europe for the second time in twenty-five years!'

Monica nodded solemnly as she sipped her tea. War had been declared last September and now it was early June and very little had happened so far, hence her question. Everyone had expected the country to be bombed immediately, day and night, and that some sort of invasion force would be assembling across the Channel, ready and eager to cross that narrow strip of water to subdue yet another country. Of course there had been the tremendous effort to get all the stranded troops home from Dunkirk after the fall of France but everyone had looked on that as a major triumph not a disaster. No one said wasn't it terrible that so many men and ships had been lost; everyone said it was virtually a miracle that so many men had made it off the beaches. In a time of such need, anyone with something that would float had bravely pitched in. Even the Mersey ferries had gone to help with the evacuation, and the city was proud of them for it.

Monica pushed aside the thick blonde wave of hair that had fallen across her cheek. She'd adopted the same hairstyle as Veronica Lake, the film star – even before she'd married Rick – and though it suited her, occasionally it annoyed her, particularly when she was worried or anxious. She sipped her tea, glancing around her mam's kitchen. She'd grown up in this house in Mersey View in the Everton district of the city, and it was as spotless and comfortable as usual – if rather old-fashioned compared to her own more modern home in the more affluent area of Allerton.

'What's the matter?' Nelly asked, for she'd been watching her daughter closely and knew her so well. 'Haven't you had a letter?'

'Oh, yes! Rick is very good, he writes regularly, although heaven knows when he'll next get some leave.' She smiled wryly at her mother. 'I know "there's a war on"! No, it's Joan I'm a bit anxious about. I didn't think she looked very well last time I saw her, and I know there have been rumours about the factory closing or being converted for war work.'

Nelly nodded, understanding. Young Joan McDonald was her daughter's closest friend, and had been ever since the family had moved into Mersey View years ago. They were the same age and, like Monica, Joan was married. Jim McDonald was a young airman who was stationed in Lincolnshire but came originally from Glasgow, and Joan counted herself lucky to work at Crawford's biscuit factory, which was modern, clean and treated their workers very well, classed as one of the best employers in the city. But Nelly'd also heard the rumours. And of course sugar was scarce now, it had been on ration since January, and you couldn't have biscuits without sugar. 'Well, luv, depending on how things . . . go on, I think a lot of women will have to do war work, like they did last time, and I can tell you from experience that filling shells is no picnic even though they pay you well. And it's dangerous work too,' she added, hoping that neither Monica nor Eileen, her younger daughter, would be called upon to work in munitions factories. Thankfully, she hadn't had to work in one for very long but those few weeks had been enough. 'When you've finished that tea, why don't you go on up to Olive's house and see Joan for yourself?'

'Mam, I came to see you and our Eileen. Where is she, by the way?' she asked, looking around for her sister.

Nelly raised her eyebrows. 'Gone to some "function", as she called it, straight from work. It's being put on by the Railway Company to entertain the sailors from the convoys – apparently, it's going to be a regular thing.'

'Well, it needs to be! Anything to cheer them up, given what they have to put up with, living in fear of being blown up by those U-boats any minute of the day and night,' Monica said as she stood up.

Because Britain was an island nearly everything had to be imported, and over the last months the convoys bringing in vital supplies had suffered heavily in what was now being called the Battle of the Atlantic. Her sister was only seventeen, a clerk in the offices of the London and North Western Railway

Company, a position secured for her by their father who also worked for them as a guard – Monica didn't blame Eileen for looking for some excitement in her life. She couldn't think of anything more boring than being a clerk in the Railway Offices. She supposed it was fair to say they were not very close – as children they'd often fought and argued – but at least Eileen had improved a bit lately.

'Well, since Eileen's not going to be back, if you honestly don't mind, Mam, I'd like to go and see Joan.'

Nelly smiled at her. 'Of course I don't mind, luv. Go on up there and put your mind at rest. Maybe Olive will have heard from their Lily and Bella in London, and that will be interesting. You'll be over for your dinner this Sunday as usual?'

Monica nodded, relieved. Sometimes her mam could be a bit prickly if she felt she was being neglected. But she was grateful that she could come over regularly, for she had to admit that there were times when she did feel a bit lost and lonely in the house in Allerton. She missed Rick desperately, so she looked forward to the Sundays she spent every other weekend with her family. One week it would be with Mam, Da and Eileen, and the next with Nancy, Claude and the girls – Rick's parents and sisters.

As she walked the short distance to her friend's she smiled to herself, remembering the day she and Joan had first met, here in Mersey View. Joan's family had just moved in and at first there had been just Joan, her brother Charlie and Olive, her mam. Billy, her da, had been away at sea. The family had somewhat intrigued Nelly, who had insisted there was something strange about them after Joan divulged that they moved house on a regular basis and for no apparent reason other than

'Mam's itchy feet'. And indeed there had been something strange, as they'd found out when Bella, Joan's half-sister, turned up on the doorstep one winter's evening. Bella's existence came as a complete surprise to Joan, her mam and Charlie, and her unexpected arrival revealed that Billy had been living a whole other life while at sea, which came as quite a shock to poor Olive.

'I've come over to see how you all are, Mrs Garswood,' Monica informed Joan's mother who opened the door to her.

Olive's husband, Frederick, had a small plumbing business and as theirs was the biggest house in the street, Olive took in boarders, although at present there were only two, both older gentlemen who worked in the city. Joan, of course, lived with her mother and stepfather, for her husband Jim couldn't afford to pay a mortgage. Neither could they, she thought, not on Rick's army pay, but his dad helped out and she managed the rest on her wages – which had improved considerably, now she was qualified.

'We're all doing as well as can be expected, Monica, luv,' Olive replied as she ushered her visitor inside. 'Our Charlie has volunteered to be a messenger lad with the Civil Defence, so he's just informed me. I don't know if that's a good idea or not.'

'At least that'll keep him out of mischief,' Monica observed wryly. For when they'd first come to Mersey View, Charlie Copperfield had been a bit of a handful. The same age as Eileen, he was now an apprentice plumber in his stepfather's business.

'Our Joan's having a bit of a rest, she said she felt exhausted when she got home – she's been off colour for a few days. But I'll go up and tell her you're here,' Olive offered.

Monica frowned. That was odd, for Joan was usually so lively. 'No, I'll go up to her, if you don't mind.'

Her anxiety hadn't lifted as she knocked quietly on the door of the big bedroom at the front of the house. Joan shared it with Jim when he was home. Hearing her friend's voice, she put a smile on her face and went in. Her friend did look pale, curled up under the eiderdown. 'What's all this about, Mrs McDonald?' She sat down on the edge of the bed as Joan pulled herself up on the pillows. 'What's wrong, Joan? This isn't like you at all.'

Joan brushed back a tendril of dark-brown hair from her forehead, and a little frown appeared between her brows. 'I know, but honestly, Mon, it was so hot in work today . . . and then when I got home, I felt I couldn't stand Mr Whitworth fussing over everything. I know he means well, but he's such an old woman, and then Mam's not really very happy about our Charlie being a messenger boy and I felt so . . . so . . . tired.'

Monica reached out and took her friend's hand, scrutinising her features closely. Joan had always been very attractive in a dark, striking sort of way, very like her ma, but she did look tired today, with the beginnings of dark circles under her eyes. 'Are you worrying about Jim? It's only natural, Joan.'

'I know – and yes, I do worry. But then so does everyone else who has a husband away in the forces. I had a letter from him two days ago and he's doing fine, from what I can make out. And missing me, of course.'

'Then is it your job?'

Joan shook her head. 'No. Oh, there have been rumours,

but so far we're managing and . . . and it might not matter soon, anyway.'

'Then for God's sake, Joan, what's wrong?'

Joan twisted the corner of the floral patterned eiderdown between her fingers. 'I don't know for certain, Mon . . . but . . . I've been sick every morning this week and I've not had my "curse" for—'

Monica's eyes widened and she let out a delighted little cry. 'Joan McDonald, you're pregnant! Oh, I just knew you'd beat me to it! Rick hasn't been home for ages, and Jim got leave just after Easter!'

Joan laughed but made shushing gestures. 'Keep your voice down, I haven't told anyone yet, not Mam – although I think she's guessed – nor even Jim. I wanted to be sure.'

'Well, no wonder you feel washed out. You're going to have to take things much easier now.'

Joan nodded, her eyes sparkling, all signs of fatigue gone. She was so happy. And now that she'd told Monica, she felt more confident in herself. She dared to believe that what she'd suspected for weeks was actually true. 'I'll be able to work until I'm six months gone, then I'll have to give up.'

'You might have to give up sooner if they want to turn the place into a munitions factory. They surely wouldn't expect you to work there in your condition!'

'Sometimes, Mon, I really can't believe it. I lie here thinking . . . me . . . a mother! Oh, I know Mam will say I'm too young but, well, she was only a few years older when she had me.'

Monica nodded. 'And it will be best if you carry on living here. She can keep her eye on you, especially as Jim's away.'

That had a sobering effect on Joan and she became serious, biting at her lower lip. 'I know it's not the best of times to have a baby, Mon, what with the world in the state it's in . . . and no one knowing what's going to happen in the future and everything.'

Monica patted her hand. 'Now, stop that! You've got to look on the bright side of things. Jim will be over the moon. You have to write and tell him! Why on earth haven't you?'

Joan managed a smile. 'Because I wanted to be sure. No point getting his hopes up and then having to write and say it's a false alarm, is there? Do you think they might give him some leave?'

Monica shook her head. 'I shouldn't think so, but maybe nearer to Christmas if things are still fairly quiet.'

'Well, I hope they stay quiet. I hate that damn shelter! It's so cold and damp, even in summer, and no matter what Mam does, it smells horrible!'

'At least you've got room for a shelter of your own, like me. Poor Mam has to go to the public one, which she absolutely loathes! She says if there are ever any really heavy raids, she'd sooner take her chances under the stairs than be crammed in like sardines with all and sundry in the shelter at the top of York Terrace. But don't you go worrying about anything like that now!' she urged her friend.

'Easier said than done. But it seems to be the merchant fleet that's getting the worst of it at the moment, and at least they got most of the army back home from Dunkirk – but I just can't help worrying about the future, Mon.'

'I suppose not. But keep your mind on the present – you're going to have to write to Jim, and to your Aunt Lily and Bella in London, and tell your mam and Frederick. They'll all be delighted, just like me.'

Joan pushed aside the eiderdown and swung her legs over the side of the bed, smiling happily at her friend. 'Mam had a letter from Aunty Lil this morning, so maybe I'll let her tell Lily the news in her reply, but I'll write to Bella.'

'What will she be to the baby? A step-aunty?'

Joan shrugged. 'I'm not sure, maybe as she's my half-sister she could just be aunty? Lily says she's doing very, very well and they all think she's some sort of marvel at that college of music.'

'She is. Anyone with a voice like Bella's is bound to be a big star one day.'

'I hope so, Mon. She deserves to be.'

Monica took Joan's arm to help her up, remembering what a very hard time their budding young opera star Annabella Ferreira Silva had had when she'd travelled from her native Portugal to Liverpool at the age of twelve, after her mother's death. Her father was Joan's own father – Billy Copperfield – and eventually he'd abandoned them all. Olive, Joan, Charlie, Bella and Bella's mother, Isabella. It was no wonder Bella had dropped the name Copperfield and now used her mother's surname. They assumed Billy was still alive and living somewhere in Brazil after he'd jumped ship, but no one knew – and neither did they care now, Monica thought, with grim satisfaction. They all had more important things to think about these days. Suddenly, she grinned. 'You realise that you're going to have old Mr Whitworth fussing over you even more now? The boarders all love to think they're part of the family, so . . .'

Joan pulled a face of mock horror at Monica's mention of the gentlemen lodgers her family shared a roof with. 'Oh, no! This child doesn't need any honorary old uncles like him!'

'Why? Jim's got no family, and apart from Frederick who will be his step-grandad, and your Charlie, the poor child will only have honorary aunts – Lily and Bella and me, and Mam and our Eileen.'

Joan rolled her eyes in the direction of the ceiling. 'You're right. Well, let's go down and tell Mam and Frederick the happy news, then. Something we can at least celebrate instead of having to hear all the gloom and doom that's in the newspapers!'

Monica nodded her agreement, but as she followed her friend downstairs she felt a little frisson of jealousy run through her. She wished Rick could come home on leave soon.

Chapter Two

———◆◆◆———

Olive smiled to herself as Joan and Monica came into the kitchen, thinking Joan looked much brighter now that her best friend was here. After their lodger, old Mr Whitworth, had gone up to his room, she'd been sitting with her husband, Frederick, discussing Charlie's latest news, with Charlie's old mongrel, Rags, sprawled contentedly at Frederick's feet.

Frederick was of the opinion that the lad would do well if called upon – he had proved himself to be conscientious and reliable in the plumbing business. 'He's growing up and showing promise of becoming a decent young man, Olive, luv,' he'd reassured her.

She'd nodded her agreement, thinking it was all mainly thanks to Frederick and Arthur Savage, Nelly's husband. They had both become strong influences and mentors in her young son's life after his father had abandoned them. All Billy Copperfield had ever done had been to disappoint and hurt the lad. But she didn't want Charlie to even think about joining up, he was still so young. She pushed those thoughts to the back of her mind and concentrated on her daughter. She'd been almost sure Joan was in the family way, but couldn't be certain. She hoped the look on the girls' faces meant her hopes were about to be confirmed.

'Joan's got some news for you both,' Monica announced, unable to contain her excitement.

'Mam, you're going to be a granny!' Joan announced, a little shyly, wishing that Jim was here with her at this important and slightly daunting time.

'Not that you'll ever really *look* like a typical granny!' Monica added. Joan's mam had always been as stylish and smart as her circumstances would allow, and she had always looked much younger than Monica's own mother, although Nelly would've killed her if she ever voiced such a thought. Of course, as far as the family were concerned, Olive's older sister, Lily, had always been regarded as the more attractive and glamorous one, working as she had as Wardrobe Mistress in the Empire Theatre. That was before Lily married David Frances, Bella's voice coach, and all three of them moved to London when Bella had got a scholarship to study at the Royal College, last September. Olive had strongly disapproved of them taking the girl to what she considered a far more dangerous city than Liverpool, and there had been a huge row over it.

Frederick was on his feet now, embracing Joan and telling her that she must take care of herself.

'Oh, I will. I promise!' Joan laughed happily.

Olive embraced her daughter, smiling but thinking that in her opinion Joan was really too young to become a mother. 'It's not an illness, you know! It's a perfectly normal condition, but I have to say you've surprised me a bit, luv. I thought . . . well, I thought you'd have waited a bit longer.'

'So did I! I just knew she'd pip me to the post,' Monica added, a little wistfully.

'There's plenty of time yet, Monica. Being a mother can be exhausting, worrying and yet so fulfilling and rewarding. Your mam will tell you that,' Olive advised.

'She does, Mrs Garswood. She says you never stop worrying about your kids until you're in your grave! She's worrying over our Eileen at the moment. Well, I'd best get back and tell her the news. She'll be delighted, like everyone else.'

'And I'm going to write to our Lily tonight, then Charlie can post the letter in the morning.'

'Did she say anything about how Bella's getting on?' Monica asked, knowing her mam would want to know. Nelly liked to keep abreast of everything.

'Still working hard both at her music and her schoolwork. She hopes when Bella is eighteen she'll at least be considered for chorus work. Oh, nothing grand yet, she says. It will take time and a lot of luck before we see our Bella at Covent Garden Opera House – if ever.'

Monica nodded. 'But I'm sure she'll do it. Remember how wonderfully she sang at my wedding? It really astounded everyone, including the vicar. No one had ever heard the like before – even though no one could understand a word, it being all in Latin.'

Both Olive and Frederick smiled as they remembered that day when Bella had sung *Panis Angelicus*, her pure sweet voice holding the congregation spellbound. There were very few people around here who had had a wedding as grand as Monica

Savage's, Olive mused. Joan had insisted she didn't want all that fuss and had been married at the Registry Office.

'I'll get off then – at this rate it'll be after ten when I get home, and I hate having to go home in the blackout.'

'Everyone hates travelling in the blackout,' Joan agreed as she showed her friend out.

As she stood on the step Monica turned to Joan. 'Why don't you come and stay with me a few nights in the week, like you used to when war broke out? It's nearer for you to travel to and from work. I don't know how that arrangement sort of fizzled out.'

'I'd be happy to, Mon, you know that, I love the peace and quiet. But do you honestly think Mam will let me now, in my . . . er, delicate condition?' Joan laughed.

Monica grimaced. 'I see what you mean. They're going to smother you with attention and advice. But the offer's there, if it all gets too much.'

'I know. Now, get off back to your mam's!' Joan smiled, feeling so much better now that her news was official.

Monica found her father and sister in the kitchen with her ma when she got back to Nelly's house. She was thankful that she could at least tell them all together, before heading back to Garthdale Road.

'How is she? I didn't expect you to stay so long,' Nelly commented. 'It'll be almost pitch dark by the time you get back home. I know it stays light much longer this time of year but the light will be going soon.'

'I'll be all right, Mam. Joan's fine. In fact, she's got great news – the best ever!'

'Jim McDonald's coming home, then? Have they thrown him out or something?' Eileen asked curtly. She'd been having a bit of an argument with her mam and wasn't in the best of moods.

Monica glared at her. 'Don't be stupid! They don't "throw people out" in the middle of a war! No, Joan is . . . expecting!'

Nelly's eyebrows rose as she looked quizzically at her elder daughter. Monica seemed happy for her friend but she wondered was she just a tiny bit jealous? 'That was rather . . . sudden! He's not been home much.'

'Obviously long enough, Nelly,' Arthur remarked, grinning at Monica. 'I bet they're all celebrating up at Olive's house.'

Monica laughed. 'Not really, if you mean are they all having a drink? They're delighted, of course, and so am I. I wanted Joan to come and stay with me; it's nearer to the factory for her but—'

'She's best off at home with her mam,' Nelly said firmly, 'and not being tempted to be running around with you.'

'Fat chance of that, Mam, and I'm never "running around" as you put it! We're both happily married women, why on earth would we want to be "running around"?'

'Oh, take no notice, she's got a downer on anyone enjoying themselves,' Eileen muttered, receiving a glare from her mother in return.

'I'll not have you talking like that about your mam, our Eileen,' Arthur said, quietly but firmly.

'I offered to bring him home, didn't I?' Eileen protested hotly.

Monica was intrigued. 'Bring who home?'

'A lonely sailor!' Nelly retorted, throwing her younger daughter a scathing glance.

Arthur smiled wryly. 'And she wasn't very pleased when I told her that, in my experience, there is no such thing!'

'Someone she met at this "function",' Nelly remarked.

'His name is Harold Stevens and he's Royal Navy, not Merchant Navy, so he doesn't get much shore leave, and he knows no one in Liverpool. He's from Birmingham and he said he misses *everything*, so I asked could I bring him home for tea one day. What's so terrible about that?' Eileen demanded.

'If he's from Birmingham what's he doing in the navy? That place is miles away from the sea?' Monica pondered aloud.

'Oh, don't you start too! I don't know why he joined the navy instead of the army or airforce, but I felt sorry for him and he . . . he's . . . nice.'

'Oh, let her bring him, Mam. She's growing up, and it's not as if she's sneaking off to meet him somewhere behind your back, is it?'

Nelly shrugged as Arthur went back to his book on pigeon fancying. 'Oh, all right, but you can bet your life that Lily Frances doesn't let Bella go fraternising with all and sundry, even though she's in London!'

Monica grinned at her sister. Bella and Eileen were the same age and had been quite friendly, but everyone knew, including Eileen, that Bella was destined for a very different life. She'd have liked to meet this Harold Stevens but knew her sister wouldn't want her there when he came for tea. She'd hear all about his visit in due course, from her ma.

* * *

When she arrived home it was almost ten thirty. She'd waited ages for a tram but eventually one had trundled out of the deepening dusk, its headlights reduced to pinpricks by their leather coverings. The house always seemed so still and quiet, she thought, as she picked up the mail and took it through into her sitting room. First things first, she told herself, drawing all the curtains and making sure there were no chinks before she switched on the lights. Mr Harris from two doors down was in the Civil Defence and took his duties very seriously – too seriously, in her opinion. He was a pompous little man at the best of times but this bit of power had completely gone to his head. He seemed to spend his evenings prowling the neighbourhood looking for carelessly drawn curtains and then taking great pleasure in upbraiding the offending householder.

She sat down in the easy chair beside the modern, empty fireplace. The summer evenings didn't merit a fire, so that was one less expense. She'd loved this house as soon as she'd set eyes on it. It was in a quiet road and had a garden front and back, which she was doing her best to keep tidy, although she did struggle a bit. It also had a garage for Rick's car – it was all a world away from the narrow streets of Everton with their rows of soot-blackened terraced houses.

The thought of the garage brought back the realisation that tomorrow night her father-in-law was coming to give her a driving lesson. Claude, who she got on very well with, had said it was a terrible waste for that car to be parked in the garage – unused while Rick was away – and that she should learn how to drive it. 'It might well be a very useful skill in the future,' he'd assured her, and so with a bit of trepidation, she'd agreed. She'd had a dozen lessons before she'd eventually passed her driving test. They'd usually been at a weekend, when at least she hadn't been trying to drive in the blackout, but Claude had agreed to show her a few tricks for parking now that she could drive by herself. She'd said to Rick's dad that it would be great to be able to take Joan out for a spin, and maybe even her mam or da, until he'd reminded her that petrol was both expensive and getting scarce. She'd written and told Rick about it all, of course, and he'd replied that he was so proud of her and that his dad was right, it didn't do a car any good at all to be laid up. Best get some use out of it.

There were only two letters that must have come in the late post, for she'd already been home straight after work. One was a bill, which she put to one side, then with a little cry of joy she ripped open the envelope of the other, instantly recognising Rick's writing.

The paper was very thin, and as the letter was in pencil it would be hard to read, so she got up and took it closer to the lamp on the sideboard. Her heart leapt and began to beat rapidly as she read the wonderful news that he had been given leave, though only forty-eight hours. It would take him almost all of that time to get home and back with the unpredictability of the railways, but she didn't care. She hadn't seen him for months and months, and she'd missed him so much!

Oh, she had so much planning to do now. She wanted to make things so very special. Special meals, special drinks, special outings, although that didn't seem very feasible, given the short amount of time he'd actually be home. And she wanted something special to wear! She was determined to look her best and wondered whether the dress shop she and Joan had frequented before the war was still open for business. It wasn't really a dress 'shop' but rather what Joan's Aunty Lil termed 'a dress exchange'. You could get fabulous outfits there, at a third of the price you'd pay in the posh shops in Liverpool and London. Yes, she'd definitely pay a visit to 'Felicity's Wardrobe' – and maybe Joan would go with her to see if she could find something too, for very soon the clothes she had wouldn't fit.

That made her think again about Rick, and she hugged the letter to her. Maybe, just maybe, after this visit she too would be pregnant. Oh, she hoped so, she really did. She knew it might seem foolish to long for a baby when everything in the world was so uncertain. It definitely wasn't the safest time to have a child, but she couldn't help feeling excited at the thought of becoming a mam.

Chapter Three

———❖———

She hadn't had much choice – Felicity McKenzie's stock had been somewhat reduced because, heeding government warnings about wartime shortages, women were hanging on to their clothes for far longer. But Monica had found a lovely pale-blue-and-white floral dress with a matching bolero, edged with a darker blue braid, perfect for the warm summer weather they were experiencing. Joan had been disappointed to find that there was nothing suitable to disguise her increasing girth, but Felicity had suggested she get a couple of lengths of fabric from Blacklers or Lewis's to make a couple of loose smocks that could be worn with skirts. That hadn't cheered Joan up much, for she'd quickly realised that she'd have to find a dressmaker to make them up, which would add to the cost.

'It's just a pity your Aunty Lil and Bella aren't here. They're both good at sewing – Bella would have made them in no time at all,' Monica had remarked. Bella had started an apprenticeship as a seamstress at De Jong et Cie in Bold Street and had shown signs of being very gifted, but she had hated it and her fellow workmates – who had bullied her terribly – and after a serious incident, Bella had left with both Olive and Lily's approval. Of course, that had been before anyone had imagined that young Bella might have another and even greater gift – her voice.

The day after she'd bought the outfit, Monica decided to have a 'try on' after work as she wanted to co-ordinate it with her jewellery and shoes. She'd already decided what food they would have for Rick's homecoming, but rationing was beginning to make itself felt. What were now classed as 'luxury goods' – and the list seemed to increase by the day – were simply no longer available, even if you had the coupons and the money. But her da had persuaded Mo Clancy at the George and Dragon to let him have a half-bottle of decent whisky, which she had paid for herself, and she had a syphon of soda water on the tray with her best glasses on the side-board, so at least Rick could have a whisky and soda. She had looked in the paper to see if there was anything on at the theatres but soon abandoned that idea when Nancy, her mother-in-law, hinted subtly that she doubted Rick would feel much like going to the theatre after all that travelling, and with so little time at home.

She scrutinised herself in the long pier glass attached to the door of the wardrobe in the bedroom. Yes, she looked well, the colours suited her, and the earrings almost matched the braid on the bolero. Of course she'd wash and set her hair and do her nails before he got home. She felt the fluttering of excitement in her stomach. Oh, this time tomorrow, with any luck, he'd actually be home! She couldn't wait, really she couldn't! She frowned as she heard the sound of the door knocker. Glancing hastily out of the window, she caught sight of Claude Eustace's maroon Austin A40 parked on her driveway. She wasn't having a lesson tonight, she thought. So, what did he want? A horrible thought struck her. Oh, what if he'd had news that affected Rick's journey? No, Rick would have contacted her first, surely?

As she opened the front door she smiled with relief, realising that Nancy Eustace was with her husband.

'I just wanted to call to see if you'd heard anything more . . . definite, Monica,' Nancy Eustace said as she settled herself on the sofa beside Claude.

Monica smiled at her. Nancy was slim and always smart in a classic sort of way. Good dresses, skirts, blouses – and always her pearls. Nelly had been rather in awe of her when they'd first met, particularly daunted by Nancy's fashionably furnished home and fine china and glass, but when she'd learned that Nancy had actually grown up in Blackburn and that her whole family had worked at the Britannia Street Cotton Mill, her reservations had disappeared and now they got on well.

'No. Just that he hopes the train will get into Lime Street without being too late. But these days it's impossible to pin down arrangements, or take any notice of timetables. We're having a salad with ham, so at least that won't spoil if he's late. I could only get four ounces of ham each, though – rationing. And no doubt he'll be starving. Still, I had a couple of tins of peaches in the larder already, so hopefully it will be a decent meal, and there's plenty of bread and butter to go with it.'

'I've got some tins of evaporated milk. Claude, you can run

over with them before you go to the station tomorrow,' Nancy said, turning to her husband.

Monica had naturally wanted to go to Lime Street to meet Rick, but both Claude and Nancy – and indeed Nelly and Arthur – had advised her to stay at home, as it was almost certain that the train would be late, and the station concourse was bound to be packed with people waiting for loved ones. After a couple of hours of being constantly jostled, she would end up tired, impatient, cross and probably grubby, and that wasn't how she wanted to greet her husband. Besides, there would be no privacy either, so reluctantly she'd agreed that Claude would go to meet his son alone and bring him home to her. They would have the evening and night together, and then on Sunday morning they both would go and see Nancy and his sisters, Ruth and Beverley, and then on to Mersey View to see her mam and da, and if there was time, Joan and her family. He had to be back at Lime Street by four o'clock, so it was all going to be a bit of a rush, but she didn't care – she would have him home and to herself for a short time at least, and that was certainly better than nothing. She was lucky, she told herself. Poor Joan had no idea when her Jim would be home next.

'Do you want to drive him back to Lime Street yourself, Monica?' Claude asked, grinning. 'You're more than capable now, you know.'

She smiled at him but wouldn't admit that she not only felt far from capable of dealing with the traffic and trying to park but that she would probably be so upset she'd be blinded by tears, and that would help no one. 'No, I really don't think I could cope – not just yet.'

'I agree, and you'll be better off saying your goodbyes here, luv, not with half of Liverpool gawping at you at that station,' Nancy added.

'There's another thing I wanted to mention to you, Monica,' Claude said, looking a little concerned. 'Oh, it's nothing to get upset about. I just want you to give it some thought, maybe discuss it with Rick while he's home.'

Monica looked at him anxiously. 'What?'

'It's about the salons. I don't know if we can keep all of them running. It's going to be harder to get supplies, and women will have more demands on their time, especially if – like last time – everyone's required to do war work of some kind. That'll put paid to most of my staff, too. I've been wondering how we'll manage and if maybe it would be wise to ask permission to set up a small salon in a couple of the factories, which would be so much more convenient for everyone. Have a think and, as I said, talk it over with Rick. I don't want to put people out of work, if they aren't obliged to do war work, and I don't really want to see everything I've . . . we've worked so hard to build up just close down, but we have to be realistic. I think there will be some very hard times ahead – for everyone. Food, oil, war materials will become vitally important and will have to come first. Clothes, make-up and hairdressing are not going to be top of women's priority lists, feeding the family will be—'

'I don't agree at all, Claude!' Nancy interjected. 'I think women are going to put a lot of effort into their appearance, as a statement of pride and defiance against the Hun. I know we did last time.'

He nodded slowly before getting to his feet. 'Well, it's

something we'll all have to think about. Now, we'll leave you in peace, luv. I'll see you tomorrow when I bring Rick back here to you.'

Monica rose and hugged them both. 'Thank you, both of you.' She turned to Nancy. 'I know how much you're longing to see him too, so I owe you a double thank you. And I'll see you on Sunday morning.'

She stood at the door and waved as they drove off. Then she turned and, closing the door behind her, leaned against it. Claude's words had disturbed her but she had no intention at all of mentioning the future of the salons to Rick, not this time. His visit was too short for them to be bothered with things like that. She'd think about the future of the salons in the weeks to come, when he'd be back at his base.

The following afternoon she was a bundle of nervous excitement; she just couldn't sit down or be still. She'd dressed and applied her make-up with care and had spent hours doing her hair and nails. The dining-room table was set, complete with a vase of roses from the garden as a centrepiece. The ham salads were laid out under clean, damp tea towels on the marble slab in the larder. She'd spooned the tinned peaches into cut-glass stemmed goblets, and the evaporated milk, which was substituting for cream, was in a little jug beside them, also on the marble slab. She wished she had some ice for the soda, but she didn't, and there was nothing she could do about that. Anyway, it certainly would have melted long before Rick got home.

She couldn't help running to the sitting-room window every few minutes, to see if there was any sign of Claude's car.

Oh, why were they taking so long? The hours dragged by. Surely the damn train must have arrived by now? But she remembered her father's comments about the appalling irregularity of the trains as a result of diversions, blackouts, troop and freight movements and the like. And Rick would have had to change trains frequently, which meant waiting for connections that would probably be delayed, too.

She examined her hair in the mirror for what must be the twentieth time, she mused. She was anxiously checking that all the cushions on the sofa and chairs were plumped up – surely for the twentieth time, too – when she finally heard the sound of a car engine. So few people had cars that she knew it must be them. Uttering a little cry of relief, she smoothed her skirt and ran into the hall to fling open the door.

Oh, he looked just the same – well, actually better, she thought. He was tanned and she was sure he was taking more exercise. His hair had been lightened by the sun, which made the colour of his eyes seem a deeper blue, but there were fine lines now at their corners. She ran the few steps down the path and flung herself into his arms.

'Oh, Rick! Rick, my darling! You're home! I've missed you! I've missed you so much!'

He held her tightly as he looked down into her face. 'You've no idea how much I've missed you too, Monica!'

'Right, let's get the pair of you inside. Every lace curtain in the road is twitching!' Claude laughed, pulling Rick's kitbag from the boot and guiding them towards the open front door.

'I don't care. And besides, nearly all my neighbours know and are delighted for us!' Monica replied.

Claude dropped the bag in the hall, looking proudly at his tall son. 'I'll get off now and leave you two alone. You've little enough time together as it is, without me hanging around playing the wallflower. I'll see you tomorrow morning.'

Rick smiled at his father. 'Thanks for the lift, Dad, it's much appreciated.'

'Oh, let me have a good look at you,' Monica cried, after Claude had gone, ushering her husband into the sitting room.

'No, let me have a look at you!' he said quietly as he drew her into his arms. 'You were always beautiful, Mon, but now you're even more . . . stunning.'

She kissed him, her heart beating wildly.

'You must be starving, I've everything ready,' she said when she finally drew away.

'Oh, I am, but to hell with the food – for now! I'd much rather have you, my darling wife!'

She giggled – like an overgrown schoolgirl, she thought – but it didn't matter. He was right, the food and the whisky and soda and all the news could wait until later – much later.

It was nearing midnight when she finally came back downstairs, wrapped in the best embroidered lawn negligee she'd bought especially. Her hands were shaking slightly as she poured the two glasses of whisky. She couldn't love him more! Oh, the last hours had been wonderful, so passionate and at times wild, at others gentle and tender. She never wanted to be apart from him again, but she had to resolutely push that thought away. Strangely, she didn't feel in the slightest bit hungry, and he swore he didn't either. At this precise moment she really couldn't care less about the rationed ham and the

28

substitute cream, still residing in the larder. Most of it would be wasted, she thought idly as she headed back upstairs, but she'd much sooner spend the hours ahead wrapped in his arms, for all too soon the first fingers of the summer dawn would start to creep across the sky.

She propped the pillows up behind them both and then curled up beside him, her head on his chest, the glasses held tightly.

'Oh, this is a real treat, luv. It's been so long since I had even the whiff of a decent scotch, it's the end to an almost perfect day.'

She looked up at him, making a little moue with her mouth. 'Almost?'

'Well, I wouldn't call that train journey "perfect". It took hours and hours – there were times when I thought it would be the middle of the night before we ever arrived.'

She sighed. 'I know, that's why they all persuaded me to stay at home. I don't suppose you know when . . . or if . . . you'll get back again?' she asked tentatively.

He kissed her forehead. 'No. I expect that these forty-eight-hour passes will get scarcer and scarcer, and then . . .'

'What?' she asked, although she really didn't want to know.

'Well, they let me come home this time because I'm being transferred.'

She sat up, startled, and took a sip of her drink, feeling she might need it. There was obviously news he needed to tell her. 'Transferred? Where to?'

He finished his drink, put the glass down on the bedside table and held her close. 'I can drive, Monica. That's considered an asset, so I'm going to be trained to drive a tank. It will take about three to four months at a depot; I'm not sure where just yet. Then I'll be attached to the Royal Tank Regiment, but I don't know which division – and even if I did, I couldn't tell you yet, because of security. Every damn thing is "security" now.' He took a deep breath. 'But when I am sent to a division, I will almost certainly be going . . . abroad.'

His words made her go cold. It was something she had never allowed herself to think about, although she'd known in her heart that one day it would come. She'd allowed herself to be lulled into a false sense of security by him being in the south of England, and also by Jim McDonald being posted to RAF Skellingthorpe, in Lincolnshire, both of them still safely on home soil. Not even after Dunkirk had she allowed herself to think that he, too, might soon be going somewhere 'foreign'.

'Are you all right, darling?' he asked, seeing her expression change and feeling her tremble slightly in his arms.

She nodded. 'Yes. I . . . I knew it would come – one day. I just thought that . . . not yet. And with Jim McDonald down in Lincolnshire still . . .'

He managed a grin. 'Playing the trumpet professionally isn't considered much of an asset for war work, not these days, anyway. He'd have been in great demand in the last war, though. From what I've heard, every aspect of military life then was accompanied by trumpet blasts.'

She bravely smiled back. 'I suppose so. Oh, I have some news about them. Joan's expecting a baby.'

'Well, that's great! Jim might get some compassionate leave for the birth. I'll definitely make time to see Joan tomorrow to congratulate her!'

Monica nodded. 'Not tomorrow, Rick. It's "today" now,' she said sadly, pointing to the window.

'Then let's not waste any more time, Mrs Eustace,' he murmured, pulling her down beside him in the softness of the bed.

Chapter Four

She stood on the doorstep watching and waving as her father-in-law's gleaming maroon Austin drove off down the road, the afternoon sun glinting on its back window, Rick's hand visible through the side window waving. As it disappeared around the corner she suddenly felt terribly bereft. The few hours they'd spent together were over – he'd gone – and it was as if the clouds had blocked out the sun and the warm afternoon had become chilly and grey. She shivered as she went inside and closed the door. Their time alone together had been so very short that, to her eternal shame, she'd even begrudged the hours he'd spent with anyone else, his parents and sisters, and her and Joan's families. Yes, she knew that everyone wanted to see him – indeed, Claude and Nancy had a *right* to see him – but still . . . he was her husband, and there was so much they hadn't had time to discuss. Who knew when he'd be home next? And now there was his transfer to the Tank Regiment hovering in the future.

She looked around her sitting room, feeling depression

wash over her at the now untidy room, the half-drawn curtains, the pages of the Sunday newspaper strewn across the sofa, two empty tea cups on a side table. The dishes were still on the table, where she'd managed to pick at some bits of the ham salad, and toy with the peaches. She'd insisted Rick eat everything else, despite his protests.

'God knows when you'll get anything to eat next! I don't suppose there'll be such a luxury as a buffet service, let alone a restaurant car, on those trains! I just don't feel hungry, and if and when I do, I can make myself some toast later on,' she'd urged.

He'd told her she was right in her assumption that there would be no refreshments of any kind on the train. So she had been relieved when, before he took his leave of her, his mother had produced a tin box that once held OXO cubes, inside which was a neatly wrapped packet of sandwiches, a slice of plain sponge cake, also wrapped in greaseproof paper, and a bottle of pale ale.

Rick had been grateful. 'Mam, you're a wonder!' he'd said as he hugged her.

Monica had smiled at Nancy over Rick's shoulder. How she wished she'd been as organised and far-sighted.

'Just don't ask where I got the cold meat from – and you owe your father a drink!' Nancy had replied, laughing, but surreptitiously wiping away a tear.

The memory only served to reinforce Monica's increasingly miserable mood. With an effort, she squared her shoulders. 'Right, Monica Eustace!' she scolded herself aloud. 'The last thing he would want is for you to be moping around being miserable. Let's get this lot cleared away for a start and tidy the place up.' Then, she thought, she'd actually drive that car down to Mersey View to see Joan.

The two friends hadn't had much time together to chat earlier on. She knew she'd have to drive home in the blackout, but that was something else she was going to have to get used to, and a few hours with Joan would do her good. Then it was work tomorrow.

'Life has to go on,' she told herself. 'At least I don't have to face the journey poor Rick has in front of him, and a whole new training course and regiment.' She caught sight of herself in the mirror and managed a smile. She looked pale and a bit washed out. But then she hadn't had much sleep last night, had she?

She found it a pleasant experience, driving through the fairly quiet streets in the late afternoon and then up St George's Hill to Mersey View. It was such a treat, she thought, with the warmth of the sun on her cheeks, a bit of a breeze lifting her hair. The fact that she was actually driving herself was a hugely novel experience, and by the time she pulled up in Mersey View her mood of loss and depression had lifted somewhat. She couldn't arrive in the street and not call in to see her mam – even though she'd seen her family earlier that day – but she wouldn't stay long, remembering vaguely that Eileen had mentioned something about bringing the sailor she'd met home for tea that day. If it was indeed today, Mam wouldn't want her under her feet as well.

She'd been right, she realised, as she kissed her mam and da, smiled at her sister and said, 'Hello, nice to meet you,' when Eileen introduced Harold Stevens to her.

She shook his hand, then gave her mother a knowing glance, before departing.

'She's brought the boyfriend home for tea and for Mam's inspection,' Monica announced as she entered Olive's kitchen behind Charlie, who had shown her in and now disappeared. Of Olive and Frederick there was no sign, so she surmised that they were taking advantage of the good weather and had gone for a walk – Sunday tea was obviously over.

Joan grinned at her and indicated for her to sit down. 'I wouldn't like to be in his shoes then, he'll be getting the third degree! You must be a mind-reader; I'm just making a pot of tea.'

'Should you be doing that at all? Shouldn't you be sitting with your feet up or something?'

'No! I'm trying to keep life as normal as possible.'

'I bet that's not easy, with Mr Whitworth and the rest of the family all fussing.'

Joan nodded and pulled a face as she poured the tea and handed her friend a cup. 'He's gone, then?'

Monica gazed miserably at her over the rim of the cup and nodded. 'And I miss him so much already. Oh, Joan, I felt so utterly wretched as I watched them drive away.'

Joan put her cup down on the table and put her arm around Monica's shoulders. 'I know, Mon, it's like being up on a cloud for the time they're home with you and then suddenly . . . bump! You're back down to earth again, back to this drab and dangerous world. I know that's the way I felt when Jim was home last. And none of us have any idea when they'll be home again, probably not for months and months, maybe even years. Oh, take no notice of me; I'm not doing much to cheer you up, am I? Fine friend I am!'

Monica smiled at her. 'You're a great friend. Now drink your tea before it gets cold. I've some news, some things I didn't get time to tell you earlier. In fact, I forgot about every-thing except . . . him leaving.'

Joan reached across the table and squeezed her hand. 'I know. Well, what's this news?'

'The first bit I'm not very happy about at all.' She looked pensive. 'In fact, I'm not really happy about any of it.'

'Any of *what*, for God's sake?'

'Rick is being transferred. He's going to be trained to drive a tank, and then he'll be attached to the Royal Tank Regiment and then . . . then he . . . he'll have to go abroad. He said they told him that being able to drive is considered an asset in the army.'

Joan nodded slowly as she digested this news. Obviously, Monica had hoped that Rick would be kept somewhere closer to home, like her Jim, for as long as possible, but that wasn't going to happen. 'I suppose any skill is considered an asset.' She managed a wry grin. 'Not that being a musician comes high on that list,' she added, for that was what Jim had been before the war. He'd played in the orchestra of the Empire Theatre and she'd met him through her Aunty Lil. But now she was glad that he would be staying down at that air base in Lincolnshire. He wasn't a pilot or a navigator or a gunner, just ground crew, but it was better than being sent to the front line, as Rick Eustace was obviously going to be in the not too distant future. 'He'll be fine, Mon. He's not a fool, and he knows how to take care of himself.'

'I know that, Joan, but it won't be easy when he'll be

having bombs dropped on him . . . and enemy artillery fire to face.'

Joan didn't say that they themselves could well be having bombs dropped on them before long – this 'phoney war' couldn't last forever, as Dunkirk had shown. The Nazi forces were now gathering just across the Channel, and the way they had so rapidly charged across Belgium, Holland and France had put the fear of God into everyone – herself included – for they seemed to be unstoppable. She decided to change the subject. 'What other news do you have?'

'Rick's dad was talking to me the other day about the salons.'

Joan frowned. 'Is he going to have to close them? Will you all lose your jobs?'

'I hope not! He really doesn't want to put anyone out of work, but he knows most of us will have to go and do war work at some stage anyway, and supplies are getting harder to obtain. They're not a priority – not in the way that food, fuel, steel and stuff like that are. He's talking about keeping the Chester salon open, because it's the least likely of the three to be bombed, and opening small salons in factories instead, with maybe just one qualified stylist and an apprentice. That's the bare minimum of staff we could manage with – there'll be no more employing stylists who specialise in perming or tinting or bleaching or manicuring. Everyone will have to muck in.'

'That's a good idea, Mon. If the government send us all to work in munitions and the like, wouldn't it be really great to have somewhere on site to have your hair done? So convenient! You could go in your lunch break, or before or after your shift. He could well pick up far more customers than he has now.'

'I hadn't thought about that,' Monica mused.

'Well, think about it now. They'll be getting very well paid. Mam said in the last war they were earning three, sometimes four times what they got in peacetime. And no husbands, fathers or brothers to have to cater for or account to either, so you'll get women who wouldn't have been able to afford it before treating themselves – and why not? Mam says it's horrible – dirty, smelly and dangerous work – so if you can have a little bit of luxury, you'll grab it with both hands. There'll be damn well nothing nice in the shops to buy, so why not get your hair done regularly? If I were you, Mon, I'd have a word with Claude about it at the earliest opportunity.'

'You're right! He'll have to see people, I suppose, and get all kinds of permissions and stuff like that—'

'And we all know how long *that* takes,' Joan interrupted.

'And knowing Claude, he'll want to get in first before other businesses have the same idea. No use waiting until your shop is reduced to a smouldering ruin before thinking about other alternatives. I'll see him at work tomorrow. I know he's worried.'

'I would be, too, if I'd built up such a successful business.' Joan paused as an idea came into her mind. 'I wonder if Crawford's would consider opening a hairdressing place – they do take our welfare more seriously than nearly every other employer, factory or otherwise, in this city. I think it would be a great success – I know I'd use it, and I'm sure they must have some spare space. Not that I'm going to be working there for much longer. Or going out anywhere in the near future.'

Monica was turning all this over in her mind. It was an excellent idea of Joan's, to approach Crawford's, and she'd definitely mention it to Claude. It could be his first work-place salon, and Joan was right. Crawford's did take the welfare of their employees seriously, they got all kinds of benefits others could only dream about – a sports and social club included. She wondered how Joan would manage financially when she had to finish work. Jim, like everyone else, gave his wife an allowance deducted from his pay, but it wasn't much. But at least Joan would be staying here with Olive, so there was no rent to pay. Her train of thought led her to her own position. Rick, too, sent money home, but she had a mort-gage to pay and her own expenses, as well as the car, and if she was really truthful she could at times be rather extrava-gant, having become used to being more affluent since she married. As Joan had said, the increasing shortages did put the brakes on that, but she needed her job. She needed it, too, to keep her mind occupied all day – when she was work-ing she didn't think of Rick as much. That was another thing Joan would have to get used to, trying to fill her days, to stop worrying about Jim – worry was bad for her and the baby.

'Lord, what's the matter now? You've gone all quiet and thoughtful.' Joan's voice held a note of concern.

Monica smiled. 'Just thinking about things. Work, paying bills . . .'

'I know, it's all a bit depressing, but I've had another idea for you to think about.'

'What? I hope it's as good as your last one.'

'Well, you said the army considered being able to drive a big asset. Why don't you put your driving skills to some use? There aren't many women who can drive, you know. Who else do you know with a car?'

Monica thought quickly and shook her head. 'No one. But, Joan, I've not been driving for very long. In fact, coming down here is the first time I've driven without Claude beside me, and I've got to get home safely yet – in the blackout.'

'Well, don't leave it too late and you'll be just fine.'

'What could I volunteer for? I'll only be free after work and on Sundays, and I do my housework and washing then.'

'Oh, to hell with the housework! There's only you in that house, and how much washing do you have? Why not try and see what's on offer. Ambulance or post and messages, or delivering stuff,' Joan suggested.

Monica nodded slowly. 'It would keep me from sitting moping every night, just listening to the wireless – that's not a lot of fun. I can't come up here or go and visit Nancy and the girls every night – everyone would be sick to death of me. And I won't go to the cinema on my own. It's the evenings when I miss Rick the most. I'll definitely think about it, but I've no experience of driving big vehicles.'

'You'll soon learn, or they'll teach you. And it's not as if anyone is going to let you loose with a tank, is it?' Joan laughed.

Monica laughed with her. 'No, I'd do more damage than good with one of those.' She got to her feet. 'Maybe Claude will be able to point me in the right direction about that, too.'

Joan became serious. 'You get on well with him, don't you? And you seem to rely on him a lot as well.'

'I do. He . . . well, I hate to say this, but he's better educated and has more of a business head than my dad, bless him.'

'But he's the salt of the earth is your dad. He helped our Charlie no end after *he* deserted us. I really don't think our Charlie has ever forgotten or forgiven the things Billy Copperfield did.'

'Has anyone, Joan?' Monica replied, knowing that her friend had never forgiven her father's behaviour either, or the fact that he had never married her mother, despite her having his two children. To be born illegitimate was shameful. But as far as Monica was concerned, she barely remembered, let alone cared about, the facts surrounding Joan's birth. And there was a bright side to Olive never having been legally married to Billy Copperfield – it had left her free to marry Frederick Garswood, who was now Joan and Charlie's step-father. A good, kind, generous man who idolised Olive – and who was affluent to boot, having his own business and owning his own house.

'Are you going to call in to see how the "interview" went?' Joan asked, lightening the subject. She never liked to be reminded of her father.

'No, I'll hear all about it on my next visit. And if I don't go now, I'll never get home in daylight!'

'Just have a chat to Claude tomorrow, Mon. And take care driving home,' Joan said, getting up to see her friend out.

The evening air was still warm as Joan stood at the front door, waving goodbye to her friend and listening to the sounds of her neighbours settling down for the evening.

Monica waved back as she started the engine, put the car into gear and began slowly to pull away. She did have plenty to think about now, which was no bad thing.

Chapter Five

—◆◆✕◆◆—

Claude had thought it a great idea to approach the senior management of Crawford's Biscuits about opening a salon before he had to deal with all the relevant government departments. To his relief and satisfaction they agreed with him, and so he'd begun the tedious business of filling in all the paperwork and seeing it got to the right department. To his surprise, within six weeks he was organising the opening of his first 'ladies' hairdressing room', a name Monica had suggested, reminding him gently that 'salon' was a bit too grand for what they were providing, which was a medium-sized room on the ground floor at the back of the Despatch Department, previously used as some sort of storeroom.

It had all been a bit frantic, Monica thought, as she finished cleaning the last mirror the day before they were due to open. Most of the fittings and fixtures had been removed from the salon off Bold Street, and items had been brought over from the New Brighton salon, too. Both were still open but with greatly reduced staff – and indeed customers, as more and more women were recruited for war work.

'It all looks great now, Mon! Who would have thought a dingy storeroom could be transformed with a lick of paint, some nice lighting and a few plants,' Joan remarked admiringly when she called in at the end of her shift.

Monica smiled and nodded. 'It does. Mr Beddows himself has been to inspect it and said he knew it would be a great asset and well used by "his ladies", as he calls his employees,' she informed Joan, with satisfaction. Mr Beddows was the managing director no less, and his secretary had already booked a regular weekly appointment. 'The diary is filling up fast so we're going to be very busy, I just hope this apprentice – Stella – has some gumption. I won't have time to be constantly telling her what to do.'

'Didn't Helen Marshall interview her?'

'Yes.'

'Well then, stop worrying. She hasn't been the manageress at La Belle Coiffure for the past eight years without learning a thing or two about people. She interviewed you, remember,' Joan reminded her.

Monica looked thoughtful. 'I just hope I'm going to be able to manage it all.'

'Of course you are,' Joan replied firmly.

Monica smiled at her friend. 'You're great for building my confidence.'

Joan grew serious. 'It's me who needs confidence. I'm beginning to wonder what kind of a mother I'll be. I'm going to have to give up work at the end of this month.'

'I know, but Mam says you should make the most of the rest, and try to enjoy the peace and quiet, because once you have the baby all that goes out of the window. You'll be on your knees with exhaustion until it's at least a year old.'

'Oh, I won't mind that. I just want to get the pregnancy over with, and get on with my life. Jim's hoping he'll get some Christmas leave and be here when his son or daughter arrives, but I'm not holding out much hope of that happening, not with the way things are going now.'

Monica frowned, knowing what Joan meant. In the south of England another battle was shaping up to be fought, one as big and as vitally important as the Battle of the Atlantic, except this time it was being fought not at sea, but in the air. Over the past weeks, wave after wave of Nazi aircraft had filled the skies above the Home Counties and even the Midlands. People had stood in the streets, roads, lanes and fields and watched the deadly conflict playing out in the skies above them, between the Luftwaffe's Messerschmitts and the RAF's Hurricanes and Spitfires. Being ground crew and stationed in Lincolnshire didn't guarantee Jim McDonald's safety, and he was never far from Joan's thoughts. Monica hadn't heard from Rick but she assumed he was all right and in the middle of his tank training with the army, although she didn't know quite where. 'Careless Talk Costs Lives' was an instruction that was becoming so familiar she was beginning to get fed up hearing it.

'Come on, I've finished here now. I'll run you home,' Monica offered. 'It's still too warm to be standing waiting at the tram stop after a day on your feet, and you look tired, Joan.' These days, she drove more often, although she was careful not to use too much of her precious petrol allowance.

'Oh, thanks, Mon. I have to admit I do feel exhausted by the end of the day.'

Monica gathered up her handbag and her light summer jacket and, after glancing around to make sure everything was in order, ushered Joan towards the door. She locked it carefully after them, put the key into her handbag and extracted the car keys.

Joan smiled at her. 'I hope tomorrow goes really well.'

'Thanks, we're starting at seven thirty, so it's going to be a busy day. Now, let's get going. I hope your mam will have the kettle on, I'm dying for a cup of tea, and Frederick may have heard some news – more than we have, anyway.'

'Do you really think so?' Joan enquired as she followed Monica out of the building.

'Well, he heard about the Nazis invading the Channel Islands before we did, remember – he deals with so many people that he gets to know things quickly.'

'Sometimes they're only rumours, but I know what you mean,' Joan answered.

Joan knew there was something wrong as soon as she walked into the kitchen of the house in Mersey View. No preparations for the evening meal were in progress, and her mother was sitting at the scrubbed deal table with her head in her hands while young Charlie was standing beside her, looking afraid and helpless. Her stepfather was obviously still down at the yard and offices; she remembered vaguely that it was Charlie's night to attend the Mechanics' Institute, where he was learning the theoretical side of heating and plumbing, but she pushed it from her mind.

'What's the matter? What's happened, Mam? Are you ill?' When Olive didn't reply, she stared hard at her brother.

'Charlie, what is it? Should you go and fetch Frederick? Will someone tell me what's wrong, for God's sake?' she cried out as a cold little dart of icy fear seemed to prick her heart and she reached instinctively for Monica's hand.

Olive raised her head and Joan saw that her mother had been crying, something she'd seldom seen her do. Olive had shed a few tears, mainly of shock and anger, when Bella had arrived out of the blue and when Billy had deserted them, but now her eyes were swollen and red. She was clearly deeply upset about something.

Monica, too, was shocked by Olive's eyes and tear-streaked cheeks. Olive Garswood was one of the strongest women she knew. She gently pushed Joan towards her mother, praying silently that nothing had happened to Joan's stepfather; she knew his work had its dangers, and sometimes there were explosions with heating boilers or gas pipes.

Joan went and put her arms around her mother's shoulders, and it was then that she saw the telegram lying on the table beside her mam's hand. It was open.

'I . . . I opened it, Joan. I . . . I . . . just *had* to. It's addressed to you, but I couldn't let you . . . not in your condition.'

Fear was beginning to paralyse Joan now. She felt cold and she realised she was beginning to shake as Olive pushed the buff-coloured envelope towards her. 'Me! It . . . it's for me? Jim! Oh, Mam, no! It . . . it's not Jim!'

Olive pulled herself together and stood up, gathering Joan in her arms, while Monica took the single sheet of paper out of the envelope and scanned the words none of them had ever wanted to read. Jim McDonald had been killed in an air raid on the RAF base at Skellingthorpe. Joan would receive further information from his commanding officer in due course. She couldn't believe it, didn't *want* to believe it. And why were they so bloody *formal* about it? 'In due course' indeed! Poor Joan was distraught, shocked and – oh, dear Lord – pregnant, too! Her eyes swimming with tears, she glanced at Olive – she couldn't begin to imagine how she would feel if it had been Rick.

Olive bit her lip as she eased Joan into a chair. 'Monica, luv, put the kettle on. She needs hot sweet tea – we all do – in fact, we could do with something stronger, but I'm afraid of giving her spirits in her condition.'

Monica nodded her agreement and, like an automaton, reached for the kettle.

Olive was beginning to gather herself, now her daughter was there, needing all the support she could give her. She'd known trouble, hardship and loss in her life, and now she had to be strong for Joan and for the rest of the family. 'Charlie, go down to the yard and tell Frederick to come home,' she instructed her son.

'What will I tell him, Mam? He was waiting for someone to come to give him an estimate for some repairs that need doing to the office. That's why he sent me home.'

'Well, that will have to wait! Tell him . . . tell him what's happened. He'll understand and know what to do.'

Without another word, the lad turned and left, closing the door behind him as quietly as he could. Joan looked terrible; Monica feared she was going to faint any minute.

While Olive made the tea, and spooned as much of their precious sugar ration as she could spare into Joan's cup, Monica sat beside her friend holding both Joan's icy hands in her own and trying, without much success, to stop crying. It frightened her that Joan so far hadn't shed a single tear. She hadn't collapsed in hysterics or begun wailing in grief, and Monica didn't think this strange *quietness* was normal.

'Joan, luv. I'm so, so sorry. Please, let it all out and have a cry! Don't feel as if you have to hold it all in. I'm your oldest and dearest friend, and I'll always be here for you. I just wish to God there was *something* I could do to help you *now*!'

'It's the shock,' Olive said. 'Here, Joan, drink this, luv, and then I think I'll get you to bed. It . . . it's all just too much for you, what with the . . . it's all too much for all of us,' Olive finished, trying not to think of the months ahead before Joan's baby was born and what the poor girl's life would be like after it. Oh, why Jim McDonald? Why? Why? Why? He'd been such a good, quiet, caring lad, he'd had no family, and she loved him as a son. She might have been more prepared, better able to accept it, if he'd been a pilot or air crew, for they were losing so many of those young men every day. They were the ones who faced death each time they took off, but Jim had been ground crew, a mechanic. Oh, how could she have been so naive as to think he'd be safe? Clearly, no one was safe in this blasted war!

Joan sipped her tea obediently but it didn't help, nothing would help, she knew that. She still couldn't take it in that he'd gone. That she'd never see him or hear his voice or have him play music for her ever again. He was dead. The pain in her heart seemed to be enveloping her totally. She couldn't think about the future, couldn't even think about the next few minutes, she could see nothing ahead of her except darkness, the total blackness of despair, loss and grief.

'Monica, will you help me get her to bed, please, luv?' Olive asked quietly when it was obvious that Joan wasn't going to finish the tea. She could barely hold the cup, her hands were trembling so much.

'Of course, then should I go and tell Mam, or should I stay with her? I really don't want to leave her like this.'

'I think she'd like you to stay, Monica, I know I would,' Olive sighed heavily and rubbed her swollen eyes. 'Oh, I hoped I'd never have to see the day when such tragedy would fall on this house.'

'I know. You always hope it won't be you.'

Between them, the two women managed to get Joan upstairs to her bedroom, where they gently coaxed her on to the bed.

It was like undressing a doll, Monica thought, as she and Olive got Joan out of her day clothes and into her nightdress, before tucking her into the bed she would never again share with her husband. That thought tore at Monica's heart more strongly than anything else. When they'd settled Joan, Olive went downstairs to wait for the return of her son and her husband whilst Monica sat beside the bed, clasping Joan's cold hand but saying nothing. For what on earth could she say now? Joan's eyes were closed, but Monica knew she wasn't asleep, indeed she wondered when Joan would ever sleep again. Suddenly, her friend turned her head and opened her eyes.

'Joan! What is it, luv? Can I get you anything?'

'No, Mon, but thanks. I feel strange, as if this isn't happening to me, as if I'm looking down at myself and thinking, why am I in bed? I'm not ill, so why do I feel nothing when I

know I *should*? What's the matter with me, Mon, that I don't
... *can't* seem to understand that he ... he's ... dead! I'll
never see him again, Mon. I ... I thought he'd be safe. He
patched the planes up, he ... he didn't fly them. Oh, why
him? Why wasn't he in a shelter? Why did he not hear them
coming, hear the sirens and run to safety? What *happened*,
Mon?' And then the tears came, racking her body, and as
Monica gathered her in her arms and made sympathetic noises,
tears slid slowly down her cheeks, too. She had no answer to
Joan's questions. They'd both assumed Jim would be safe
and now, now he ... he was ... gone. So what chance did her
Rick have when he was sent out in his tank to fight?

A few minutes later, when Olive came back into the room,
she found them both with their arms around each other,
sobbing. Thinking it for the best, and thankful that Joan was
now giving way to her feelings, she left them and went back
downstairs. She'd heard the front door open and close, and she
thanked God that Frederick was now home to help her with
her grief.

Chapter Six

It was Nelly, not Frederick, Olive had heard downstairs. She'd seen Monica's car stop outside Olive's house and watched both girls go inside, but she'd become a bit anxious when Monica didn't seem to be making any effort to call on her own family. Then young Charlie Copperfield had left hurriedly, looking pale and shocked. All her instincts told her something was wrong. She'd been Olive's closest friend ever since the family had moved here years ago, and now she was worried.

'Eileen, keep your eye on that pan of potatoes and don't let them burn – if you can tear yourself away from that magazine!' she'd instructed her younger daughter, taking off her apron and shaking her head, wishing the girl was not so taken up with her appearance and this young naval rating, Harold Stevens.

To her surprise Olive's kitchen was deserted. But when, barely a minute later, her friend hurried down the stairs, she was shocked by her appearance. 'Dear God! Olive, luv, what's wrong?'

'Oh, Nell! It . . . it's the worst tragedy that could fall on us all, but especially our poor Joan. I've sent Charlie for Frederick.'

Nelly's hand instinctively went to her throat. 'Oh, no! Oh, luv. She . . . she's not lost . . .'

Olive shook her head quickly as she sat down heavily opposite her friend and neighbour. 'No, the baby is all right, I hope. It's Jim.' She covered her eyes with her hands.

Nelly was instantly on her feet. 'What's happened to him?'

'He's been killed, Nell. There was an air strike on his base, we don't know exactly what happened. How, when or why . . . we don't know, but . . . but he's gone.' Olive wiped her eyes with the corner of her apron. 'Charlie went to tell Frederick. He should be home any minute.'

Nelly hesitated. She could see Olive needed support and comforting, but surely that was Frederick's role as her husband? She didn't want to push in. 'I'll stay with you, luv, just until he gets here,' she offered. It was the least she could do for her friend. 'Is our Monica with her?'

Olive nodded. 'At first she was in such a state of shock – well, we all were – that our Joan couldn't cry. She didn't break down, Nelly, although Monica did.'

'Definitely shock, Olive.'

'We got her to bed, and then I left them together. I thought Monica might be able to help. Better than I could, anyway.'

'And?' Nelly prompted quietly.

'When I looked in last they were both sobbing. So, I left them to it. Thanks, Nell, for . . . for . . .'

'I've been with you through nearly every crisis in your life, Olive Garswood, and we'll get through this – somehow, and together.' She stood up as Frederick Garswood, accompanied by his stepson, came into the room.

'Send our Monica down to me, Olive. It's her family Joan needs now, and you've enough on your plate without having her under your feet as well. I'll try and talk her into going in to work tomorrow. They are opening that first factory hairdresser's at Crawford's, and it will be best if she keeps busy. I'm beginning to think this "phoney" war is over and that we've got dark days ahead to face. But we'll manage, we always have, Olive. You and me together against anything fate can throw at us.'

Olive nodded slowly, feeling Nelly was right to be fearful of what the future might hold, but wishing she wasn't. 'I . . . I'll have to write to our Lily later on. In the meantime, I'll try to get everyone to eat *something* at least. I've got the lodgers to think of, after all.'

That reminded Nelly of her pan of potatoes. She squared her shoulders; she'd better get back, there was little she could do here now, and food was becoming too scarce to waste. They'd have to eat the spuds, even if Eileen had let them burn black. And she'd insist that Monica stay tonight, she was in no fit state to drive back to that empty house in Allerton. 'If you don't feel up to it today, luv, leave the letter until tomorrow, your Lily will understand,' Nelly advised as she left.

It was much later when Olive finally cleared the table and took a pen and the writing pad from the drawer in the dresser. It seemed as if the very air in the house was pressing down on her like a great ominous thundercloud, but she knew she'd have to write to her sister eventually, so she might as well get it over with. Her gentlemen lodgers had been very distressed and full of sympathy. Charlie hadn't wanted to go to his evening class, and had become quite adamant about it, but between them, she and Frederick had gently and tactfully persuaded him to go. They'd pointed out that it would at least be a little thing Charlie could do in memory of Jim McDonald whom he'd admired so much, and Frederick had promised to walk down with the lad.

Her husband had been as shocked and upset as herself, for Frederick Garswood cared deeply for his stepchildren and hated to see them upset. As he'd walked back home from the Mechanics' Institute, he'd reflected on how much poor Joan had already suffered in her short life. She didn't deserve such grief and loss. Her father had let her down terribly, not once but three times, yet she'd somehow managed to put it all behind her and been so happy with young Jim McDonald. He'd wondered sadly if this would be the last death in action they'd have to face, but he was realistic enough to know it probably wouldn't be.

Joan was finally sleeping. Olive had struggled through some dire crises in her life – including the loss of a man she had loved – so she'd help her daughter through this in every way she could. She wasn't going to let anything bring harm to this unborn child; it was even more precious now and would have the very best that she and Frederick and Joan could provide. She couldn't bear to contemplate what the days, months and years ahead held for her daughter and grandchild. It would be such a blessing if this damn war would be over quickly and life could return to some semblance of normality, but there didn't seem to be much hope of that.

She took the top off the pen, pushed her thick dark hair back from her forehead and began to write.

6th September 1940

My Dear Lily, David and Bella,
    It is with such a heavy heart that I am writing to tell you that today we received the terrible news that . . .

Lily already had the beginnings of a headache when she sat down wearily at the table beside the window, with Olive's letter in her hand. It had arrived in the lunchtime post and it was now early evening, but beams of bright sunlight still penetrated into the sitting room of the small, first-floor flat in Great George's Street, just off Marylebone High Street. It was plainly furnished, as it was rented accommodation, but she'd added a few ornaments, cushions and rugs of her own to brighten the place up, and it suited them all. David, her husband, was working late at the Royal College of Music where he was a voice coach, and seventeen-year-old Bella – the girl she now looked on as a daughter, although she was actually no blood relation at all – was with him. Both would be home shortly, so she'd read her sister's letter while she had some peace and quiet. The flat was so small that sometimes it felt like living in a sardine tin, she mused irritably.

She herself had enjoyed a day off from the theatre – which, despite the desperate times, was still open – although she seemed to have spent most of it standing in queues for the pitiful amounts of food that could be had. She sighed, thinking back to the days when she'd been able to walk into a shop and buy all manner of food and – just as importantly, in her view – clothes, hats, shoes, stockings and make-up. She'd always taken a great deal of care with her appearance and was rewarded by knowing that she was considered to be a very elegant and fashionable woman, even though now fast approaching middle age.

She had married late, after devoting herself to her career in the theatre. In recent years, she'd been wardrobe mistress at the Empire in Liverpool, before finding a position down in London once they'd decided to relocate there so that Bella could have the best training possible to enable her to hopefully have a successful career in the world of grand opera. For Annabella Ferreira Silva had the finest mezzo-soprano voice Lily had ever heard.

She smoothed out the pages of Olive's letter but as she began to read it, the words became blurred by tears. Oh, hadn't both her poor sister and niece suffered enough in life already? She brushed away her tears with the back of her hand and gazed out of the window, but saw nothing. Joan had loved that Scottish lad so much, and Lily had been so delighted at her niece's happiness. After all, it had been she who had introduced them when Jim had joined the orchestra at the Empire and had asked for her help in finding lodgings. Joan hadn't wanted the big, grand wedding her best friend Monica Savage had enjoyed. She'd been happy with just a simple ceremony in the Registry Office, but she'd looked as radiant in her elegant navy and fuchsia outfit as Monica had looked in white lace. And when she'd heard that Joan was pregnant . . . well, David had insisted they open the very last bottle of sparkling white wine they had, to celebrate the good news – even Bella had had a glass.

Lily closed her eyes and dropped her head in her hands, unable to continue reading. Poor, poor Joan. How would she cope? How would she bear it? She'd had a lot to deal with in her twenty years, but this . . . Oh, this! And with a baby on the way – due in three months' time. She thanked God that Joan lived with Olive and Frederick, they would look after her.

At the sound of voices on the stairs Lily raised her head and folded the letter, tucking it back into the envelope. She knew that both David and Bella would be terribly upset by the news, but Bella in particular, as she had been very close to Joan. When Bella had first arrived in Liverpool as a twelve-year-old stowaway on a cargo ship from Lisbon, it had been Joan who had taken her under her wing, and the girl loved Joan as a full sister. A dawning realisation that had been niggling away at Lily these past weeks began to resurface – this war had arrived on her doorstep and was starting to take its toll. She didn't like it one bit.

She'd managed to wipe away her tears and tidy her fashion-ably styled blonde hair before her husband and Bella came into the room, good-naturedly arguing about why it was that so many famous operatic sopranos were in fact very large women – particularly as they so often had to portray thin, dying young waifs – but one look at Lily's face and they both became serious.

'Lily, my dear love, what's happened?' David asked, dropping his music case on the sofa and taking her in his arms.

'Aunt Lily, you look so sad. What has happened?' Bella cried, impatiently brushing strands of her long, dark curly hair away from her cheeks.

Lily detached herself from her husband's embrace and

handed him the letter, then went and put her arms around Bella. As David read Olive's words aloud, and he and Bella absorbed the terrible news, the young girl began to sob. Lily gazed helplessly at David over Bella's shoulder.

'Let her cry, Lily. It . . . it's such a terrible shock for everyone. We never expected . . .'

'No, we didn't!' Lily cried, all her grief and fear bubbling up inside her.

But before she could utter another word, the first rising notes of the air-raid siren split the air, making them all jump. It got louder by the second, rising to its blood-chilling crescendo, until it seemed as if the entire flat was shaking.

'It's a raid! Oh, dear God, David!' Lily cried, while Bella looked up with sheer terror in her dark eyes.

'Keep calm, Lily! Get the coats, gas masks, bags . . . the things you've packed in that little case, Lily, for emergencies, and I'll get the blankets,' David instructed, firmly but calmly.

For the moment everything was forgotten as they all rushed around their small home, gathering up the necessities, while the siren continued its piercing wail and people could be heard shouting in the street below. They picked out the shrill sound of a whistle, either from a policeman or a Civil Defence volunteer, as people were directed through the streets towards the public shelters, which were mainly in the Tube stations.

'Hold on tightly to me, Lily – and you too, Bella, we don't want to get separated!' David shouted over the din as they reached the street, where people were running everywhere in a state of panic and confusion.

'I knew we couldn't go on escaping this forever! I just *knew* it! But why now? Why the hell now of all times?' Lily shouted back, her voice shrill with fear. But she felt anger, too, that they couldn't even begin to take in the news of Jim's death, let alone begin to grieve for him, for already the drone of the approaching aircraft could be heard and then the *thud, thud, thud* of the anti-aircraft batteries opening up in the park.

Chapter Seven

———◦•✦•◦———

It had never been as bad as this before, Lily thought to herself, as she sat on the bitterly cold platform clutching Bella tightly while David's arms encircled them both. The blankets they'd brought didn't seem to help at all; both she and Bella were shivering, and not just from the cold but with the fear of what was to come. This first heavy raid on London had been going on now for almost five hours, and it was like nothing that had gone before. There seemed to be no end to it in sight, for the planes that droned on above them kept on coming in endless waves.

There had been a couple of raids over the past two months but none so serious or lasting so long. Lily, like many people, hadn't taken a great deal of notice of them – they'd just been an inconvenience for maybe an hour. When people had emerged from the depths of the Underground station they'd even managed to joke with each other, but no one was cracking jokes now. She glanced around, taking in the huddled groups of people; families, friends, neighbours and even strangers sitting close together with fear in varying degrees written all over their faces and in their eyes, the men and boys trying not to show it. The station was damp, badly lit and horribly uncomfortable, she thought, as she smoothed Bella's hair in an attempt to calm the girl. Bella was terrified as they endured the hours of explosions above them, preceded by the faint whining, whistling noise the bombs made before they hit their targets. Even this far underground, the walls shook. She couldn't begin to imagine what it was like for all the police, firemen, Civil Defence workers, ambulance drivers and crews working up there on the surface. She hated it, she *hated* it all!

'Oh, Aunt Lily, when will they go away? They must have no bombs left . . .' Bella sobbed into her shoulder.

Lily bit her lip, glancing up at David for support. It was the question they all wanted the answer to.

'I'm sure it can't be long now, Bella,' David replied. 'You're right, they've *got* to run out of bombs soon, and then we can go home.' He was trying to sound as confident as he could but he was wondering just how many of those damn planes were up there. And were more on the way – God forbid?

Home. The word seemed to stick in Lily's mind. She longed to just get up and go home this very minute, leaving this crowded, damp, dismal place behind her, a place that reeked of fear.

What she hated most, even more than her terror of the bombs, was the total lack of privacy. They, like everyone else, had been allocated a 'pitch' on the platform with just a few feet between themselves and the next family. Here they were expected to sit, or even try to sleep, on the hard, cold concrete for hours on end. Yes, they were probably safe from the terror that flew over London, but that was all. The authorities had done their best, she thought grudgingly. At intervals along the platform there were curtained-off areas that provided woefully basic sanitary facilities, which gave little privacy and after an hour began to smell. She wrinkled her nose in disgust; after five hours, the stench was becoming unbearable. As well as the sounds from above there was the constant hum of noise, with people talking, praying, swearing, singing softly and even laughing at times. Babies and young children cried sporadically, and the 'neighbours' to the right of them on the platform tonight seemed a rough lot – far from clean, thoughtful or polite.

Home. The word seemed to take over her thoughts. Not the flat in London, which she didn't really class as home, but Liverpool. Olive's large, comfortable, clean, warm house in Mersey View even had the luxury of its own shelter in the yard. If she was back home she'd be away from these crowds of people, life would be as 'civilised' as it possibly could be, and she wouldn't even mind all the shortages or hardships. She could support and help her sister, comfort her niece, but was she being selfish? She'd insisted – against Olive's wishes – that they come to London for Bella's sake, Bella's career, but was it good for the girl to be subjected to all *this*? Bella was a quiet, sensitive girl, and these days she was troubled by so many things. She ate like a bird, and Lily knew she was finding her time at the Royal College increasingly hard, even though Bella insisted she was enjoying the music and her studies. She knew the girl missed Olive and her family. They were all things she would have to think about in the future. But oh! Would this damn bombing never end? she prayed through gritted teeth.

Two hours later, her prayer was answered as they heard the first notes of the 'All Clear' siren. They thankfully gathered up their belongings and began to file towards the exits, guided by the Civil Defence volunteers, until at last they were above ground and took the first breaths of fresh air they'd had in seven hours. It was far from fresh, Lily thought, glancing around as they walked towards the corner of the road. The sky was almost as bright as day, with the glare from hundreds of burning buildings, firefighters visible amongst them, hoses still trained on the flames. Some buildings were already beyond saving, and many were mere ruins silhouetted against the livid sky. Fire engines and ambulances made their way down the road, trying to avoid the huge craters, broken gas and water mains, electric and phone cables that twisted like huge black snakes across roads and pavements, hindering people who were trying to get back to see if their homes were still standing.

Bella stood rigid, clutching David's arm tightly and shaking with what Lily assumed was both fear and shock. The heat was intense, and beads of perspiration stood out on Bella's forehead. Bella had never been as afraid in her life as she was now; after all those terrible hours they had survived underground, only to emerge to face . . . *this!* This inferno of noise and devastation, a vision of hell like the one she remembered the nuns in the school in Lisbon showing her as a very young child in a religious instruction class. That image had stayed with her for years. She hadn't even been as afraid as this when she had stealthily boarded a cargo ship, that dark night so long ago, to come to Liverpool and find her father. She thought she had managed to put that terrible voyage behind her; she had almost forgotten the sheer desperation and grief that had driven her at the time to make such a perilous journey. But the sight of this magnificent city – a place she'd begun to look on as 'home' – in blazing ruins brought everything back to her.

'It's all right, Bella, luv. They've gone now. I know things look terrible, and *are* terrible, but we're safe, we've survived, and we'll get back to normal very soon,' David comforted her, feeling far less confident than he appeared. Was it going to be possible to get back to normal – ever?

To everyone's relief the building that contained their flat was still standing, and seemingly undamaged, although some of the buildings further down the street had suffered damage, including the hotel and church at the top end. 'Oh, thank God! At least we've still got a roof over our heads,' David announced, thankfully shepherding his little family towards home.

Bella managed a smile as Lily put her arm around her, but she was still afraid. 'Will they come back, Aunt Lily?'

'Not tonight they won't! Now, let's get inside,' she urged, 'and I'll make a cup of tea. We could all do with one after the last few hours, and then we'll make the most of what's left of the night to get some sleep.'

She bustled around, drawing the blackout curtains over the taped-up glass of the windows, while Bella sank thankfully down on the sofa, utterly exhausted by the ordeal.

To everyone's dismay that night was just the beginning. The Luftwaffe continued their raids on the capital, night after night, without respite. Thousands of homes, businesses and many old and famous buildings were destroyed or badly damaged, including St Paul's Cathedral and Buckingham

Palace. But the Londoners began to develop a heroic resilience to the terrors of the darkness. There were makeshift signs on hundreds of buildings pronouncing 'BUSINESS AS USUAL' after every night of destruction, and everyone worked hard to keep things running. Like so many women, Lily felt her nerves were being shredded, stretched out like piano wires, as they battled daily to try to make life bearable, if not normal.

She was getting more and more worried about Bella. The 'Blitz', as it was being called, was taking its toll on the girl and her studies. 'I can't concentrate, Aunt Lily! How can I sing when every night . . . there is no rest from them?' she'd pleaded.

Lily at last decided to discuss it all with David, as she should have done in the first place, she told herself sternly. It would have to be this afternoon, she determined, because as Bella had said, there was no rest from them at night.

David looked thoughtful when she broached the subject, pointing out the effect it was having on Bella. 'I know, Lily, and I have to admit it's worrying me, too. She tells me she can't practise, that she is afraid to sing, that people will think her insensitive in such terrible times and . . .' He paused, frowning, 'I don't think the college can remain open much longer. It's getting harder and harder for everyone.'

'I know. Most of the theatres don't open now. A lot have been damaged, people are afraid, people are spending hours and hours in the shelters. So, I was thinking . . . would it be wise for us to go back to Liverpool?'

David shrugged. 'I don't honestly know, Lily. Who knows what that madman across the channel in Berlin has planned? Will he give up on London and turn his attention to other cities? Liverpool is the biggest and busiest port, second only to London, after all. The docks are vital to the survival of the country. We've all witnessed how badly the convoys have suffered, and Liverpool is their main port. Have you mentioned any of this to Bella herself, Lily?'

Lily shook her head. 'No, I wanted to hear what you thought first, but maybe we should. We came here for her sake, so should we leave now for her sake, too? Perhaps she is too young, David, to realise what this move could do to her career.'

'If she's unable to sing, Lily, she won't have a career at all.'

Lily knew the truth of this. Oh yes, they'd considered America, it had proved to be the land of opportunity for many, but the country couldn't compare with the centuries-old classical music colleges and conservatoires, opera houses and concert halls in Europe, even though most of them were now under Nazi occupation. And then there was the huge problem of just getting to America now that immigration had ceased, and the huge passenger liners no longer crossed the Atlantic from Southampton or Liverpool.

She sighed. 'Then let's see what she has to say. I'll fetch her.'

These days Bella kept a small case, in which she had packed everything she held dear, ready beside her bed. One of the things she treasured was a programme from Covent Garden for the opera *Tosca*, which she carefully leafed through almost every day. It was her greatest ambition to one day sing that demanding lead role, but she was beginning to fear that her dreams would never come true, that there would be no opera houses or theatres left standing in the entire world and all the beautiful music would be lost forever.

'We want to talk to you, Bella – David and I,' Lily announced, popping her head around the door of Bella's minuscule bedroom.

Bella's large, dark eyes widened with anxiety. 'I am not in trouble?'

Lily laughed. 'Of course not! We would just like to discuss something with you.'

Bella's features relaxed as she followed Lily into the sitting room.

'David and I have been talking about us all going back to Liverpool, Bella,' Lily announced quietly, watching Bella's face for her reaction.

'What do you think, Bella?' David asked. 'Would you be happy to go, or would you prefer to stay here in London? There is no guarantee that they won't bomb Liverpool in the future but—'

'You know that your career and your happiness are very important to us,' Lily interrupted, not wishing to think about Liverpool being bombed. 'And we want the best for you.'

Bella's face lit up with her eager smile, and her eyes danced as they had not done in weeks. 'Oh, Aunt Lily, Uncle David, I would be so happy. I didn't think I would miss everyone so much but it makes me so sad not to see them all, and now poor Joan . . .'

'What about your music, Bella? It's your future, it's so important to you, that's why we came here,' David reminded her.

Bella nodded slowly. 'I know, but we did not expect this

bombing, and if it goes on and on . . . what will there be left? All the theatres, concert halls, music halls, places to make music and sing will have gone! And . . . and we do not know anything about the future. If there will even be a future for us.'

'That's very true, luv. We can't plan a future until this damn war is over and that lunatic Hitler and his armies are defeated – no one can – but you *must* continue your studies, Bella. A talent like yours should never be wasted. It would be criminal! I could continue to coach you,' David offered. 'But I'm not as well qualified or experienced as your coaches at the college.'

'I would like that very much, Uncle David – and do not say such things, you are as good as any of them. And I will work hard, I promise.' She turned to Lily, her dark eyes still sparkling with excitement and relief. 'When can we go, Aunt Lily? Can I write to Stepmama and Joan?'

'Of course you can. But perhaps it would be better to wait until I have told them first, and see if they will be happy to have us back. And there are other things that will have to be sorted out, like giving notice on this place, packing up, finding out about trains – and even the prospect of work for me and Uncle David. We can't live on fresh air, and we won't depend on Olive and Frederick's charity, no matter how hard up we are. But I can't see that finding work will be much of a problem; women will be doing men's jobs now, like they did in the last war.'

'Then I will wait until you have heard from them before I write. But I too will get work when I get back to Liverpool, there must be *something* I can do that will not interfere with my music studies.' She could always go back to sewing, she thought, although she would hate it – but she was sure it would be better than a munitions factory.

Both Lily and David smiled at her, knowing that they had made the right decision. The smile on her young face and the dancing light in her dark eyes told them that. Lily hadn't realised just how much Bella had missed everyone.

'I'll write now,' she said, spurred on by Bella's enthusiasm, and getting to her feet. 'I should be able to catch the late post.'

Chapter Eight

⸻

It had taken far longer than Lily had anticipated to organise their return. For one thing the raids continued without let-up, and the disruption to life and business was causing huge headaches for everyone. And so it was the beginning of October before they finally boarded a crowded train that would take them first to Rugby then north to Crewe, where they would have to change again for Runcorn, and finally to Liverpool. God alone knew how long it would all take, Lily commented acidly, as they managed to find seats.

'But, Aunt Lily, "there's a war on",' Bella laughed, settling happily into her seat and clutching her little cardboard case of treasures tightly on her lap. Amongst the many small keep-sakes – carefully wrapped – and the papers and programmes in the case was the little copper figure of the Barcelos rooster, a symbol of her native Portugal and good fortune that Charlie had made for her when she'd come to London. She wondered how he was getting on. Her stepmama had mentioned in a letter that he was keeping busy with work, night classes and his duties as a messenger boy. As the train slowly began to pull out she wondered if there might be something similar that she could do to help the war effort, for they were the same age. She thought of Monica's sister Eileen – she had her full-time job in the offices of the railway company, which would be considered very important now, she was certain of that. More important than studying music and voice at college.

Oh, how she longed to see them all again. It would be so sad that Jim would not be there, but she would do everything she could to help Joan, who was very dear to her. And it would be good to see Monica and her family again. Monica was always so stylish and glamorous – she doubted that the war had changed that. She envied Monica her fair skin, blue eyes and shining blonde hair. Wouldn't it be great to have Monica cut and style my hair? she thought. She was getting older; she'd be eighteen next birthday and felt she needed to take more time over her appearance. Eileen Savage was the same age as herself and Charlie, and she went to dances and even had a boyfriend, much to her Aunt Lily's disapproval. She wondered what it would be like to go to dances and meet young men?

She wasn't sorry to be leaving London behind; though she was a little concerned that Liverpool might be bombed, too. But at least she would be with her family – and as Aunt Lily had said, it wouldn't be half as bad sitting out an air raid in the shelter in the yard with just family around you and not half the population of Marylebone.

Bella had fallen asleep with her head on Lily's shoulder by the time the train finally pulled into Lime Street Station. Lily and David had both dozed, on and off, since they had left

Crewe, and Lily vowed that it was the last time she was going to travel by train if it was always going to be as slow, uncomfortable and unreliable as this journey had been. She was stiff, cold, hungry and longing for a cup of tea, but there would be no chance of that until they got to Olive's house in Mersey View. And they would have to get a taxi, as the buses and trams would have stopped running hours ago, and they couldn't possibly walk, not with all their luggage. The fare would eat into their small savings.

'Come on, Bella, luv. Wake up now, we've finally arrived,' Lily urged the sleepy girl as David gathered their cases from under the seats and the rack overhead. Their other luggage was in the baggage car and they would need a porter to help them with it – that's if it had been transferred safely, or even at all, David thought grimly, remembering all the changes of train. He was inclined to agree with his wife that it had been something of an epic, not to say challenging, journey.

When they finally arrived in Mersey View they were both relieved but a little startled to see the tiny crack of light that spilled from the edges of Olive's curtains in the front room. There would be hell to pay if the ARP warden saw it, David thought as he paid the cab driver, but to Lily it was a shining beacon of hope and relief – she'd tell any warden just that, if one dared to appear and start huffing and puffing in complaint. She was in no mood for officious little upstarts – which is what many of them were, in her experience.

Bella virtually fell into her stepmother's arms as Olive opened the door and ushered them all inside. 'Oh, I'd almost given up on you! You're so late! What took you so long?' Olive cried, hugging Bella to her and smiling at her sister and brother-in-law.

'Don't we know it? It was a shambles, Olive! A complete and utter shambles!' Lily said, dropping her case on the hall floor and taking off her hat. 'We had to wait for hours at both Rugby and Crewe for the connections, and then we were stuck in some sidings or other for ages and ages. We didn't know where we were, there was no information on *anything*! It was a miracle we got on the right train at Crewe – and that the luggage did, too. Oh, they've done a magnificent job at that station to confuse the enemy, should they ever invade – but at the same time they've managed to confuse the entire travelling public! There were three people we spoke to who were on the wrong train and couldn't get off until Runcorn! Oh, I could murder a cup of tea, Olive!'

Frederick appeared behind Olive, looking relieved, and David shook his hand. 'This is very good of you to take us in – and I'm sorry we've kept you up so late. I couldn't help noticing, by the way, that you've a crack of light showing in the sitting room.'

Frederick nodded. 'Oh dear, I'll see to that. And no need to apologise for being late, come in and take your things off. Olive's got soup and sandwiches and tea ready for you.'

As they followed him into the comfortable but dimly lit room Bella stared around, smiling tiredly. Everything was so familiar and she felt much safer now. 'I am so happy to be here again, Stepmama.'

Olive patted her cheek. 'And we're happy to have you, we've all missed you. I sent Joan to bed hours ago, she gets very tired and she's still trying to get over . . . things.'

Lily nodded her sympathy as she sipped her tea, thinking the finest champagne couldn't have been more welcome or tasted better. 'It must have been a terrible, terrible blow for her, Olive. For you all – I know we were very upset. How is she coping?'

'She's getting better, she has good days and bad days. Monica has helped her a lot, but it took her weeks to even begin to accept the fact that he . . . he isn't coming back. His commanding officer wrote her a beautiful letter, Lily, so sympathetic and really kind. He explained that it was just a stray machine-gun bullet that hit him in the back as he was diving into the dugout. He was killed instantly, he would have felt nothing. They . . . those devils were strafing the runways with their machine guns. A few feet to the right and it would have missed him. It was just a terrible turn of fate, but she can't seem to accept that, and it breaks my heart to see her trying.'

Bella's eyes filled with tears and she reached over and patted Olive's hand. 'I will try to help her, Stepmama. I promise.'

Olive smiled at the girl. She realised Bella had grown and matured in the time she'd been away. 'I know you will, luv, and she'll be so glad to see you. Now, Lily, finish your tea and we'll get your things and Bella's upstairs. I've had to do a bit of swapping around but you're in your old room, and so is Bella.'

'We'll try not to make a noise and disturb either Joan, Charlie or your gentlemen lodgers,' David said, getting to his feet.

'You'd have a hard time disturbing our Charlie, that lad can sleep through almost anything—'

'But not an air raid that goes on all damn night,' Lily put in.

75

'No, and I know you haven't had it easy, Lily, but well, I think you've done the right thing to come home now. We'll all manage – we've had a few light raids but nothing much really, and let's hope it stays that way,' Olive said firmly.

Monica bit her bottom lip to stop herself from screaming, and glared at Stella, her apprentice. This was the fourth time today that she'd had to tell her to sweep up the hair from the floor. The girl was so slow, and virtually useless; Helen Marshall must have had a brainstorm or something when she'd taken her on. And what's more, the girl was left-handed, which, though no fault of Stella's, made teaching her most things – and especially how to create finger waves – more of a challenge. They were always busy, for the small salon had proved very popular, 'a real godsend', so many of her customers swore. It was so successful that Claude had re-employed Madelaine, one of the girls from the now closed Liverpool salon. However, Monica had made up her mind that Stella Wainwright would have to go – and soon. She and Madelaine couldn't carry Stella for much longer. The girl was totally unsuited to the job; she'd be better off in a factory, though she doubted Crawford's would take her on, she was so dilatory. It would be a good foreman indeed who could get a decent day's work out of *that* one.

'Do you think we might be finished a bit earlier tonight?' Madelaine asked, to break the hostile silence, as Stella began to sweep up with very bad grace.

'I hope so, if we can get the salon cleaned up ahead of time.' She looked pointedly at Stella. 'I want to go and see Joan – her Aunty Lil and family were arriving from London last night.

We're all hoping it might help Joan, cheer her up a bit. She was always fond of Lily and Bella. And then I'm going around to see Claude and Nancy, no matter how late it is,' she finished ominously, with another pointed stare at Stella's back.

Madelaine nodded and went to greet her next client, Miss Smythe, the managing director's secretary.

Despite her hopes Monica didn't manage to get away until almost seven o'clock, but she was thankful that today she'd brought the car. She gave Madelaine a lift home and then went on to Mersey View, looking forward to seeing Lily again and wondering if she'd managed to pick up some decent clothes or beauty tips in London – there was virtually nothing in the shops here, and she'd not had a new hat for over a year.

'Oh, Monica, it's so good to see you again!' Lily cried as she hugged the girl.

Lily had spent the morning unpacking and helping Olive, and then almost the whole afternoon sitting with Joan, trying to get her to talk about how she felt, and if she would go back to work after the baby was born, but it had been hard work. She'd been upset at her niece's appearance, but told herself it was only to be expected after what the girl was going through. Joan's dark eyes seemed to have lost their sparkle and there were dark circles beneath them. She looked drawn and she'd lost the vivacity that had always characterised her. Despite her pregnancy, she'd lost weight. David had gone off to see some friends and colleagues, taking a reluctant Bella with him, but she had insisted the girl go – there would be plenty of time for Bella to be with Joan, and her career was important. They'd both returned half an hour ago with good news. David was to resume his position as a voice coach and music tutor at the Philharmonic Hall, as well as also joining the Civil Defence as an Air Raid Protection volunteer – something suggested by Frederick, who himself was an ARP warden. Bella was to resume her studies, but at the Bluecoat School, off Church Street. They had very generously waived her fees in view of the fact that the headmaster was a good friend of David's and had been absolutely stunned by Bella's voice and repertoire. 'So, I will have some time to do something else to help with the war effort, like Charlie is,' Bella had announced.

Lily and Olive had exchanged glances. Lily was aware that her sister was not particularly happy about her son charging around the streets on a bicycle carrying messages in the middle of a raid, although Frederick always backed the lad up when there were 'words' over it.

'Will you stay for your tea, Monica?' Joan asked, smiling rather wanly at her friend.

'No, that wouldn't be fair, Joan, luv. I'm not going to deprive you or anyone else of their rations when I've got my own, but a cup of tea wouldn't go amiss.'

'Won't your mam expect you for tea, Monica?' Lily enquired, knowing from experience that Nelly Savage was a bit on the domineering side, although she doubted that Monica took much notice of that. The girl looked well and was still very stylish, even in the plain pale-lilac cotton overall that she wore under a short black jacket.

'I'll pop in for five minutes before I head off back to Allerton, although I'm not in the mood to listen to Mam and our Eileen rowing over that lad she's taken up with.'

'I thought your mother would have been quite happy with

78

him,' Lily remarked as she set the table. 'He's Royal Navy, isn't he?'

'He is, but his rank isn't what Mam would like. You know her, now I've married "well" in her eyes, she'd prefer it if Harold Stevens was third or even second Officer, and from a naval background, not just a plain common-or-garden able seaman from Birmingham. No, I've had enough "contretemps", as Claude would say, for one day.'

Joan sat down beside her. Monica's visits were always the high point of her day, and only to her friend would she pour out her grief and heartbreak. Monica seemed to understand far better than anyone else, even her Mam. 'What's the matter at work?' she asked.

'Stella Wainwright is what's the matter at work. She's absolutely hopeless, she'll never make a hairdresser in a hundred years! She has to be told to do *everything*! She shows no initiative at all! If I didn't nag the daylights out of her to brush up, we'd be knee deep in hair by lunchtime – and as for shampooing, she drowns everyone! I'm going to see Claude later tonight; she's got to go, and we'll just have to manage until he can find me a girl to at least clean up and shampoo.'

Bella was gazing at Monica intently, her eyes bright with determination. 'Monica, me . . . me! I could do that. I can clean and polish mirrors and bowls, and brush floors, fold towels – and if you show me how, I will shampoo. I . . . I want to help. I want to do something useful.'

'But, Bella, what about your studies? We didn't bring you back to work in a hairdressing salon,' Lily protested, before remembering that it was Monica's chosen profession. 'I mean it's an excellent profession, but your voice, Bella . . .'

'Your Aunt Lily is right, Bella, your studies must come first. But if you could come in, say, after four o'clock each afternoon, and on Saturdays,' Monica suggested. 'That might suit us both, and I think Claude would agree to pay you. No one would want or expect you to become a full-time apprentice, Bella, I just need someone to help out until Claude can find someone more suitable than the disaster we have now!'

Bella looked in some confusion from Monica to Lily, and then at Olive and Joan for their support.

It was Joan who settled the matter. 'She could do that, Aunt Lily, it wouldn't interfere with her studies, and she'd be earning a bit of money of her own. I think she'd get on well with the customers, and we all know she's a hard worker.'

Bella nodded vigorously. 'I am! And I will be doing something for the war effort, too. Uncle David has joined the air-raid wardens, so I can do this! Please, please say yes, Aunt Lily,' she begged. She would work very hard, but it would be such a pleasure to be with Monica – and she would be earning money of her own, too, which would be a real bonus. It wouldn't be much, but she'd never had any money of her own before.

Lily nodded. 'All right, Bella, just as long as you don't go getting any ideas about abandoning your music.'

Bella hugged her tightly. 'Oh, thank you, Aunt Lily! I won't let my studies suffer, I promise.'

Chapter Nine

Bella settled down very well in the salon, and with her attractive dark looks and slightly exotic foreign manner of speaking, she was a favourite with the customers. She worked hard and Monica was beginning to realise that, if she had been allowed to, Bella would have made a good hairdresser, as well as having the voice of an angel and being a talented seamstress and embroiderer. There seemed no end to the girl's talents. She said as much to her mother, one evening, as she sat helping Nelly to unpick a jumper. The wool would be used to make another garment – possibly a blanket for Joan's baby, or so Nelly had hinted.

'Well, I suppose that's a blessing for both Lily and Olive. God knows, Olive's got enough on her plate to worry about these days, what with Joan and their Charlie.'

'Joan's much better now, Mam, she can speak about Jim without bursting into tears.'

Nelly nodded her approval – it would all take time, but at least it sounded as if Joan was beginning to accept the reality of Jim's death. But then Joan was strong, like her mother and she supposed like herself. She frowned as she unpicked a knot where the yarn had been joined. Heaven knows, everyone has to find the strength from somewhere these days, she thought. But she reminded herself that, compared to London, Liverpool had come off lightly so far from the bombing raids, and she was thankful that Lily had brought her family home.

'So, what's wrong with Charlie Copperfield that's causing his mam to worry – apart from the war, that is?' Monica asked.

'Oh, Olive was telling me he's changed lately, he seems to be . . . unsettled with everything and everyone.'

Monica nodded her agreement; she'd noticed that, too. 'I suppose he's just growing up, Mam, as are Bella and our Eileen.'

'Don't get me started on *that* one and her antics! Not yet eighteen and talking about getting engaged. I ask you? She's only known him a few months. We don't know much about him or his family. Oh, they make a right pair do our Eileen and Charlie Copperfield – headstrong and spoilt, the pair of them!'

Monica grinned at her mother. 'Oh, I wouldn't say "spoilt", Mam. Neither you nor Olive have ever had the means to spoil them, but I'll go along with headstrong.'

A week later, Charlie burst into Olive's kitchen, his cheeks flushed from the cold wind, his eyes bright with both excitement and fear.

Olive hastily put the pan she'd been holding back on the stove. 'Charlie, what's the matter? Where's Frederick?'

Charlie clutched the back of a chair to regain his breath.

'He sent me on ahead! We've all got to get out, Mam, get to the shelter as quickly as possible . . .' he gasped.

Olive was confused. 'Why? There've been no air-raid warnings since yesterday?'

'The sirens will kick off any minute now, Mam, Frederick's seen them . . . Dorniers, hundreds of them over the river, and all heading for the docks and the dock estate. And us! Quick . . .' The rest of his words were drowned out by the rising wail of the siren, a sound they were all getting more used to these days.

With an effort Joan dragged herself out of her chair. Charlie disappeared to get the two elderly gentlemen from the dining room, where they were waiting for the evening meal, and shepherded them to the shelter in the yard.

'Joan, don't you be exerting yourself, luv. Almost everything we'll need is already in the shelter, I checked this afternoon. There's just the Thermos flasks to fill, I'll do that now. And I've made sandwiches – they're in those tins, you take them – and that's another meal ruined!' she finished acidly, glancing down at the pan on the stove. 'Why can't they damn well wait until we've had our supper? You have to queue for hours, and then *they* arrive and bloody well ruin good food. That bit of meat will only be fit for the bin by the time we get back in.'

Lily and Bella appeared, Lily with an armful of blankets and Bella with her little case of treasures. 'Joan, you go first, but don't rush, there's no panic – yet!' Lily shouted over the noise of the siren.

Already the sound of the artillery batteries in Birkenhead opening up could be heard faintly. Joan nodded as she collected up the tins containing the sandwiches. David had already rushed out to join his fellow wardens, and Olive knew that as soon as he got home Frederick would be out again, too. They should both be sitting down at the table to a decent meal after working all day, but there was no chance of that tonight.

When Bella was settled, and Lily and Olive had made Joan as comfortable as they could, Olive turned her attention to Mr Whitworth and Mr Compton, both of whom had been pronounced medically unfit for war work of any kind but who tried to keep everyone's spirits up at times like this.

'Here you are, I'm sorry there's no hot meal, but, well . . .' She apologised as she handed them mugs of tea and offered them the sandwich box.

'Thank you, Mrs Garswood, we know you're doing your best, and we both appreciate it, don't we, Albert? We'd get nothing in a public shelter, not even water, and you've made this place as comfortable as possible in the circumstances,' Henry Compton reassured her, smiling politely.

'At least it's hot,' Lily added as she sipped her drink. 'It's getting chillier now, and the cold seems to penetrate these shelters no matter how many coats and blankets we have.'

Being half underground, and the roof covered with packed soil to minimise the impact of any blast, the shelter was dark and damp. At first they had tried to heat the place with a tilley lamp, but the smell of its paraffin fuel in such a small confined space was so bad they'd given it up as a bad job. In any case, Olive had always been afraid a strong blast might overturn it, the results of which didn't bear thinking about. She was always concerned about the candles, even though they were all firmly wedged in brass or iron candlesticks and not just stuck on saucers.

Half an hour later, as Olive and Lily were growing increasingly sick of the cold, and Joan and Bella were trying to ignore the sounds of the inferno that raged above them by playing 'I Spy' with grim determination, Frederick appeared. His face was black with soot, mixed with rivulets of sweat trickling down his cheeks.

'Just called in to see everyone is all right. Any chance of a quick cup of tea, Olive? It's bad out there, and no one knows when it will be over.'

Lily stared at him, her forehead creased in a frown. 'Why didn't David come with you, he is all right? He's had nothing to eat or drink since mid-afternoon.'

'He's fine, Lil–'

'Is it the docks?' Olive asked, before Frederick could finish.

Then they all fell silent as, for a few terrible seconds, the whole shelter shook. They realised with a shock that at least one building in the street had been hit.

'That was close!' Lily cried as they all looked at each other with undisguised fear in their eyes.

'Lord, I hope it wasn't Nelly's house,' Olive said, biting her lip. Like many other people Nelly flatly refused to suffer the discomforts and humiliations of the public shelter, so she and Eileen – and Monica if she were there – sat under the stairs with cushions and blankets, hoping that the table Arthur had pulled across would take the force of any blast. Arthur himself would be out with the other wardens, or up at the railway yards and tunnels at Edge Hill. Olive felt terrible that there wasn't enough room in her shelter to accommodate her friend and her daughters, but they simply wouldn't fit, not even if they all squeezed in like sardines. It had been a push to find room for Lily and Bella. This didn't make Olive feel any better about the situation, though.

'Yes, let's hope it wasn't, but Paradise Street, Hanover Street, the Langton and Alexandra Docks have been badly hit so far,' Frederick replied, quickly finishing his tea and handing the mug back to Olive.

'Have you seen Charlie?' Olive asked, clutching his arm as he turned to leave.

After seeing the two gentlemen lodgers to the shelter, her son had taken his bicycle from the shed and gone out into the night.

Frederick shook his head. 'No, but he'll be all right, Olive, don't worry,' he tried to reassure her.

'If you see him, tell him to get home here now! He's done enough for one night, and I didn't go through all the tears and tribulations of bringing him up only to have him go breaking his neck by falling into a bomb crater! I'm worried sick about him.'

'I'll do that, Olive, if I see him. But he's seventeen, and he's needed out there,' Frederick reminded her as he quickly kissed her cheek.

Olive stared at his disappearing back and knew what he said was true, but it didn't help to have to sit here and just . . . wait, while her husband and son were out there and having to face God knows what. Her main fear was indeed that Charlie, who tended to be reckless on that bike, would drop into a bomb crater in his haste. The Lord alone knew that fire engines, police cars and ambulances had suffered the same fate, killing and injuring their crews.

She sat down beside Lily and picked up the magazine she'd been trying to read. But she only had the weak light that came from the candles to see by, and she was constantly being distracted by the worry and uncertainty and fear.

'Olive, you've read that article three times already,' Lily commented. 'What's so fascinating about trying to make a new hat from felt squares? You wouldn't be seen dead in anything you could make with *that* stuff. I know I wouldn't.'

'No, Aunt Lily, you are too stylish,' Bella put in, smiling at Lily. 'And Joan and me, we are so sick of this game.'

'We've run out of things to "spy" in here. My back is aching and I'm cold,' Joan complained. The baby kicked a lot these days, and it always seemed worse when she had to sit in a cramped position. She was longing for it to be born – and not just to be rid of all the discomforts – but she had two months to go yet.

Mr Whitworth took the blanket from around his shoulders. 'Joan, here, take this; we can't have you shivering with cold.'

Joan smiled at him and shook her head; it wasn't cold she was shivering with, but fear. 'No, really, I'm fine, thanks. I'll try walking around for a bit. That might help my back.'

'How can you do that? There's no room to swing a cat in here!' Lily protested but was cut short by a loud hammering on the door, prompting Olive to get up and open it. 'Charlie! Thank God! Get in here!' she urged her son, half pulling him down the steps that led into the shelter.

'Mam! I didn't want to come, but Frederick said I had to! I'm needed! I'm really needed, you don't know what it's like out there, and there's no sign of them going home, although we heard one or two have been shot down over the sea by our Hurricanes. I'm not a little kid who has to go home to his mam in case he gets hurt! I felt terrible; you've made a complete show of me in front of my mates, Mam!'

It had all come rushing out, and Olive was quite taken aback by his vehemence. 'Charlie, I . . . I was only thinking of your safety.'

'Of course you were, Olive. Charlie, sit down beside Bella and calm down, we're all nervous wrecks,' Lily said, attempting to smooth ruffled feathers. She could see her sister's point – but she could see her nephew's, too.

With very bad grace Charlie sat down on the bunk beside Bella, muttering to himself.

'Charlie, I understand why you'd not want to come here and sit with us, doing nothing, when you could help,' Bella whispered to him – she could see he was really angry, and it upset her.

'No, you don't, Bella,' was the sullen reply.

Bella tried again. 'Stepmama, she worries so much about you, about us all . . . It is hard for her, and she does not mean to upset you or make you angry.'

'I know, but I'm not a kid any more, Bella, and she doesn't seem to realise that!' Charlie paused. 'I don't care! It's not for much longer.'

Bella stared hard at him, beginning to feel anxious. 'Charlie, what do you mean by that? Why do you say "not for much longer"?'

He leaned closer to her. There was sufficient noise going on above so he didn't need to whisper. 'Can you keep a secret?'

She was instantly suspicious. 'What secret, Charlie? Will it upset . . . people?'

'I suppose it will – at first – but they'll just have to get used to it. I'll have to go one day.'

Bella's dark eyes widened. 'Go? Go where, Charlie? What have you done? Tell me, you *must!*'

'Only if you promise not to say anything to *anyone* yet?'

Bella felt cold fingers of fear creeping around her heart. For most of her life she had looked on Charlie as a brother. He *was* her half-brother, they were the same age, and they had grown up together and been close before she'd gone to London. She nodded slowly, glancing at Olive who was thankfully engrossed in conversation with Aunt Lily and Joan. The two gentlemen lodgers were playing cards. 'I promise,' she said.

'I've joined the Merchant Navy, Bella. I'll be going at the end of the month.'

Bella was horrified. 'Charlie! Charlie, you . . . *can't!*' she hissed furiously. 'They won't take you, you are too young! Oh, Charlie, why?' she pleaded.

Charlie glanced hastily around but was relieved to see that no one had noticed her expression. He took her hand and squeezed it, to remind her to keep her feelings hidden. 'Hush! They will take me – they already have. You can join as a junior deck apprentice at fifteen. I'm seventeen, and I've got some training at a trade, plus I go to the Mechanics, so I'm going as a second-year apprentice deck officer with British Petroleum. They need everyone they can get if they're to have enough crew to man the ships transporting oil and food supplies to where they're needed. I'll be keeping the shipments safe from enemy fire while they're being moved by BP. I'll be doing work that really helps, Bella.'

Tears started in Bella's eyes. 'Oh, Charlie! Why? You can be of help here.'

He shook his head. 'Doing what, Bella? Oh, at first I thought I was being useful, "doing my bit", but just riding around carrying messages isn't enough.' He pointed upwards. 'Out there when a raid is on, I realised I could do more. I need to do more and I want to do more, Bella! I don't think many people realise that we are fighting not just for our freedom but for our very lives, Bella, and when I see the bombs falling and buildings being blown to smithereens, fires raging and people losing their homes, being badly hurt – or worse, killed – it makes me so *mad*! I need to do something to fight back, can you understand that, Bella?'

She hadn't realised, she thought sadly. She hadn't realised how deeply he felt about this terrible war and the sights he saw whenever there was a raid. Slowly she nodded. 'I . . . I can try, Charlie.'

'I know everyone will be upset, and I suppose Mam will be furious with me, but she's just going to have to realise that I've grown up, Bella, and the world is changing.'

Bella managed a smile. 'I will keep your secret, Charlie, but I wish you were not going so soon.' She reached down and rummaged under the bunk, pulling her little case out.

'What's that?' Charlie asked, diverted for a moment at the sight of the case.

'I keep things in here – special things,' she replied, drawing out a tiny bundle wrapped in a piece of red cloth, which she handed to him.

'What is it?'

She smiled shyly. 'I keep it because it is special to me. But now, I want you to have it. It will protect you – like a lucky charm. It has been lucky for me, so I know.'

Charlie unwrapped it and then a smile spread over his face. It was the little brass Barcelos rooster that he'd made for her before she'd gone to London. 'You're right, Bella. It will be lucky for me, too.'

They sat in silence, each with their own thoughts. Bella dwelling on Charlie's safety, and Charlie on what kind of reaction he was going to get from his mother at this news – and what he would have to face as a merchant seaman at this time of great danger.

At last, to everyone's relief, they heard the 'All Clear'. Easing their cramped limbs, they began slowly to gather up their belongings.

Chapter Ten

C harlie was right to be apprehensive about Olive's reaction when he broke the news to her and his stepfather after the heavy raids of the nights of 13th and 14th October. He had been out with Frederick and David throughout the hours when the bombs had fallen, and mayhem and destruction had rained down, but in deference to Olive's feelings he'd gone home an hour before the last of the Dorniers turned its nose towards the Mersey estuary and the sea beyond.

All three of them were now exhausted, dirty and hungry, but Charlie knew he had to break the news because he was going in less than a month's time.

'I've got something to tell you all before we go to bed,' he started tentatively.

'You certainly pick your moments, Charlie, I'll say that,' Frederick stated as he slumped in an armchair. 'Well, make it quick,' he urged. 'We're all exhausted, and we won't get much sleep before it's time to get up for work.'

David nodded in weary agreement.

'What's the matter, Charlie?' Lily asked, noticing that Bella was biting her lip and looking anxious.

He took a deep breath. 'I know you won't be very pleased with me but . . . I've joined the Merchant Navy, as a junior apprentice deck officer with British Petroleum. I'm joining my ship, the *British Courage*, later this month. She's being fitted out and we sail as soon as she's ready – for Canada, I think, but no one will say very much about it.'

There was complete silence, which was not what Charlie or Bella had expected, and they glanced at each other in trepidation.

Olive sat down suddenly, still clutching a tea towel and a mug, the colour drained from her face.

It was Frederick who spoke first. 'I suppose it had to come, Charlie. You've not been happy just being a messenger lately, have you?'

'No.' Charlie ran his hands through his hair, a habit he had when he was anxious. 'Don't you see that I *have* to do something more? I'm not old enough yet to join up. They're much stricter about age than they were in the last war.'

Olive found her voice. 'And thank God for that! You might think you're grown up, but you're still only a lad. You're still too young to go! You have no idea what you're going to have to face. Oh, Charlie, you fool! Why couldn't you have waited? Don't you realise that you've just signed on for one of the most dangerous of all wartime occupations? You know those convoys are constantly attacked transporting oil back home? You'll have a target on your back every day you're at sea!'

Lily could see that her nephew was about to launch into a defence of his actions, so she put her hand on Olive's shoulder and turned to Bella. 'You knew, didn't you, Bella? He told you, I can see he did by your face.'

Tears welled up in Bella's eyes. 'Yes, I knew, but I promised not to say. I promised, Aunt Lily. I couldn't break a promise! And not to Charlie, he's my brother!'

'It doesn't matter now, Bella. They can't do anything to stop me, I've signed on and they've accepted me. I'm going and that's that!' Charlie stated determinedly.

Frederick got to his feet and went and put his arm around his wife's shoulders. She was near to tears, as well as Bella. Joan sat white-faced and obviously upset, staring from her mother to her brother. She'd lost her husband – was she going to lose her brother, too? she thought, with a sense of rising panic.

'I just wish that you'd confided in me, Charlie, we could have talked it over,' Frederick said quietly, certain he could have talked the lad out of it. 'But before anything more is said, did you honestly not consider how much your mam will worry? She . . . we . . . all know how many ships have already been lost and men drowned on the convoys—'

'And you go and join a company that ships petrol and oil, for God's sake!' Olive was so distraught that she didn't stop to think about her words. 'How many of their ships have already been blown sky high? They don't just sink, Charlie, they . . . they . . . explode, taking everyone.' She burst into tears, unable to think of such a terrible fate happening to her only son. The lad she'd struggled to rear by herself after his father had deserted them. The lad she loved even more than Joan, although she would never admit it to anyone. Joan was strong, sensible and practical – Charlie was not. He'd never got over

Billy letting him down so badly, even though he now respected and was fond of Frederick, his stepfather. But Charlie had been damaged forever when Billy just up and left – and at a time when her boy had needed him most.

Joan found her voice, even though it shook slightly. 'Oh, honestly, Charlie, trust you to do something as stupid as that! Why couldn't you have joined a company that doesn't carry such dangerous stuff? Grain, or steel, or coal and other war materials? Now we're all going to be out of our minds with worry, and it's not as if Mam hasn't got enough to worry about already. We all have!'

Lily nodded her agreement. David had said nothing so far, and she knew he was thinking it was not his place to do so, as he was only Olive's brother-in-law. But she was going to have her say, for her poor sister was too upset to do more than sob into the tea towel. 'You could have waited, Charlie. You'll be eighteen after Christmas, and that's not too far in the future. You could have joined any of the forces then, and been properly trained before being sent into action. But no, you go and do something stupid like signing on to sail on a floating bomb! I agree entirely with Joan, and I don't think you gave a single thought to how your poor mother would feel. You're a fool to think you'll make a difference by getting yourself blown up. Well, just don't expect anyone to be waving you off with hugs and kisses.' She turned to Bella. 'And as for you, miss, I'm very disappointed in you. You should have told someone – if you had, we might have been able to do something about it.'

Bella nodded as the tears trickled down her cheeks, but she truly didn't believe that anything could have been done. She was terrified for Charlie's safety, after hearing Olive's words

95

about the tankers. They were always the prime target for the U-boats in every convoy, and now Charlie was going to criss-cross the Atlantic Ocean, risking his young life each time. The reality of what he'd be doing hadn't really sunk in when he'd first told her he'd signed on with BP. But now she, too, was wishing that he'd waited, or signed on with another shipping company, but it was too late.

It was with very heavy hearts that they all went to their beds for what was left of the night.

Daylight revealed that it had been the corner shop run by Ethel Newbridge that had received a direct hit; it was nothing more than a heap of smouldering rubble now, but thankfully Ethel and her family had been in the shelter. It had been Nelly's husband, Arthur, and Lily's husband, David, who had broken the news to Ethel after the 'All Clear' had sounded.

'She was upset but mostly angry at losing her livelihood, her home and most of her stock,' David told Lily.

'She's like all the women around here, David,' Lily replied. 'Resilient and tough, as they've had to be all their lives, so I shouldn't wonder if Ethel's business will be up and running in some form very soon. What about the rest of the damage? Was it extensive?'

'North Hornby and Gladstone Docks, a block of tenements in Myrtle Gardens – that was bad, eleven dead, nine badly injured. Two surface shelters in Louisa Street, Mere Lane . . . I could go on all morning, Lily.'

'Don't! And don't tell our Olive about the shelters in Louisa Street, or she'll get more upset than she already is and insist we follow Nelly Savage's example and sit under the stairs, which in my opinion is just plain daft. What kind of protection is that? I wonder their Monica hasn't said something to her; she's got sense has that girl. I believe these salons Claude is opening in the factories are doing very well.' She sighed, thinking she was indeed fortunate that she was back at the Empire Theatre and could manage her own hair very well – except for cutting and bleaching, which Monica took care of. Of course, the raids had seriously disrupted performances at the theatre, but they were managing – with Ben Stoker, the manager, reviewing things daily. He'd confided to her that he hoped they would be open for business as usual at Christmas, because if it was one thing the people of Liverpool needed this Christmas it was some light entertainment. She'd agreed wholeheartedly and was planning to persuade the whole family – Olive's gentlemen lodgers included – to attend one performance at least. Hopefully, Joan would have had her baby by then, and she was certain that Nelly wouldn't object to babysitting for a few hours one night.

She mentioned it casually when Monica visited next, but the girl wasn't very helpful.

'Mam's not fond of babies, Lily. I know that for a fact. She always says she had enough with me and our Eileen. They disrupt her routine – not that she has much of one, these days, what with the raids and the queues and the like,' she replied.

Lily let the subject drop. But the talk of raids and routines niggled at a problem Lily had been trying to ignore due to the simple fact she didn't know how to solve it. Bella was singing less and less – what with working at the salon with Monica and having nowhere to perform – and the way the war was going, who knew how long it would be before she'd have the

97

opportunity to be onstage and gain the experience she needed? She exercised her voice whenever she could, but it wasn't enough. Her career could disappear before it had even begun if they stayed put in Liverpool. But where else could they go? Lily pushed the thought to the back of her mind, where it would have to stay until a suitable idea presented itself to her.

All too soon, October was drawing to a close and it was time for Charlie to go. He was due to join his ship on Friday. Frederick hadn't wanted Olive to go to the docks to see him off. But despite her fears and anxiety, she was insisting.

She had also insisted on going with her son to Greenburgh's, the naval outfitters at the bottom of Park Lane, and Joan had decided to go, too.

'I'm perfectly able to get on and off a tram, Mam,' she'd said when Olive protested, 'and it's not all that far to walk from the stop – I know, because Monica's driven past it a couple of times.'

Olive, though, was having none of it. 'That's as may be, Joan, but after all these raids who knows what obstacles and diversions we'll encounter? The roads are a mess, you know that, and all the tram and bus routes have been affected. Now, I'm having no more arguments from you. You've not much longer to go now, and we don't want anything happening.'

Joan had given up; she felt her mam needed some moral support, but she didn't want to start a major argument.

By Thursday evening after supper was over, Charlie had packed his sea bag and hung his uniform on the back of his bedroom door. His nervousness had grown with each passing day, but he told himself that he was doing the right thing. Jim

McDonald and Rick Eustace hadn't seemed at all nervous when they'd joined up and had gone off to start their training. Rick was somewhere in the south of England, learning to drive a tank, and Jim . . . well, Jim hadn't shown any fear, and to Charlie he would always be a hero. It was one of the reasons why he'd joined up. He ran his hand down the sleeve of the black doeskin jacket with its brass buttons and single gold and maroon stripe that denoted his lowly rank. In a way, he was glad that Frederick and his mam would accompany him at least as far as the dock gate. He wouldn't be going off alone. He turned at a quiet knock on the door.

It was Bella. 'They won't let me come with you tomorrow, Charlie. Aunt Lily says we must carry on with our work as normal, to show we are not afraid of *them* and their bombs, so I have come now to say goodbye.'

He smiled down at her. She'd grown into a very pretty girl, although she seemed totally unaware of the fact. To listen to her sing, as she sometimes did in the house, was better than going to any theatre, and he was very proud of her. Now he was older, he understood better just how brave she had been when, after her mother had died, at the age of twelve she'd made the long and hazardous journey from Lisbon to Liverpool, all alone, to find her father, with very little money and just a scrap of paper with the address in Mersey View.

'Thanks, Bella. I'll miss you, I'll miss everyone.'

She nodded. 'This is your uniform? You will look very smart, Charlie.'

He grinned. 'It's only for "best" really. I'll have work to do, so I've got boiler suits for that. Not nearly as smart.'

A frown creased her forehead. 'You will be careful, Charlie?

It is true what Aunt Lily says about Stepmama worrying, and it is a very dangerous place to be on a ship carrying oil.'

'I'll take care, Bella. I know the risks, but we need that oil so badly.'

'I know, Charlie. You have packed the little rooster?'

'Of course I have, and I promise I'll have it in my pocket day and night.'

She smiled. 'Good. So I go now and let you get some sleep, it is good that there has been no raid tonight. Take care and good luck, Charlie. I will pray for you, but I know the Barcelos will keep you safe.'

He found it hard to get to sleep, filled as he was with conflicting emotions, but he did at last, clutching the little brass figure he'd made for her and wondering what kind of a bed he would be sleeping in tomorrow night.

Next morning, Olive could barely keep back the tears as she kissed Charlie on the cheek and hugged him tightly, before he left her and Frederick and walked through the dock gate to where the grey-painted hull of the tanker was visible.

It didn't look big enough to brave both the ferocity of the North Atlantic at this time of year or the U-boats, Frederick thought, as both he and Olive watched the lad present his credentials to the policeman on the dock gate and turn to wave a final goodbye.

'Oh, Frederick, he's so young, despite looking so smart and grown-up in that uniform . . .' Olive dabbed at her eyes with her handkerchief.

'I know, luv, but he'll be fine, and he *is* grown-up now. We're both proud of him.' He paused as they both watched the lad disappear into the entrance to a dockside warehouse.

'Do you think, Olive, that . . . well, that his father would have been proud, too?'

Olive looked up at him; she'd been thinking that herself but had pushed it from her mind, not wanting to remember Billy Copperfield. 'All he should feel is guilt. I don't think he even remembers that he's got a son, never mind one old enough and brave enough to do what our Charlie's doing. I don't even know if Billy is alive or dead, Frederick, and I just don't care. Charlie is ten times the man his da was, and always will be.'

Frederick bent and kissed her cheek. 'He is, Olive, and we've every right to be proud of him. Come on, luv, let's go home,' he urged.

Chapter Eleven

C harlie hung over the ship's rail, watching the heaving grey-green water and wishing he were dead. Oh, it hadn't been so bad at first, while they were still in dock; in fact, it had been exciting. Everything had been so new, and he'd been kept very busy working out his way around the ship, finding his allotted muster station in case of emergencies, as well as his 'watch' station, then meeting the members of the crew that he'd be working alongside daily. As they'd left Liverpool on that cold, dismal late October afternoon he'd stood on deck as they sailed out towards the Mersey Bar lightship and marvelled as the captain, officers and engineers had manoeuvred the massive tanker into its place in the wedge-shaped convoy. He'd never been on a ship as big as this before, he'd only ever been on the Mersey ferries, and he'd stood watching and feeling proud of his city as the familiar skyline faded in the distance and dusk fell rapidly over the waterfront.

When they'd left the Mersey they had been joined by the warships that would sail with them across the ocean to Canada and hopefully protect them. Then he'd begun to feel apprehensive as he realised how very different and dangerous his life was about to become. But his newfound mate, Will Taylor – like him an apprentice deck officer but, at twenty, with three years' experience under his belt – had told him that the whole situation was getting better. The planes of RAF Coastal Command could venture further now, so they often met the convoy on its way back in mid-Atlantic, to see off the Nazi subs. And the Royal Naval U-boats and frigates – or 'hunter killers', as they were coming to be known – were taking their toll on the enemy submarines. That had boosted Charlie's spirits no end, until they'd left the comparative shelter of Liverpool Bay and sailed out into the Irish Sea, when it got far rougher and the tanker wallowed in the heavy swells. The night of the second day, when they'd passed the Fastnet Rock off the south coast of Ireland and sailed into the Atlantic Ocean, it had got worse. He'd literally fallen into his bunk, thankful to lie down at last, and hadn't wanted to get up for his watch. It had been Will Taylor who had dragged him out and made him come up on deck, but he had needed to summon every ounce of willpower he could to stay upright, scanning the grey murk that surrounded them through his binoculars, when he wasn't hanging over the side being horribly sick, as he was now.

Earlier, Will Taylor had brought him a mug of tea that was still fairly hot and told him to drink it, he'd feel better, and had then laughed sympathetically, saying he'd get over it in three days. And, ill or not, everyone had to pull their weight. Charlie had tried to sip the tea but had groaned as he felt the bile rise in his throat, thrusting the mug back into Will's hands as he'd rushed to the rail again. Will said no matter how terrible you felt no one ever died from seasickness, and it was a well-known fact that even the great Admiral Lord Horatio Nelson was sick every time he went to sea, so there was nothing to be ashamed of. Charlie didn't believe him, he'd never felt so bad in his entire life!

The convoy moved slowly, sailing at the speed of knots dictated by the slowest ship; at this rate, Charlie was certain it would be weeks before they got to the coast of Nova Scotia. The way he was feeling, he was certain he'd be dead by then! At this precise moment he couldn't have cared less if they were completely surrounded by German U-boats, all he wanted to do was lie down and die. All the family were right, he thought. He should have waited to be called up, instead of rushing off like a fool to this vision of hell! He felt in his pocket for something to wipe his mouth, and his fingers closed over the cold brass figurine of the little rooster. He gripped it tightly; Bella couldn't have envisaged how bad he'd feel when she'd given him this, and he wondered how long it would be until he saw her and his family again – if ever.

The morning after, he woke with a clear head, the sickness had gone, and he found he was starving hungry. He smiled to himself with relief. He'd slept heavily and he'd survived! He realised as he washed and dressed in the cramped space that they still had at least another five days ahead of them before they reached the coast of Canada, and he was looking forward to that. Then, of course, there was the prospect of the far more dangerous return journey, when their hold would be full of the precious fuel. But he'd face that when the time came – Will Taylor had done the return crossing often, and so far he'd beaten the odds. He was just grateful that the seasickness had passed, and now his next job was to find the mess and get some breakfast. He grinned as he pulled on his jacket and felt the small lump of brass in a side pocket.

Maybe Bella was right. It would protect him.

At seven o'clock on a cold November evening, Monica was getting ready to leave home and walk to the ambulance station. She hoped she wouldn't be needed tonight, as it terrified her, driving through streets where buildings were on fire and collapsing, while the planes buzzed overhead like swarms of angry, deadly bees. Thankfully, most of the time the blazing buildings did give enough light for her to be able to see, and avoid obstacles and craters as she ferried patients to hospital. At first, she'd found it quite hard work to drive the ambulance – her little sports car was very light by comparison – but she'd grown used to it.

Neither Nelly nor Nancy, her mother-in-law, were happy about her working for the war effort, but there was little they could do about it. It was strange, she thought, while she was actually driving she wasn't frightened – it was only when the emergency was over that it hit her. She hoped that tonight, if there was no raid – and they were spasmodic – she might be able to get away and visit Joan. Her friend only had a matter of weeks now until her baby was due, and she was feeling very tired and fed up. Joan, like everyone else, was worried about Charlie. There had been no news and, of course, he was not allowed to write until they got to their destination, and then it would take forever for letters to get back.

She closed the door behind her and walked down the path,

glancing back to make sure she'd left no lights showing, then frowned as she hunched her shoulders against the cold wind. Charlie hadn't picked the best time to go to sea, she mused, not with winter coming on, when the Atlantic could be wild and dangerous, and it would all add to Joan's worries. Rick wrote as often as he could, but that was never enough for her. She was hoping that when he'd finished his course he'd get some leave; she hadn't seen him for so long, and letters just weren't the same, particularly as they were now being heavily censored. She brightened up; maybe he'd get home for Christmas. That would be wonderful, and it was only about five weeks away now. But would that upset Joan still further? she pondered. Joan already missed Jim terribly – and to see her with Rick, and especially at the festive season, well . . .

'On your way to the station, Mrs Eustace?'

The warden's voice pulled her from her reverie and she smiled at the man. He lived a few doors down from her but wasn't nearly as full of himself and his own importance as some of them were – that Mr Harris, in particular.

'Yes, Mr Simpkins, but I hope we'll have an easy time tonight.'

He shook his head and lowered his voice. 'I wouldn't bank on it; we've already been notified that a purple warning has been flashed to the batteries in Calderstones Park. Looks like they're on their way across again! Did you have any plans?'

'Not really, I was just hoping to go to see my friend. She's expecting very soon and is a bit fed up, to say the least, and she's a widow. Her husband was killed, he was in the RAF.'

'That's tough. She can't be very old to be a widow, but it's hard on everyone. Where does she live, Mrs Eustace?'

'Oh, Everton. Mersey View at the top of Northumberland Terrace, just a few doors down from my mam and dad actually.'

'Well, let's hope they'll all be fine. If I get the chance, I'll drop in and let you know if I hear any news. But if that warning is right, I expect we'll be run off our feet, too,' he concluded, touching the brim of his tin hat before he turned away.

At half past seven the sirens started to wail all over the city and its precincts. So, the warning was right, Monica thought, with rising fear. She grabbed her tin hat and her bag and climbed into her ambulance. The team of medics she usually worked with were already on board; they greeted her with strained smiles as they anticipated how terrible the night ahead of them might be. Monica began to check that everything was in order when there was a terrific explosion that shook the whole building and caused plaster to drop from the ceiling. Her heart began to race with fright as she realised that the blast must have been unusually close. This part of the city had not been targeted so far, and she prayed that her home hadn't been damaged – it didn't bode well for the hours that lay ahead of her. Maybe it was just a stray bomb, maybe the pilot had got lost, as they were miles away from the docks here in Allerton – although they did have the gas works in Spofforth Road, and really the docks at Garston were not *that* far away. She pushed those thoughts from her mind as Mr Hargreaves, the station commander, poked his head in and handed her a list.

'There are casualties already, Mr Hargreaves?' asked Burt Eaton, leaning forward to peer at the list. Burt was one of Monica's crew of medics and a man she respected enormously for the comfort and care he delivered every night she worked with him.

'Afraid so – it's shaping up to be a very heavy raid. There's hundreds of them all flying upriver and dropping their loads everywhere across the city. They've got some new type of bomb now, a "parachute mine" it's called. Drops down on a parachute, so that's why we didn't get any warning noises. Damn them to hell! As if incendiaries and high explosives aren't enough for us to cope with – and they've got plenty of those, too!'

'That's all we need. So, where are we heading, Mr Hargreaves?' asked John. He was another medic who, like Burt, was always ready to help in any way he could.

'It's houses in Durning Road that have been hit – the brigade is on its way, and wardens are already there.' Mr Hargreaves turned to Monica. 'Head off down there, and then on to Broadgreen Hospital. And for God's sake take care, girl.'

She nodded as she turned the key in the ignition, wondering how long this raid would go on for. She doubted she'd get to see Joan tonight. As she drove through the streets, heading for Durning Road, she could see these new bombs in the skies above her. As Mr Hargreaves had said, they were floating down on parachutes, their silence making them appear even more sinister, until they hit their target and then exploded like every other bomb. The sky was now bright as the fires raged, and as she drove between them she got the occasional glimpse of wardens and police clambering through the flames and wreckage to help people who hadn't left their homes in time. It was terrifying and she tried not to think about the carnage the bombs were causing, nor the broken, bleeding bodies and the serious casualties that awaited their arrival – beside her, the crew of trained medics were as grim-faced and tense as she was.

She swerved to avoid a blazing van that had been blown on to its side, shouting for her crew to 'hang on', when she saw a figure running towards them, waving his arms. She slammed her foot down on the brake as she recognised Mr Simpkins.

'Oh, Mrs Eustace, I was hoping it was you. Quickly, there's a woman and her three kids, all injured as far as I can see, and we think there are other casualties. They'd not gone to the shelter, they were under the stairs. It's Holland Street, next left – but take care, as houses are still collapsing.'

She nodded as a thought came into her mind and filled her with terror. They'd been under the stairs! Oh, God! Her mam and sister would be sheltering under the stairs! How many times had she told Nelly it was madness to hope that a staircase would protect them? A million times at least, but she wouldn't listen. Her father, along with all the men in the street, would be out in this inferno, heedless of their own safety. 'Mr Simpkins, do you know if Everton is being as badly hit as us?'

He wiped the sweat and dirt from his face and nodded. 'Afraid so, there's hardly a district that's escaped so far, and we've hours to go yet, Mrs Eustace. Sorry, but for the love of God, get down to Holland Street. Those kids are in a bad way. Here, take the list.'

As she drove off, concentrating on finding Holland Street, she could feel panic rising in her. She was virtually oblivious to the noise and the fires and the heat and the smells of broken drains and gas pipes that surrounded her. After she'd got this lot to hospital, she was going to drive to Everton. She didn't care that she would be needed for more casualties here in Allerton, she had to get to her family, to her mam. She had to make sure they were safe. And if they were, she didn't care how much her mam might protest, she was going to drive them to the nearest air-raid shelter, for this could go on for hours yet, and at least she was used to driving through this mayhem now.

By the time they finally reached the hospital, one of the children had died and the poor mother was unconscious. Monica felt anger and frustration bubble up as she watched the nurses and porters get the pathetic little family inside the building. What had those poor little kids ever done to deserve this? What had anyone done?

She turned as Burt came around to the side of the vehicle, his face full of suppressed fury. 'God help them, but at least they'll get looked after now. Where are we headed next, Monica?'

'I don't know, Burt, but wherever it is I'm not going! Get in, or stay here with the others and Alf, but I'm going to Everton to make sure my mam's all right. She won't go to the damn shelter either; she'll be under the stairs like that lot, poor things.'

He stared at her hard, though he knew she was doing her best under circumstances no young girl should ever have to face. 'Monica, I know it's difficult, luv, but you . . . we've got to keep going, keep to this area where we really are needed. We can't just abandon all these people, girl. While I'm out doing my bit, I don't know if our Maisie and the girls are safe either. I could find out when the raid is over that they . . . they're injured – or worse, God forbid. Or that the house is gone. But I can't go off to find out, no matter how much I want to. No, girl, you can't go. Just think what your husband would think or say if he knew you'd left people to . . .'

She didn't want to hear his words but, although she didn't want to admit it, she knew he was right. In her heart of hearts she realised that she was being selfish – she couldn't just abandon people when she was so desperately needed – and that Rick, who would be risking his own life before long, would be ashamed of her. And what about Joan whom she'd been hoping to see? Joan's beloved Jim had already made the ultimate sacrifice, so what would her dearest friend think of her selfishness?

Slowly, she nodded. 'You're right, Burt. I . . . we . . . can't leave here.'

She glanced, through tears of disappointment and fear, at the piece of paper Mr Simpkins had thrust at her before she'd driven off.

'It's Ardleigh Road next. Get in, Burt, I've already wasted too much time with my daft ideas.'

He smiled at her and she managed a bitter smile back. No matter what the hours ahead would bring, she felt that tonight she had grown up.

Chapter Twelve

That raid on Liverpool was the heaviest of the war so far. Three hundred and fifty tons of high-explosive bombs, thirty land mines and three thousand incendiary bombs were dropped on the city. Three hundred people were killed, and thousands more were injured or made homeless. The raids went on for three weeks, but to Monica's huge relief both her mother and sister survived them, although the houses further down the road were badly damaged by incendiary bombs that the overworked fire-watchers – men, boys and even some girls – failed to put out before the fires took hold. There were so many that it became impossible to deal successfully with them all, and Nelly was very thankful that neither her home nor Olive's sustained any damage, apart from the soot that came down the chimney as a result of the explosions. But that was easily cleaned up, she stated firmly to Monica when she called round the night after the first raid. Nelly simply refused to admit they'd been in any danger.

Monica gritted her teeth to stop herself from screaming.

'You know, Mam, I could kill you sometimes, you're so stubborn! During that last raid I was terrified for you and our Eileen, huddled under the stairs. What kind of protection is that? None! Believe me, I've seen the results of people sitting under the stairs – or worse, the kitchen table – I've driven them to hospital, and not all of them survived their injuries! I was all for driving here to see that you were all right, until Burt Eaton talked some sense into me. Thank God Joan was sitting it out in a shelter.'

'Yes, and if we were fortunate enough to have a shelter, we'd be doing the same!' Nelly replied acidly, determined not to be swayed from her decision, although at the height of the bombing she'd begun to doubt the wisdom of sitting under the stairs as bits of plaster and dust had fallen on them. And twice the house had shaken menacingly.

Monica gave up and went to see Joan. 'She's just so pig-headed, there's no reasoning with her at all!' she said, the frustration clear in her voice.

Joan, who was sitting with her feet raised on a stool, and a cushion at her back, nodded her agreement. 'I just wish there was room in our shelter, Mon, and then at least you wouldn't worry so much.'

'I know, but these days I worry about *everything*! I worry about Rick, Mam, Dad, our Eileen, Claude and Nancy, whether the factory will still be standing or if my little salon will be buried under a pile of rubble so I'll have no job and won't be able to pay the bills. I worry about you, and when the next raid will come. Oh, Joan, life is one long worry.'

'You can say that again, Monica,' Lily agreed, coming into the room and catching the end of Monica's sentence. She carried her sewing basket, a dress draped over one arm. 'Bella's going to help me alter this – I've managed to get some braid to trim it, brighten it up a bit. There's nothing to be had in the shops – and anyway, I don't think I've got enough coupons left. I've used what I had, trying to get little gifts for Christmas.'

Joan looked wistfully at the dress her Aunt Lily had spread across the table. 'I can't tell you how great it will feel to be able to get back into my clothes. I seem to have been wearing these same two smocks forever, and I'm sick of them! I swear I'll burn them after I've had the baby!'

'No, you won't, Joan, material's too precious to burn. We can make something else, or use it to trim things,' Monica said firmly.

Lily smiled at her. 'Well, not long to go, Joan. Now, I've an idea that I want to run past you two girls before I speak to our Olive and your mam, Monica.'

They both looked at her with interest, as did Bella who had joined them, a pair of tailor's scissors in her hand. 'What kind of idea, Aunt Lily?' Bella enquired.

'Well, everyone is fed up to the back teeth with all the shortages. We're living in a more or less permanent state of anxiety, and it's not doing anyone's nerves any good at all to be constantly living on a knife edge, wondering when the blasted sirens will sound again. So, I had a word with Ben Stoker, and as he's decided to go ahead with the Christmas programme, I've asked him for a block booking of tickets – for all of us. Well, for those of us that want to go and be entertained and forget our worries for a couple of hours and be cheered up for Christmas. I thought the twentieth of December would be best.'

Monica and Joan looked at each other with some trepidation, but Bella was smiling and clapped her hands. 'Oh, Aunt Lily, that will be wonderful! It's so long since we had any kind of musical entertainment – I've missed it so much!'

'But Lily, what about Joan? The baby is due that week. Is it wise to be dragging her on and off trams?' Monica voiced Joan's feelings.

But Lily wasn't to be deterred. She'd had to do a serious amount of grovelling to get those tickets, and it was the only night that was available for a block booking – even for herself. 'Oh, don't first babies always come late?' she remarked airily.

Joan frowned. 'Not necessarily, sometimes they're early.'

'Well, either way, Joan, it will do you the world of good to go out. I'm determined that everyone is going to have some kind of a festive Christmas – despite everything those damn Nazis can throw at us. We're not giving in to the likes of *them*!'

Bella was beaming with anticipation, while Monica looked at Joan and shrugged.

Monica knew that Lily Frances was as stubborn as her own mam, and once she'd made up her mind there was no shifting her. 'So, who will you ask to join you then, Lily?' she asked.

Lily frowned with concentration as she began to unpick a dress seam. 'Well, all the family, of course, and the two gentlemen lodgers, although they may not want to join us—'

'Charlie might be home by then,' Bella interrupted.

Lily smiled at her but doubted that would happen. 'You, of course,' looking across at Monica, 'your mam and dad and your Eileen – I'm not sure that the tickets will stretch to that young man of hers . . . Harold, is it? But if Mr Whitworth and Mr Compton don't want to come, he'll be welcome.'

'That's a lot of tickets, Aunty Lil,' Joan put in.

'Harold Stevens might not be home; his ship is on escort with the convoys, so no one knows *anything*. But I'm sure Mam and Dad would love to go,' Monica added, her spirits rising at the prospect of a night out.

'Well, the first thing to do is ask people, and then I can give Ben a definite number. It wasn't easy to get him to agree to a block booking, I can tell you, I had to do a lot of persuading. But I do want to give everyone a Christmas treat – especially you, Joan.'

Joan smiled at her aunt, but Lily's round-up of who might be able to go brought memories of Jim to mind – he should have been on the list of possibles. And as the baby's birth was imminent, she was very unsure of her part in the plans.

After a lot of discussion within both families, it was finally decided that Lily, David and Bella plus Olive, Frederick and Joan would all go, together with Monica and her parents and sister. To Lily's relief the two gentlemen lodgers declined, saying it would be just wonderful to have a quiet, comfortable evening at home with a couple of hands of whist, which meant of course that she had spare tickets for both Charlie and Harold, should they both be home, which was still doubtful.

Frederick had made one stipulation about which he was adamant, and that was that Lily, Bella and Joan would travel to the theatre by taxi, and damn the expense. Monica was insisting on driving, with Eileen as her passenger, but Nelly was just as adamant as Frederick that she and Arthur would go by tram or bus, as would Frederick and David – and the two lads, if they were home.

'Well, a taxi won't be as bad as having to get a tram or bus,' Monica said to Joan.

'I know, but it's all adding to the expense for Frederick and Lily – she's got good seats, right in front of the stage. If I wasn't the size of a house, I could have gone with you, but I'd never fit into your little sports car now, Mon.'

Monica grinned at her. 'We'd need a shoehorn to get you in and out, and you're safer in a taxi. My little car is so low to the ground, it can be very bumpy – and we certainly don't want to set anything off!'

Joan was optimistic. 'It might be all over before then, Mon. I really, really hope so. You've no idea just how tedious and tiring it all is.'

Monica looked pensive. 'No, I don't, Joan, but I wish I did.' Then she grinned. 'Oh, take no notice of me; we're all going to enjoy this Christmas treat.'

To Lily's dismay the raids started again the night before their planned trip to the theatre. The bill boasted a host of famous acts who were only too glad to do their bit for the war effort. Even Tommy Handley, from the popular radio show *ITMA*, was appearing.

'Oh, perhaps they won't come tomorrow night, Aunt Lily,' Bella said hopefully as they all sat in the shelter, feeling cramped, cold and filled with fear.

'They often don't come on consecutive nights, Lily,' Olive added, knowing how much her sister was looking forward to an evening at the theatre, even though she personally thought it was the height of irresponsibility to insist on taking Joan, whose baby had so far shown no signs of being in any hurry to appear.

To everyone's relief and delight, both Charlie and Eileen Savage's young man, Harold, had arrived safely in Liverpool two days before. Both were very grateful that, for once, the convoy had not been attacked on the return crossing. Olive had her precious son home again – and in time for Christmas, too.

The following afternoon, they decided they would take their chances – their night out was too precious to miss if there was no sign of a raid, and there had been no rumours of alerts so far. Lily had worked so hard, with Bella's assistance, help-ing all the women to smarten up their hats, coats and jackets, while putting in extra hours behind the scenes at the theatre. The taxi had been booked, and they had all agreed to meet in the foyer of the theatre.

When they assembled, done out in all their finery, Lily gave out the tickets and ushered them all upstairs to the Dress Circle.

An air of excited anticipation hung over the little group as they settled themselves into their seats. Bella's eyes were sparkling with happiness and pleasure – she was so looking forward to tonight, and the best thing of all was having Charlie at home. She was so glad her brother was back safe. Eileen Savage looked just as happy as she sat beside Harold, with her mother on the other side to make sure the pair behaved. Joan, too, looked flushed with excitement, Monica thought, as she settled herself beside her friend. It was the first time since Jim had been killed that Joan looked animated about anything. She was so relieved that Joan was still capable of enjoying herself, for her friend still struggled with her grief and maintained that she was certain it would never really leave her. Monica was glad, too, that both the lads had made it home safely; if only Rick had been here with her, the night would have been just perfect. She glanced around quickly. The Empire was a beautiful theatre with heavy, gold-fringed, red velvet curtains framing the stage and swags on the boxes. There was lots of gold leaf everywhere, comfortable red plush seats and deep-pile carpeting in the Dress Circle. Above them hung the most enormous crystal chandelier she'd ever seen, and the place was packed. The performance was obviously a sell-out, despite the risks.

The curtain had gone up, and the orchestra was in full flow, heralding the 'warm up' act, a minor comedian. Suddenly, the laughter ebbed away, as over the music came the rising wail of the sirens.

The girls looked at one another in alarm. Both Charlie and Harold had gone pale, and Nelly was clutching Arthur's arm tightly. Slowly, the lights went up and they could see that no one had moved. Not a single person had risen and left their seat, and the orchestra continued to play, despite the increasing racket. Before any of them could speak, Ben Stoker appeared on the stage and announced through the microphone that the show would go on, but that those who wished to leave should do so now, and in an orderly fashion. He would have no panic in his theatre.

Monica gripped Joan's hand tightly, knowing how vulnerable they all were and that she really should leave to make her way to the ambulance station.

As if reading her mind, Joan squeezed her hand. 'Don't go, Mon! Don't leave us . . . me!'

'I won't, Joan, but we're in for a rough night.'

Fifteen minutes later, they heard the sound of the first planes and then the explosions as the bombs hit their targets, which seemed to them to be very close. Still no one moved, and the show went on – although they were all having trouble concentrating.

An hour and a half later, when the plaster started to fall from the ornate ceiling and the massive chandelier began to sway dangerously, Ben Stoker again appeared onstage and announced that it was just too dangerous for people to stay and that everyone should make their way to the foyer and then to the shelters. He begged for a calm and orderly exit, so no one would be hurt. Both Olive and Monica helped Joan to her feet and began to make their way towards the exits, all three of them white-faced, subdued and shaking with fear but determined not to show it. People around them wore the same grim-faced masks of determination, although some girls and young women were in tears.

After what seemed like ages, they finally reached the doors that led out on to Lime Street, but as they emerged on to the pavement both Olive and Nelly cried out in horror before quickly clamping their hands over their mouths. What had they all walked out into?

Surely it would have been safer to stay inside? Lily thought in panic. The whole of Lime Street seemed to be on fire. On the opposite side of the road St George's Hall, the beautiful neo-classical building which housed the Law Courts, was a blazing inferno. The winter sky appeared almost as bright as day and was streaked bright orange and scarlet through the smoke and flames. The air was thick with smoke, too, and it was difficult to breathe. David, Frederick, Arthur and the two lads, who were both in uniform, began to hustle everyone along the crowded pavement. Two air-raid wardens were pointing the way to the nearest shelter, but suddenly Joan stopped, bent forward and cried out in pain.

'Oh my God! Joan, what's wrong?' Monica cried, clutching her friend's arm, her fear of the raid pushed aside.

'Joan, is it the baby?' Olive demanded, trying to stay calm and think what would be the best thing to do. Joan going into labour and being caught in a raid that might well go on all night was an appalling prospect.

'I don't know, Mam, but the . . . pain . . .' Joan gasped.

'Lily, we've got to get her home! We've all got to get home, I'm not having her give birth in a bloody public shelter with half of Liverpool looking on – including God knows how many men and boys! That's just not going to happen! I doubt we'll even be able to find the midwife. Joan needs privacy and some peace, although . . .'

Lily, badly shaken, nodded. 'No, she's not going to be subjected to that, Olive.' She knew just what those places could be like.

'It might be hours yet, Lily. All labours are different.' Olive turned to Frederick. 'How are we going to get home?' she shouted as part of a building down towards the junction with London Road collapsed. 'It's absolute bedlam!'

'Well, luv, there's not going to be any buses or trams,' he said, looking grim. 'And no taxis or private cars.'

'She can't walk all the way to Everton!' Nelly cried.

'She's not going to walk anywhere. I'm going to get my car, I'm driving her home.' Monica sounded more confident than she felt. Heaven alone knew how she was going to get Joan into her low-slung sports car – but the alternative was unthinkable.

'Monica, you can't! Not in this!' Nelly protested, clutching her daughter's arm.

Monica shook off her grip. 'I can, Mam. I'm used to driving an ambulance in all *this*! Don't worry, I'll get her home in one piece. Why don't you all go to the shelter until it's over, and then get home in safety? I'm sure you'll be there in time to help. Come on, Joan, luv,' she urged, 'it's not far to where I left the car.' She prayed that the vehicle was still driveable and was not a smouldering mass of tangled metal.

The last the little group saw of the two young women before they all turned towards the direction of the shelter was them walking slowly through the smoke and noise, illuminated by the lurid glow of the flames, heading towards Lord Nelson Street where Monica had left her car. They all prayed, too, that they'd get to Mersey View safely.

Privately, Olive cursed her sister for yet another act of irresponsibility. Oh, she'd have a few words to say to Lily when, or if, they all got home.

Chapter Thirteen

To Monica's relief the car wasn't badly damaged. Oh, the lovely dark-green, shiny paintwork was blistered and blackened by the heat coming from the burning buildings all around them, but somehow her little sports car had escaped destruction. She'd be able to get them home – hadn't she driven through nights like this before? she told herself. But then she realised that the people she took to hospital were all strangers – this was Joan, and it was different.

'Oh, thank God! Joan, try your best to get into the passenger seat,' Monica coaxed. 'I know it's not going to be easy or very comfortable but . . .'

As she unlocked the door she realised her hands were shaking. She fought down her rising panic – that wouldn't help her friend in this perilous situation. She had to stay calm.

With some awkward and painful manoeuvring Joan got herself in, although her belly was pressing hard against the dashboard and her hat had slipped and was almost covering one eye, so she could barely see. She fought down the groan as another contraction tore through her. 'Oh God! Mon, I don't know which is worse – the pain or the rest of it!' She indicated the surrounding destruction with a hand that shook.

Monica took a deep breath and pushed back the thoughts of what would happen if Joan's contractions speeded up before they got home. Maybe she should drive straight to Mill Road Maternity Hospital, but she decided it was too far. 'Hold on, Joan, I'll go as quickly as I dare, but it's going to be a bit bumpy to say the least. Just don't forget that I'm used to driving through . . . the rest of it!'

Joan managed a wry grin as the pain of the latest contraction faded. 'I won't. Just get us home, Mon, please?'

Frederick looked at his watch as the 'All Clear' sounded. Ten forty. The raid had started at half past six but, despite being late-comers, they'd all crowded into the already packed shelter and managed to find enough space to sit down, the women and the two girls at least. They'd all been aware of what was going on overhead and outside – you couldn't ignore it – and they'd all prayed that Joan and Monica had reached Mersey View safely. No one in here had seen them, so the car must have been undamaged and driveable at least, Lily had remarked as she'd tried to bolster Olive's spirits.

Frederick had felt so helpless – and he knew the other men in their little party did, too. Usually they were out in this, helping people – and the two lads were, of course, constantly facing the twin dangers of the weather and the U-boats to get the vital cargoes home – but there had been nothing any of them could do until the raiders had gone home. Relieved the raid was finally over, he bent down and pulled Olive to her feet as she groaned with the stiffness of cramped limbs.

'We'll get home as quickly as we can, luv,' he urged, knowing she would be worried sick about Joan.

She nodded. It would be a long walk and likely to be nearly midnight when they eventually got there.

She'd calculated correctly; it was ten to midnight as, worn out, they at last turned into Mersey View. The street was in complete darkness, except for the glow in the sky from the damaged and still burning city, but thankfully there seemed to be no new bomb damage to any of the houses.

With relief Nelly picked out the shape of Monica's car parked outside Olive's house. 'They made it home safely, Olive, luv, thank God!'

'I just hope your Monica had the sense to get them both into the shelter in the yard.'

'She will have, Olive, but they'll both be in the house by now, it was hours since the "All Clear" went.'

'Well, depending on how far along our Joan is, she'll at least be able to have the child in her own comfortable bed and not on the concrete base of a damn public shelter,' Olive replied, fishing in her handbag for her house keys.

She'd just inserted her door key when the siren sounded again, and they looked at one another in horror.

'Oh, not again! Oh, dear Lord, not again! Haven't they done enough damage for one night?' Lily cried in fury.

Frederick looked at David and Arthur. 'Obviously not!

125

We'd better get down to the warden station,' he said, as Nelly hastily began to shepherd Eileen and Harold towards her house.

'No, luv. The two lads will be more useful with us,' Arthur announced.

Olive turned to her friend and neighbour. 'Well, I for one am not spending any more time in a shelter tonight! Our Joan isn't, either. Those two girls haven't driven through hell to get home only to spend God knows how many more hours in that horrible, cold shed in the yard. Nelly, you and Eileen can have Lily's place and mine with the two gentlemen . . . you're not sitting under the stairs tonight! And I'm going to take my chances in the house with Joan. It just can't be any bloody worse than the shelter.'

Nelly nodded and made her mind up. 'Olive, I'll stay with you in the house, you'll need all the help you can get. But the two girls can't stay, they'll have to join the others. Eileen, you and Bella go straight through into the yard,' she instructed. It was going to be a long – not to say terrifying – night, with just herself and Olive having had experience of childbirth. Lily could either stay and make herself useful, or join Eileen, Bella, Mr Compton and Mr Whitworth. She wasn't at all sure that Monica should stay with her friend. Yes, she was as close to Joan as anyone was, and she was a married woman, but there was nothing pretty about giving birth – and it might just put her off for life.

Olive found the two girls at the top of the stairs, Monica's arm around Joan's shoulders. 'We're just coming, Mrs Garswood, but she's in a lot of pain now,' Monica informed Olive. She was relieved to see her own mother in the hall behind Olive, for she'd been terrified of having to help Joan all by herself after the sirens had gone again.

'Well, Monica, you can take her back to her bedroom. We're staying put here! The men and lads have all gone out to help.' Olive's voice was grim as she took in her daughter's white face, the pain in her dark eyes and the beads of sweat on her forehead. 'I'm not having her sitting out there in the yard, not now, not in this state.'

'Shouldn't you try to get back to your ambulance, Monica? Your car's still outside,' Nelly urged.

'Absolutely not, Mam! If you're staying then I am, too. Even if I won't be much help with other things, I can hold her hand, fetch towels, things like that.'

Monica was firm, and so Nelly gave up. They got Joan back to bed and made her as comfortable as they could in the circumstances.

Monica sat on the bed beside her friend, holding her hand. They could already hear the drone of approaching aircraft, but she didn't care. She felt strangely calm and unafraid. It was a popular saying these days that you never heard the bomb meant for you. So if it was fate that they would all die tonight then so be it! She wasn't leaving her friend – and by the look of it, neither were the other three women, Lily included.

'Lily, would you go down and bring up as many old newspapers as you can find? And there's some old remnants of towels in the airing cupboard that I keep for Frederick's hands when he gets home from work. Bring them too,' Olive instructed her sister.

Without a word Lily left. She knew what they were for, even though she had never had a child herself, and she didn't envy poor Joan one bit at this moment. No woman should have to endure the agony of childbirth with bombs raining down from the sky in their hundreds, and she felt stricken with guilt that she'd insisted they all went out tonight. All she'd wanted was to give everyone a treat. Now all she could do was run errands, make tea, and try to keep all their spirits up despite the carnage that would soon surround them.

The time seemed to drag interminably, Monica thought, as she wiped the sweat from Joan's face again with a flannel. They had all silently cursed the planes that had circled for hours like a plague of banshees above the city, accompanied by the continuous screaming of descending bombs and the sound of explosions – some far away but others much too close for comfort.

Oh, poor Joan, she was having a terrible time of it, she thought with sympathy. She'd never in her life witnessed someone she was so fond of in such pain. Through gasps of agony, Joan had told her that the midwife at the hospital had warned her that labour would be tough, but she'd never dreamed it was going to be quite like this – the relentless, wringing pain that had already seemed to go on for hours and was getting worse. Monica had tutted sympathetically and smoothed damp wisps of Joan's dark hair off her forehead. She'd not believed it could be so bad, either. No one had ever said that giving birth was like this! No one had told her what to expect when, or if, she got pregnant. But if this was it then she doubted that she would ever want to have a baby. No wonder Mam always said two were more than enough, and that if the men had to go through it there would be far fewer children ever born.

Another spasm of agony tore through her friend's body and made Joan scream as the sweat stood out on her forehead. She clutched her hand so tightly that Monica was certain her fingers were broken. Joan's whole body must be drenched in sweat, for her nightdress was creased and sticking to her swollen belly. Her dark hair was stuck to her scalp but at least she seemed oblivious to the bombing. Monica felt so utterly helpless, as she knew Lily and both Joan's mam and her own must be feeling. All they could do was try to comfort Joan, tell her it wouldn't be long now, that her contractions were coming very close together. Olive had cried out that she wished she could bear the pain for her, but it didn't seem to help Joan at all. She cursed everything and everyone in her agony, and Monica just wished it was all over and that the damn raiders would give up and go back to Germany – or better still, get shot down by RAF fighter planes.

Lily had never personally witnessed such agony, either: she would never complain about not having children now. She had Bella whom she looked on and loved as a daughter, and that was enough.

Fleetingly, she wondered how Bella was coping in the shelter. The girl was terrified of the bombing, as they all were, but Lily was afraid that it would scar Bella for life. The fear was something none of them would ever forget – should they survive this terrible war – and it was this fear that finally showed Lily what she had to do, for Bella's sake. An idea had been taking shape in Lily's mind and tonight she was certain this was the leap they would have to take.

It was just a matter of when.

* * *

Bella was desperately trying not to show how afraid she was, but she couldn't stop shaking. The two elderly gentlemen were seemingly quite calm and playing cards, whilst Eileen was sitting next to her on the bunk with her knees drawn up to her chin. Bella realised that the other girl was as frightened as she was but, like her, trying not to show it.

'I'm so afraid for Harold, Bella,' she confided. 'My da should have let him come in here with us, instead of dragging him off out *there*! Doesn't my poor Harold have to live in constant danger for days on end when he's at sea? It's not fair. It's bad enough his leave is being spoilt by these raids!'

'It's not fair on Charlie, either. And when he's at sea I think he is in more danger than Harold. Harold is at least on a warship, they have guns and mines, they can fight back,' Bella reminded her.

Eileen decided to change the subject, for Bella had a valid point, although talking was better than sitting here in silence listening to the sound of the bombs dropping. 'I just wish they would go home so we can get back into the house. Do you think Joan will be in labour for much longer?'

'I don't know, Eileen!' Bella replied irritably, her nerves on edge, her thoughts again on what Joan was going through. The one evening she had been looking forward to had turned into a really terrible night so far. It had been awful when they had to evacuate the theatre, though she'd been amazed at how calm everyone was. Then there were the uncomfortable hours in the shelter in Copperas Hill, worrying if Joan and Monica had got home safely, followed by the long walk home through scenes of complete destruction. And never before had the raiders come twice in one night. She was tired and she was frightened and she had little patience for Eileen's questions. '*I know nothing about these things. Aunt Lily won't even discuss anything like . . . that. She says I am too young and I must concentrate on my career.*'

Despite her fear Eileen was intrigued. She lowered her voice to a whisper. 'Don't you even know how babies get inside?'

'Of course I do, but I don't want to talk about such things, Eileen.' She lowered her voice, too. 'When I was on the ship from Portugal, something . . . I won't talk about it! I just won't!'

'Oh, suit yourself, Bella. But one day it'll be different. You'll be happy enough to think about all that. When you find someone and fall in love. Like me and Harold.'

Bella turned to Eileen, her dark eyes wide and questioning. 'Eileen, you and Harold, you haven't . . .'

'Oh, don't be daft, Bella, when would we ever get the chance? Besides, my mam would absolutely kill me! If I got pregnant I'd be thrown out on the street for bringing disgrace on the family.' She had completely forgotten that Bella's father had not been married to Bella's mother, so the girl was illegitimate, as any child would be who had the misfortune to be born outside marriage. It was the ultimate sin in the eyes of decent society, for both mother and child – and she had to be honest, the sole reason she curtailed Harold's advances in *that* direction.

Bella said nothing; old memories were rising up and she was too tired to fight them down. She must do as Aunt Lily advised and concentrate on her career. When she had risen to the dizzy heights of a professional soprano, only then might she possibly think about marriage and babies. But definitely not yet.

A little doubt nagged at her as she watched Eileen pull a blanket around her shoulders. She wasn't sure that she actually believed Eileen's words. These were very precarious times and Harold's life was in danger every time he went to sea – as was her half-brother Charlie's. But that was something else she didn't want to dwell on. She tried to get some sleep.

It was five fifteen on the morning of December the twenty-first before the 'All Clear' sounded and, after waiting for another fifteen minutes in case there were any stragglers dropping the last of their bomb load, Bella and Eileen scrambled to the door of the shelter, determined now to find out how Joan was.

The house was still standing and there appeared to be no damage as they threw open the kitchen door and headed for the hall. Lily met them at the top of the stairs. She was smiling, although Bella knew she must be exhausted.

'Oh, Aunt Lily! What . . . Joan . . . ?' Bella blurted out.

'She's fine now. Utterly exhausted, of course, but very, very happy. Little James – Jamie – Alexander McDonald finally decided to put in an appearance half an hour ago. Just a couple of minutes before the "All Clear", and he's beautiful. If you can call a baby boy "beautiful". He's certainly got a fine pair of lungs.'

Bella hugged her tightly. 'Oh, can we see her . . . them?'

'Not yet, we need to tidy things up, but very soon. You can both go and make us all a cup of tea,' she urged, 'and then we'll call you.'

She was so thankful the ordeal was over, not only for poor Joan but for herself, Olive and Nelly – and Monica, too. But it all seemed to be forgotten now. As soon as Olive had placed the baby, wrapped in a clean towel, in Joan's arms, her niece had said it had all been worth it. Despite all the pain, the hard work and the terrors of the bombing, she was so happy she couldn't find the words to express it all. Monica, too, appeared to be over the moon and had cooed over baby Jamie – even though, like nearly all newborns, he wasn't really a very handsome sight.

Her sister and Nelly Savage were just exhausted, but delighted too, while she . . . well, it would be a long time before she would forget this night, and she was determined never to see another like it. Twice in one night the city had been heavily bombed. Things were getting worse, there was no safety anywhere. She'd had enough of this damn war already and the effect it was having on her little family. Enough was enough, in her opinion.

Chapter Fourteen

The raids continued right up to Christmas morning, so that year's celebrations were another quiet affair, with the city badly damaged. Many families were homeless and living with relatives, having been bombed out two and even three times before. Shortages were increasing, but no one in Olive or Nelly's houses seemed to mind. They may not have had much with which to rustle up a festive feast but what they did have they enjoyed together, determined not to let the enemy rob them of Christmas altogether. And it was little Jamie's first Christmas, after all, so for that reason alone it would be a special one.

To everyone's delight the raids meant that neither Charlie nor Harold were going back to sea until the following week. Little Jamie McDonald was thriving and Joan was recovering her strength. It didn't matter that this was the first Christmas she had experienced as a widow. Yes, Jim was gone, but she had Jamie and her family, and that was some consolation.

Monica spent as much time as she possibly could with her

friend, for Joan had insisted that she be her son's godmother.

'I'd be delighted, you know that, Joan,' she'd replied. She'd already written to Rick with the news but there was no sign of him getting any leave. The memories of Joan's traumatic labour were fading and she was again beginning to wish for a child of her own.

On Boxing Day morning, Joan was looking thoughtful as she nursed her baby and chatted quietly to her friend. 'There's something else you can do for me, Mon. And I don't want a list of excuses, if you don't mind – I'll get that from Mam.'

Monica looked at her with curiosity. 'What? What are you planning to do that isn't going to make your mam very happy?' Joan clearly had something on her mind.

'Well, I've been thinking, Mon, that when I'm properly back on my feet I want to do something really useful. I don't mean just going back to work in a factory. I think we'll all be conscripted for war work soon, anyway, and Mam will be happy to look after Jamie, although I don't want to be parted from him.' She smiled as she stroked the downy little head of her sleeping son.

'Surely that won't be until he's weaned? You can't leave him before then, and they damn well shouldn't expect you to! There are plenty of single girls, or married women like me, before they start calling young mothers up.'

'I know, but . . . will you teach me to drive, Monica? Then I'll be able to drive an ambulance like you, after work and at weekends. I feel as if I should be doing more. That Jim would want me to do more.'

'He certainly wouldn't want you risking your safety, Joan, not now you've his son to think of, too.'

'I won't be doing anything just yet, Mon. Will you teach me, please?'

Monica considered it, then slowly nodded her head. She tried not to use her car very much now, as petrol was in short supply, and when she thought of the risks Charlie Copperfield and his shipmates ran in order to get it to port, it always had a sobering effect on her. 'All right, just as long as we don't start until you're really fit and ready. God knows what your mam – and mine – will say about it, though, I don't know.'

Joan grinned. 'Oh, I've a fair idea, Mon, but I don't care!'

'On your head be it, then, Mrs McDonald!' Monica laughed. She could understand her friend's desire to do more. She wished she could, too, but she didn't view the prospect of working in a munitions factory with delight. Wasn't she doing her bit in the salon, on top of driving the ambulance?

Olive really didn't have much to say when the girls broke the news to her. She was preoccupied with the surprise announcement Lily had delivered the night before, like a bolt from the blue, and she was still fuming about it.

The previous evening, after supper was over and the chores for the day done, Joan had taken Jamie up to bed with her. She still tired easily, and Olive worried that she was not getting enough to eat for a nursing mother – though, really, no one was these days. The two gentlemen were in the parlour playing cards, and she and Frederick were sitting in the kitchen having a cup of tea, when Lily walked in, with David and Bella in tow, sat herself down and announced quite calmly that she had made a decision.

'What sort of a decision, Lily?' Olive demanded, thinking

that Lily's 'decisions' usually spelled some kind of catastrophe, like the night out at the Empire.

Her sister nervously patted her already immaculately styled hair, a sure sign that she was anxious about Olive's reaction.

'Now I don't want you to get upset about this, Olive, we've discussed it long and hard, haven't we, David?'

Her long-suffering husband nodded his agreement, but Olive knew he wouldn't have had much to do with this decision, whatever it was. She'd long ago realised that Lily was a force of nature. Her sister was a law unto herself, and when she put her mind to something you couldn't shift her. Olive was apprehensive but, to a degree, resigned to whatever was about to unfold.

Lily took a deep breath. Better to get it over with. 'This war is getting worse, you can't deny that, and God knows how long it will go on for and . . . well, David and I don't want Bella wasting these years, missing out on her training, being denied the chance to fulfil her potential. There might not be a single concert hall or opera house in Europe left standing at the end of it all! London is being so badly bombed that I doubt Covent Garden will survive. We're doing this for Bella and her future.'

'Doing what?' Olive probed.

'We've decided to take Bella and go to . . . Portugal.'

Both Olive and Frederick were stunned into silence. Oh, of all the mad things Lily had done over the years, Olive thought this was the craziest. She could see that Bella herself wasn't very happy about it, either, for the girl looked positively miserable, but so far she had said nothing. Bella knew Lily's views on her career only too well.

Before either of them could speak, Lily plunged on. 'It's a

neutral country; they are not at war, so Bella can continue her training, hopefully at the Teatro Nacional de São Carlos. There will be no danger of us all being blown to kingdom come at any moment, and it's Bella's native country, she speaks the language and . . .'

Olive was on her feet, her eyes flashing with temper. 'For God's sake, Lily, are you mad – both of you? This is far worse than when you all went to London, against everyone's advice and straight into the heart of the bombing! Lily, have you really *thought* about all this? Neither you nor David can speak Portuguese, what will you do for money and jobs? How the hell will you get there in the first place? You know how dangerous it is for shipping around this coast, and further afield too, right into the Mediterranean!'

'The fact that it's a neutral country is a big positive, though, I must say,' Frederick broke in, seeking to lower the temperature of the exchange. 'But I'm sure you know, Lily, that no one trusts Salazar, and there are lots of spies from all sides. And you might not be able to get back home. But that being said, there's still a lot of good to this idea,' Frederick added, trying to see both sides of the argument, as usual.

'Where will you live, in the name of heaven?' Olive continued, immediately dismissing Frederick's more measured reaction.

Lily was unperturbed. 'Lisbon. Probably the Alfama district, Bella knows that fairly well, it's where she lived before—'

'I know *that*, Lily!' Olive snapped at her. 'But it's a long time since Bella lived there; she was only twelve when she came here!' She turned to Bella. The girl's dark eyes were wide with anxiety and glistening with unshed tears, for she hated arguments. 'Bella, luv, this is *your* life, *your* career. What do you want to do, never mind our Lily and David?'

Bella bit her lip. She had already told Aunt Lily how she felt, but to flatly refuse to go would be to let Lily down, throwing everything she had sacrificed for her back in her face. No, of course she didn't want to go. She loved her English family and didn't want to leave them. Her memories of her natural mother and the neighbourhood in Lisbon where they had lived were so faded now that she could barely remember them, and her command of her native language had diminished since she seldom spoke it these days. She would still have family in the city, she was sure – her mother had had several brothers – but since they had so coldly turned their backs on Bella and her mother when they needed them most, she would never want to seek them out. Set against all that was her terror of the bombing, and the loss of a career she'd set her heart on. A career which she knew Lily would go to any lengths to see come to fruition.

'I . . . I don't want to leave you all, Stepmama, and I don't know if I will be happy now in Portugal, but I can't stay here, it will hurt Aunt Lily so much, and I am grateful to her and Uncle David for everything they have done for me, so . . . I must go.'

'And she's terrified of the bombing, Olive, you know that, even though you would be hard put to get her to admit it,' Lily added, to press the point home.

'Everyone is, Lily. She's not on her own with that!' Olive snapped back. She was disappointed that Bella hadn't stood up to Lily and her crazy plans, but then the girl was not yet eighteen and her career was, indeed, very important to her.

Her mind didn't seem to be full of fashion, films and romance, like Eileen Savage's was – Nelly's younger daughter didn't seem to think of the future at all. But maybe she was right not to? Olive mused. Did any of them even *have* a future – except to finally accept living under the Nazi jackboot, as the people of the Channel Islands were now having to do?

Lily had been watching her sister closely. Olive's anger was fading and she felt relieved, her sister's temper was always short-lived. Now, they must get down to making her plans a reality. 'So, let's talk about the practicalities.'

'Like what?' Olive demanded, turning to put the kettle back on the hob. They all needed a strong cup of tea after all that.

David spoke for the first time. 'I've made some tentative enquiries. There are a few ships that are still sailing from Liverpool to Portugal and the Azores and beyond, but the trips are erratic and take far longer than they used to. We'd have to be sure it was a Portuguese-registered vessel, other-wise . . .' He spread his hands suggestively, and everyone knew what he meant. In order to reach Lisbon safely, they'd have to be under a neutral flag, but there was still no guarantee they would not come under attack. 'So, it's a matter of waiting until we can get a passage – it could be weeks or months.'

'Of course we'll have to take as much luggage with us as we possibly can, and then we'll have to find somewhere to rent.' Lily smiled at Bella and patted the girl's hand. 'But first, we'll have to stay in a hotel – a very cheap hotel,' Lily finished.

'Well, good luck with that one, Lily. I would imagine that it won't be easy. I'm sure thousands have flocked to Portugal to escape the war, and even come over the border from Spain to escape General Franco's fascist regime. But I'm certain you'll make it work,' Frederick said. He, like his wife, thought they were mad, but he wanted to be helpful if they were as determined to pursue this plan as they seemed to be.

Lily was not to be deterred. 'Then we will all go to see whoever is in charge at the Opera House, to find out if there is a possibility of work for David and me. We both have considerable experience, even if we're not completely fluent in the language – yet! Thank goodness Bella has been teaching us Portuguese when she can. Then we will be in exactly the right place to get Bella a position, even if it's only in the chorus. Oh, I know she's not fully trained yet, but surely they will understand why she couldn't continue her studies. She will be able to explain exactly why, in full, and far better than we can.' Again, she smiled at Bella. 'I'm certain that once they hear her sing, there will be no problems at all. We'll all settle in, Olive, I'm sure of it,' she finished firmly.

Olive poured the tea. 'And in the meantime?'

'Life goes on as usual, whatever else Herr Hitler has up his sleeve! We'll continue to work, and Bella will carry on with her studies at the Bluecoat School and work with David, too. We'll just have to sit tight until we can get a ship.'

'I take it that's your department?' Frederick stated, looking at David.

He managed a wry smile. 'That's right. I don't think it's going to be as quick, or as easy, as Lily would like.'

Lily shot her husband an icy look but she was quite relieved that this first little hurdle to her plan had been surmounted – finally, it was all out in the open and being discussed.

* * *

Joan totally agreed with her mother and stepfather that she'd never heard anything so utterly irresponsible as to choose to go sailing through U-boat- and warship-infested seas to another country in the middle of a world war. True, neutral Portugal was Bella's homeland, but . . . it was madness, and she said so to Monica.

Monica, however, could see Lily's point of view. 'I have to agree, to an extent, Joan. But once they get there, life will be more normal than it is here, and your aunt is only thinking of Bella. The way things are going, there won't be a theatre left standing here. In fact, there won't be much left standing at all!'

'Bella doesn't want to go,' Joan insisted. 'She told me so, but Lily's been piling on the guilt. But in her heart, I know she really does want an operatic career, and that's something she won't get here, not for years and years – if ever.'

'She must be looking forward to it, in a way? Oh, not the travelling there, naturally. It will bring back memories of how she got here in the first place. Do you remember that night in February, Joan, and how bitterly cold it was?'

Joan nodded. 'As if any of us could ever forget! She was terrified, freezing cold in just that thin dress and jacket, with no stockings or decent shoes. Poor kid, her mam just dead. No family, no money, just a bit of paper with our address on it, and then . . .'

Monica nodded, wishing now she hadn't brought the subject up; it was a sad story, and not one she wanted her friend reminded of. She knew Joan had never forgiven Billy Copperfield for deserting the family.

'Well, there's no stopping Aunty Lil once she's made up her mind, so that's that!' Joan pronounced with resignation.

'Maybe one day, Joan, we'll get to hear Bella sing as a famous opera star, somewhere like Milan – or Rome, or Paris.'

Joan managed a smile. 'Maybe. Once this flaming war is over – whenever *that* might be!' She grimaced. 'We might be too damn old to travel by then, Mon.'

Monica pulled a face. 'Oh, don't say that, Joan! I'd love to travel, but there's not much chance of that for the foreseeable future.'

Chapter Fifteen

―――・◦◆◦・―――

February,
1941

Even though he had visited the various shipping offices at least three times a week, it was well into the new year before David managed to secure three berths on the *Rio Tagus* sailing from Liverpool to Lisbon and then on to Horta in the Azores. It seemed to Olive that Bella had become resigned to them leaving Liverpool. She had even begun speaking Portuguese to both David and Lily as much as possible, to build on their basic grasp of the language. To Olive's great surprise Lily seemed to be mastering it far better than David, despite his musical background, which she had been certain would give him some idea of foreign words and phrases. Maybe, she thought, as she assembled the meagre ingredients for a vegetable pie for supper, and listened to her sister reciting the names of the different types of shops and services to Bella, they would indeed all settle down in Lisbon

– or *Lisboa*, as Lily insisted they now call their future home.

She was more concerned about Joan these days; she was doing far too much around the house, and took her turn standing in the interminable queues in the freezing cold for food. She was as thin as a rail, and Olive tried to make sure that she surreptitiously gave her daughter most of her own share of the weekly milk, egg and butter ration. Jamie was a placid baby and was no trouble at all, which Olive viewed as a blessing, and twice a week Monica came after work to give Joan a driving lesson – if it could be called that, or so Frederick had remarked. All they did was drive up and down the street for half an hour, which at least provided the neighbours with some entertainment, but Joan seemed to be mastering the skill. Just last week, Monica had announced that she thought Joan was now ready to move on to a larger vehicle, namely an ambulance.

'Hopefully, she'll get plenty of practice driving a bigger vehicle, Mrs Garswood, before there are any more raids. There are always people who seem to have to go to hospital urgently these days,' Monica had informed Olive, to try to allay the woman's concerns for Joan. She was always so glad she hadn't tried to drive Joan to Mill Road Hospital, the night she'd gone into labour with Jamie, for it had taken a direct hit during the air raids.

'Please God, there won't be any more raids. We've been lucky this month; they seem to have turned their attentions elsewhere,' Olive muttered as she started to rub in her pastry ingredients.

She was relieved that the sirens hadn't sounded for weeks now, although that fact hadn't changed Lily's mind at all. Her sister was now doing the last of her packing, and David had

145

acquired all the necessary documents. At least Bella wasn't looking so downcast these days. Hopefully, Charlie would be home before they left, and she knew Bella was looking forward to seeing her brother before she left for Lisbon. Maybe the girl was now looking forward to going back to her homeland to live. She hoped so; she wanted the children to be as happy as possible under the circumstances. The one fear that haunted her was that this small freighter Lily and her family were to sail on would be sunk at sea and that they would never, ever see them again, or even hear any news. She wasn't sure just how efficient the Portuguese were with official things like that. After all, Bella had arrived in Liverpool with no papers, and no one had queried the fact – and there hadn't been a war on then. Oh, it just didn't bear dwelling on! she thought, as she watched Monica take the baby from Joan and begin to sing softly to him. He looked up at her with his big dark eyes and a grin she put down to wind. He was too young for it to be a proper smile, but it was lovely all the same.

Nelly had told her that Monica was longing for a child. There didn't seem to be much prospect of that at the moment, she thought, watching the young woman. Perhaps that was a blessing in disguise when you looked at what had happened to her Joan, having to give birth in the middle of a raid, and already widowed. But at least it had brought little Jamie into their lives, and that was something they'd always be grateful for.

At last the day arrived when Lily, David and Bella were due to leave. Charlie was home safely and had insisted that he go with them all to see Bella off, although earlier that morning there had been an argument between them when Charlie wanted to give her back the little brass rooster. Bella, however, had been adamant.

'No! You will not be safe without the Barcelos, Charlie! Once we get to *Lisboa* we will be safe, so I do not need it, but you do! You still have many more times to cross the ocean . . . and with the weather and the U-boats . . .'

'But it will bring you luck, Bella, with your singing and your career. You *must* take it! After all, I made it for you.'

'No! No! I will not, Charlie! I will make my own luck – even if it is only in the chorus to start with, then one day . . .' Bella had stamped her foot with impatience. 'Oh! I insist! If you do not take it, I . . . I will leave it here! I will give it to Stepmama to keep for you! I will! I will!'

Generally, neither of them were really superstitious, but Charlie had reluctantly agreed, tucking it back into the inside pocket of his uniform jacket. She was right: once they reached Lisbon they at least would be safe, but he'd miss her, he'd miss all three of them. But Charlie knew Lily was making the right decision for Bella. He'd done two trips now with BP in the convoys and felt he had grown up. He certainly understood things better and had learned to master his feelings; he'd be happier knowing that Bella would be safe from the air raids, even if the rest of his family wouldn't be.

They all arrived at the damaged but still useable dock gates at the entrance to the Gladstone Dock. While David and Frederick spoke to the policeman on the gate and David produced the relevant papers, Olive turned to her sister in undisguised shock at the sight of their means of transport to Portugal, the *Rio Tagus*, tied up alongside the dock.

'Good God! Don't tell me you've spent a small fortune to sail on . . . *that thing!*' she cried.

Lily, too, was looking with dawning horror at the black hull of the battered freighter which seemed to be covered with more rust than paint. There was a gangway of sorts leading up to the deck. From a flagpole at the stern of the vessel a grimy, ragged Portuguese flag hung limply in the damp morning mist coming in from the river and swirling around the rail of the open deck – a rail that was also rusted and twisted in places, and with one stretch missing entirely. There was no sign of life at all aboard.

'Oh, Olive! I . . . I never imagined . . . it's . . . terrible!'

'It is! It doesn't look as if it will get you much further than the Mersey estuary, Lily! Can't you get your money back and stay?' Olive added hopefully. The ship reminded her of one of the old rust buckets Billy Copperfield had worked on as a stoker, many years ago, when he'd lived with her here in Liverpool.

David had heard her. 'It's not nearly as bad as it looks, Olive.' He turned to his wife. 'Lily, when I first came down to see the captain about looking at our accommodation, I was really surprised. They can carry up to six passengers, but this time there will be just the three of us. The cabins are basic but clean and comfortable, there is a small dining room – mess – we'll share with the crew, and also a lounge area. He assured me the food will be good, and plentiful, too – and there will even be wine, should we wish for some. When the weather gets better, we will be able to take walks on deck – and when we arrive, Lisbon will be warm and sunny.' The two women were still looking unconvinced, so he carried on resolutely.

'It looks so battered because they encountered rough weather crossing the Bay of Biscay. Not unusual at this time of year, the captain assured me, but it's a sturdy little vessel and doesn't pitch and roll too much.'

'I just hope you're right, David,' Frederick added. He could see that Lily and Bella were both looking very apprehensive. If the sea had been rough enough to tear away the railings on deck on the way here, then just what were they in for on the return voyage?

It was a thought that had occurred to Charlie too, as he remembered his first few days at sea, but he had no intention of mentioning it. 'Oh, you'll all be fine; don't worry, Aunty Lil, or you, Bella. Looks aren't everything, she's not an ocean liner, but it takes less than a week to get there – if that. It's not as if you'll be at sea for weeks on end, and it's great if you can get up on deck, even if it's only for a couple of minutes each day. It helps . . . and with warm, sunny weather to look forward to, too . . . well . . .'

Lily didn't look convinced but there was no going back now. They'd paid their money – and quite a bit of it, too, in fact most of their savings – so now they would have to get on board and cope with whatever lay ahead of them. She devoutly hoped they wouldn't be seasick. Olive had confided in her that Charlie's seasickness was so bad at first, he had just wished he was dead – and that was no way to start a new life. Despite David's reassurances, the *Rio Tagus* didn't seem to offer much in the way of comfort, let alone what could be called luxury, but from what her husband said it was at least safe.

She turned to him, nodding slowly. 'Well, you'd better go and see if you can find someone to help us with these cases, we can't carry them up that gangway by ourselves. And then . . . well, we'll just have to wait and see.'

Monica hadn't gone with them to the dock; she'd had to work in her little salon in the factory. She'd miss Bella's help but at least she'd managed to find a decent girl to replace her, as they were always busy. Joan was coming this evening; they were going to get her friend enlisted in the voluntary ambulance service, so she needed to rustle up a decent meal from what she had at home. She was always tired at the end of the day, but it was a 'satisfied' sort of tiredness, she thought to herself, as she walked from the tram stop and up Garthdale Road towards her home.

It was a good job she knew the way by heart, she mused, as she opened the gate and turned up her own path, for there wasn't a chink of light to be seen anywhere. The blackout was still being rigorously enforced; even though she, like so many others, hated it, everyone knew it was a vital defence against incoming bombers, and essential for their safety. She frowned as she clasped her keys in one hand, ready to open the door: surely, surely that tiny pinprick of light couldn't be coming from behind her sitting-room curtains? She was always so meticulous about making sure they were drawn tightly before she left for work, and she was sure she had switched off all the lights; even though the days were slowly beginning to lengthen now, it had still been dark when she left.

She stopped and peered more closely. It was a chink of light. Suddenly, she felt cold. Had someone broken in? Had she been burgled? Was the intruder still inside? Wartime didn't stop the criminals. In fact, she'd heard that the looting of bombed-out houses and businesses was on the increase, which she considered a despicable act. People had little enough, without what was left of their homes being robbed for the bits that remained, and the few pennies there might be from damaged gas and electric meters. She stood debating what to do. Of course she was apprehensive, but during the raids she'd faced far worse than some low-life rifling through her belongings. Should she go and look for Mr Thompson, one of the local ARP wardens, just in case whoever it was turned violent?

She was still dithering when she heard footsteps coming up the path behind her, and she sighed with relief. The warden must have seen the light, though God knows how, it was so small.

'Why are you standing here in the dark gazing at your house, Mon? What's wrong?'

Monica turned to see Joan, and clutched her arm, relieved that at least now there were two of them, even if it was her friend and not the warden who had arrived. 'Oh, am I glad to see you, Joan! Look, just at the right-hand corner at the bottom of the window, there's a light on inside, and I swear I switched everything off this morning. Someone is – or has been – in the house.'

Joan's voice was grim. 'Well, standing here isn't going to do anyone much good. Have you got your keys handy?'

'Yes. But do you think we should make a bit of noise, chat loudly or laugh in case there's someone inside? It might scare them off,' she suggested, although realising it was a bit of a weak idea.

'Why give them the chance to leg it out of the back door,

Mon? If there is anyone in there, you can bet your life they're bent on pinching your things.'

'I've not got much. I don't keep money in the house any more. Rick and his dad talked me into putting what I don't need in the bank, and what bits of jewellery I've got aren't that valuable, except my engagement ring, and I always wear that – except at work, when it's in my handbag in its box. All the chemicals in the bleach and perm lotion would ruin it.'

'Right then, Mon, go ahead and open the front door, and we'll go in together – regardless. We can always yell for help if we need it. And we've both got handbags – they'll do to start with!' Joan urged firmly.

Taking a deep breath, Monica opened the door – as usual, the hall was in darkness. Still clutching Joan's arm, she ventured inside while Joan managed to find the small torch she carried in her handbag and started scanning the hall with it.

As the thin beam of light settled on the bulky shape of an army-issue kitbag, Monica uttered a scream of both relief and delight. 'Joan! Joan! It's not a burglar! It's Rick! It's got to be Rick!'

Joan began to laugh and followed her friend into the sitting room. A drowsy-looking Rick Eustace was getting to his feet from the sofa, where he'd obviously been sleeping, and Monica flung herself into his arms, laughing and crying at the same time.

'Why didn't you tell me? Oh, Rick, why didn't you write or even send a telegram? Oh, I've missed you so much! I've hardly anything in the larder, and I must look a mess! Joan and I were going to go to the station and get her enrolled as an ambulance driver tonight but—'

She would have gabbled on if he hadn't stopped the flow of words with his lips.

Tears pricked Joan's eyes as she witnessed the happy little scene. She would never again come home to find her husband safe and well, but she was happy for her friend. 'Welcome home, Rick. Believe me, we are both very relieved it's you and not some no-mark bent on making off with the family silver!'

Rick tore himself away from his wife's embrace and smiled sadly at Joan, remembering that she was a war widow now. 'Thanks, Joan. It's good to see you. Don't worry, the family silver's at Mam's house.'

Monica's eyes were shining, her happiness evident in every line of her body as she clung tightly to Rick's arm. 'I should be very cross with you, Rick Eustace, giving us both a fright like that!'

He grinned down at her. 'But of course you're not. I wanted it to be a surprise. I meant to open the door to you, but I was so tired after that journey I just fell asleep,' he explained. 'I've got forty-eight hours and I intend to make the most of it,' he informed Monica, although there was other news he also had to impart and he wasn't looking forward to that. He'd finished his training and was now, with his new battalion, going out to join General Montgomery's forces in North Africa. This time next month, he might well be facing Rommel's Panzer divisions somewhere in the desert.

Joan pulled her gloves back on determinedly. 'Well, there's no use me staying here and playing gooseberry, I'm off home. You can take me to join up another night, Mon, after Rick's gone back.'

Rick had been aware that his wife had been teaching Joan

to drive, but he'd not known of her intentions to drive an ambulance, like Monica. He'd always liked Joan and Jim, and now he felt deeply sorry for her, a young widow with a baby to bring up – alone. He admired the fact that she was still determined to do something for the war effort. He pushed his disappointment down inside him as he made up his mind. 'No, Joan. Why don't we all go down to the ambulance station and then go for a quick drink? And then I'll drive you home. You're not standing waiting for a tram in this weather – I know Monica will agree.'

Monica tried to hide her own disappointment, for she desperately wanted to spend every minute with her husband, but she nailed a smile to her face. 'And you've worked so hard preparing to join up, we have to do it tonight.' She was trying to remember if her best nightdress was in the pile of ironing waiting to be done – but well, if it was, so what? He wouldn't notice, and she didn't care. She wouldn't be wearing it for very long, anyway.

Joan looked from Monica to Rick and wondered what to do. She obviously didn't want to come between them, especially when he had such a short leave, but the return journey home wasn't appealing either. She'd steeled herself for this interview and had had two rows with her mam about it. These days she seldom, if ever, went out at all. It would be a treat to sit in a pub with a small port and lemon, or whatever they could provide, in the company of her friends.

'It's settled, then! I'll get my greatcoat. I suppose it's still bitterly cold out there?' Rick asked, thinking that very soon these cold, damp, dark winter days and nights would be just a memory for him.

'It is,' Monica assured him. She didn't want her friend to think she'd come out on a wild goose chase. And what kind of a friend was she if she couldn't spare an hour to have a drink with Joan? It must be tearing Joan's heart in two, just to see them both so happy and in love, when she'd lost the love of her life forever, at the age of twenty.

Chapter Sixteen

———◦→◦←◦———

Lily just couldn't believe that it was so warm at this time of the year. It was a sunny April morning as she walked down the narrow cobbled street towards the small market square. It would still be cold, and maybe even wet and windy, back home in Liverpool; sometimes the miserable weather went right through until early June, but here it never got as cold as it did back there, not even in winter. It was so good to feel the warmth of the sun on her face as she came out of the narrow street and into the square. This morning she would get what shopping she needed, and then she was going to meet David for a glass of wine at the Hotel Palacio Principe, one of Lisbon's better hotels, followed by some lunch at a tiny café where the food was good and very reasonably priced.

They had both been very, very fortunate in finding work, he as a voice coach and she as an assistant in the wardrobe department at the Opera House. Of course Bella's voice had helped a great deal, and the girl was well thought of. David worked from early morning until lunchtime, when almost everything closed down for three hours, and then carried on later into the early evening, while she started work in the afternoon. It was often after midnight when she got home, so they didn't really see much of each other, but they were both finding ways to work around that.

Her shopping done, she caught the tram down into the city and then walked to the hotel. David was sitting in the foyer and she was surprised to see that Bella was with him.

'No training this morning, Bella?' she queried as she settled herself on the ornate brocade sofa beside the girl.

Bella had settled in very well and was popular with almost everyone. She had asked if she might undertake small jobs for Senhora Pereira, the wardrobe mistress – mainly sewing repairs to earn some money so that she could contribute to their living costs when she wasn't singing. But she had already twice been singled out to sing in the chorus. Lily smiled at her; she had to admit that eighteen-year-old Bella was developing into a very beautiful and confident young woman, and she was aware of the admiring glances she attracted whenever she accompanied them on their occasional jaunts.

'We finished early, Aunt Lily. We will be staging our first production of *The Magic Flute* in two weeks, and so there is much to do.'

'Oh, don't I know it,' Lily replied, rolling her eyes to the decorated ceiling.

'Shall we go into the lounge bar? It's more comfortable than here,' David suggested.

The room was getting rather crowded as people arrived and waited for their lunch companions. Most of them were men, David noted, and was well aware from the way they were dressed and their mainly fair complexions that they were not native Portuguese. In fact, he was certain that most of them were spies: German, British, Italian, Dutch and other nationalities. They made him uncomfortable, and Lily positively hated them – all of them – but the city was known to be full of spies; generally they tried to avoid them. The Hotel Palacio Principe was different – and not to be confused with the more famous Hotel Palacio which attracted the writers, painters and poets who had escaped from repressive regimes in their own countries but which was also notorious for the Gestapo spies who congregated there. Yes, they frequented this hotel, despite its sometimes dubious clientele, because the very first time they had ventured across the threshold, both the manager and the maître d' had been friendly and welcoming – a fact David had put down mainly to both Lily and Bella's attractiveness and friendly demeanour. Of course, it helped that Bella spoke the language fluently, having quickly picked it up again.

The lounge bar was decorated in the Art Deco style of the last decades, but the large room was looking a little shabby in places. The potted palms, vibrant hibiscus plants and high glass-domed ceiling hid the rough edges, though, and added a bit of style, Lily thought. A white-jacketed waiter placed the small dishes of *petiscos* down on the table in front of them and took David's order for drinks: a bottle of vinho verde for Lily and himself, and a glass of fresh orange juice for Bella.

Lily glanced around, frowning slightly at a party of people who had just come into the room. She hoped they wouldn't stay long; they spoiled the atmosphere, in her opinion. Foreigners, all of them, judging by their dress and manners. 'That's the only fly in the ointment about this city,' she

commented, looking pointedly in the direction of the group.
'The place is full of foreigners.'

David laughed. 'That does include us, Lily, my love!'

'Oh, you know what I mean. We're here for a genuine purpose – Bella's career – and it is her native country. We're not here to try to glean any scrap of information we can on military or naval matters. They give me the creeps!'

'But like us, Lily, they're enjoying themselves away from the dangers of war,' David reminded her.

The waiter brought their drinks and David paid the bill.

'Well, yes, I have to agree with you there, David. It is pure heaven to be away from all the terror of the bombing and the chaos,' Lily said, with feeling, 'and the shortages of virtually everything. But I do still miss home and, of course, family.'

She meant it. It was wonderful not to live in fear of the sirens and the bombers, and the telegrams that were arriving with ever-increasing frequency. Wonderful not to have to stand in a queue for hours in freezing weather just to get a few ounces of this or a few ounces of that. Here, the shops were well stocked and you could buy nearly everything – provided you had the money – not to mention the wine, something she had never drunk frequently at home, whereas here everyone drank it as if it were water – and she'd been told it was safer. And then there was the weather. It certainly did help, and Bella seemed to positively glow with the advent of a warm spring. Lily even loved the little house they rented up near the Castelo de Sao Jorge. It was tiny by comparison to Olive's house in Mersey View, which was far from being a mansion, but it was never cold or damp, and everything seemed to thrive in the pots in its small backyard. You could have fruit and

159

tomatoes and vegetables all year round, and her neighbours had freely given advice on how to grow them.

'Do you think a letter might get through soon from Olive, Lily?' David asked, popping a *bacalhau* into his mouth. He, too, loved the food, wine and lifestyle of their adopted country.

Lily shook her head, looking thoughtful and sipping her wine. 'I really do hope so, David. I miss hearing all the news about . . . well, about everyone! Our Olive is good at writing letters, she doesn't miss things out, and she knows just what I will want to hear. But well, who knows what the post is like over there, never mind letters getting over to other countries? It's almost six weeks now since I wrote, and we've heard nothing, nothing at all.' She had written as soon as they moved into their little *casa*, telling her sister about their journey – which, to her surprise, had been both comfortable and pleasant – as well as the good news that she and David had both got jobs. She'd described the city and the customs and the friendliness of the people towards them, and told her sister how she'd learned that Portugal was Britain's oldest ally. But when she'd taken her letter down to the *Correios*, she'd been told not to hold out much hope of it arriving at its destination. She'd also been told that she could, of course, telephone – but that could also be erratic and very, very expensive. It had been out of the question, anyway, since Olive didn't have a telephone, and nor did anyone else in Mersey View.

Bella's forehead creased in a frown. 'I worry so much for them all, particularly Joan and Charlie. Has there been any more news of how things are going at home?' she queried.

Occasionally, they heard bits of news, and Bella in particular managed to pick up scraps of information from the people who worked in the Opera House. There were no posters here telling people 'Careless Talk Costs Lives', and some speculated openly about what was happening in the occupied countries, as well as Great Britain and America. There were daily newspapers and there was always talk that America would soon join the war, on the side of the British, and she hoped they would, but that's all it had amounted to so far – talk.

David shook his head. 'Not much, Bella, but there don't seem to have been any more bombing raids – at least, not on Liverpool – but that could change any day, and we'd not hear of it.'

Bella sipped her drink and nodded, her dark eyes full of sadness. 'That, I think, is the worst part, Uncle David. That we will not know, we will hear nothing . . .'

He reached over and patted her hand. 'We will hear, one day, Bella. And one day, it will all be over and then we can go home. But until then, we have to get on with our lives and do what we can to follow our plans.'

Lily nodded her agreement. 'You're right, David. I just wish I could send our Olive some of the food we can get here, but I can't.'

'And do not forget the sunshine, Aunt Lily,' Bella added, brightening up. 'Soon there will be the Festival of Easter. The celebrations go on all week, from Palm Sunday, in every town and village. I remember them from when I was a little girl. Everything is so beautiful, the flowers and music and the sacred services, you will love them.'

'I expect I will, Bella – that's if we get any time off to see them, let alone take part. I swear Senhorita Renata is determined to make everyone's life an absolute misery before the first night of *The Magic Flute*. I'm worn out with her already, and I know Elena Pereira is, too. I don't know how she keeps her mouth shut. I have difficulty at times!'

Bella reluctantly nodded her agreement. Lucia Renata, the famous Italian soprano who was to play the leading role of Pamina, daughter of the Queen of the Night, was known for her tantrums and tempers. She was fast approaching fifty and only got away with such behaviour because she had been a huge star at the opera houses in Milan and Rome before the war. No one really liked her; not Senhora Elena Pereira, and certainly not her Aunt Lily, who had remarked that the woman was arrogant and definitely needed taking down a peg or two. She was in danger of tarnishing her looks with her spite, and needed to remember that she couldn't hope to go on portraying beautiful young heroines for very much longer, even if her voice was still good.

It was the first week in May when Lily's letter finally arrived. The envelope was torn and stained and had obviously been opened and stuck down again. That wasn't unusual, Olive thought; all mail was censored. What was unusual was the fact that her sister's letter had got here at all. It had been postmarked weeks ago, and in Lisbon.

'Well, thank God they arrived safely at least,' Olive announced as she sat down at the kitchen table to read Lily's letter. Only she and Joan and baby Jamie were in the house; all the men were at work, and Charlie was away.

Joan finished changing the baby's nappy and tucked him up in his pram ready to wheel him into the corner of the yard, where there was a patch of sunlight. Everyone advised her that some fresh air each day was good for babies, as long as they were wrapped up and kept out of draughts. She herself wasn't all that sure about the air around here being 'fresh', but she'd followed Olive and Nelly's instructions without comment. 'Can I read it after you, please, Mam?' she asked as she deftly manoeuvred the pram out through the kitchen door.

'Of course! It's quite a long letter, but then I expect if you are living that far away there's plenty to write about. And also I suppose she must have been thinking that God knows if or when it would get here.' Olive scanned the lines of her sister's neat handwriting, nodding thankfully as she took in all the facts. They were safe, they had rented a house, they had jobs, Bella was happy at the Opera House, even if so far only behind the scenes, and she was so grateful for that.

Already thoughts were flitting into Olive's mind as to what she should write in her reply. Thankfully, there had been only a few spasmodic raids over the past months, and the city was slowly trying to get back to normality. Everything was still scarce and on ration, but Lily would know that. Jamie was growing and was a placid baby, Charlie was away at sea but safe, as far as she knew, and Joan, well, her daughter was becoming very adept at driving an ambulance and seemed to enjoy it. In fact, Monica had said she was a better driver by far than she was, and Joan had just this week been transferred to a local ambulance station. It was a waste of time, effort and the tram fare to go to Allerton and back, she'd declared.

Olive folded the letter and handed it over to Joan who was putting a pan of potatoes on the cooker.

'Will we write back, Mam?' Joan asked as she wiped her hands on her apron and took the letter from Olive.

'Of course we will. In fact, we can all write a page or two, but it getting there is quite another matter. Lily does say, though, that there are a lot of foreigners in the city – in fact, in the country as a whole – so they are not on their own. Although I gather from some vague remarks that she doesn't trust most of them. I'm surprised that bit wasn't censored.'

Joan nodded thoughtfully as she continued to read, which wasn't very easy because so much had been blacked out that at times things didn't make much sense. Well, at least they would have something to tell Monica when she called after work this evening, she thought, as she handed Lily's letter back to her mother.

'The main thing is that they are safe and seem to have settled into their new life, so let's pray that continues,' Olive said, thinking that safety was all any of them could hope for.

Chapter Seventeen

———◆·••◆·◆———

It was at the very beginning of May that Monica realised that what she had longed for was about to come true. She was pregnant. She hadn't been feeling well lately, she was tired all the time, her breasts had become larger, she had missed her periods, and the last two mornings she'd had to dash to the bathroom to be sick. There had been raids the last two nights; not particularly heavy ones, but it had been late when she'd at last got home. She'd felt awful and had crawled gratefully into bed, foregoing her usual cup of tea, only to wake next morning feeling sick and still tired.

She splashed her face with cold water and looked at herself in the mirror above the washbasin. She didn't look any different, she thought critically. A bit paler than usual, but a dab of rouge would sort that out; she just hoped this morning sickness wouldn't last long. As she went back into the bedroom and sat down at the dressing table a warm glow of happiness began to flood through her. There couldn't be any mistake, she was sure of that. She had longed for this to happen, and it must have been when Rick was home on his last visit. Oh, now she would no longer envy Joan having little Jamie. She'd go to see her mam straight after work. Nelly would be just as delighted, and so would her dad. Joan would be happy for her, too, and then she'd have to tell Nancy and Claude they were to be grandparents, and the girls were going to be aunts. And of course she would have to write to Rick, although she wasn't sure how long it would take for him to get her letter. A small frown creased her forehead and she paused, hairbrush mid-stroke. She didn't know exactly where he was, just that his battalion was somewhere in North Africa. Letters were addressed to an army depot in Somerset and she assumed they were forwarded on. It was a safety measure, but she wished she could know for certain that he would get to hear the wonderful news. But then they were fighting a war, they weren't off on some jaunt – something her mam was always stressing when she complained about the slowness of the postal service. Oh, how she wished this was happening in different circumstances! If only she knew where her husband was – or better still, if he could be here with her, in their home, as he should be. But almost as soon as that thought crossed her mind she dismissed it. Now was not the time to think about the negatives. Something wonderful was happening, something she'd so longed for.

She smiled to herself as she put on some lipstick – her news would cheer her mam up, for she was having a bit of a battle with Eileen over her relationship with Harold Stevens. In Nelly's opinion, Eileen was far too young to be getting so serious with a lad – and a lad who seemed too much at the beck and call of his very demanding mother at that! Nelly had heard enough about Mrs Stevens to get the measure of her, and the woman seemed to be as against sharing her son with a new bride as Nelly was against them getting married too young. Nevertheless, flying in the face of all Nelly's advice and wishes, Arthur had given his consent to Eileen getting engaged to Harold, and they were planning to get married later that year, in September. Now all Eileen could talk about was what she was going to do for her bridal outfit, how they were going to get enough food and drink for a decent wedding breakfast, and just where Harold's mother was going to stay, should she make the journey from Birmingham, she being a widow and not in the best of health and mistrusting hotels and guest houses. It was all driving her poor mam mad!

Monica had done her best in the matter of a wedding dress and veil, offering her sister her own dress to wear. But despite the fact that her dress was far finer than anything that could be found these days, even if you had the money and hundreds of coupons, Eileen had refused point blank, saying she wasn't going to wear Monica's 'cast-offs', which Monica had told her was the height of ingratitude. It had caused a huge row between them, and they were barely on speaking terms even now.

Well, she wasn't going to let anything so petty upset her, she thought, as she went downstairs and prepared to leave for work. She had to look after herself now, it was vitally important for her and Rick's baby, and as she walked down the road in the warmth of the May sunshine, she felt the tide of happiness wash through her again. Oh, she wished she could tell Rick face to face that he was going to be a father, and that he could be home in time for when his son or daughter arrived. A little shiver ran through her as she remembered that Joan had once said the very same thing, and then Jim McDonald had been killed well before Jamie was born. She pushed the memory away – no, nothing like that was going to happen to Rick. But try as she might, she couldn't get the thought out of her mind that Rick was somewhere in North Africa and facing an implacable and highly efficient enemy.

Everyone had been utterly delighted with her news, Monica thought happily, as she got ready to make the journey home from Mersey View that evening. Nelly was so overjoyed that she'd dissolved into tears and then said she would accompany her to see the doctor the following day, to make certain of the fact. Mam was nothing if not practical. Even her sister had muttered 'congratulations', accompanied by a smile of sorts, but had then added that it was fortunate that, as Baby Eustace wasn't due until November, it wouldn't take the shine off her September wedding. That had prompted a very severe telling-off from Nelly. Joan had hugged her so tightly she had hardly been able to breathe, and Olive had urged her – laughingly – not to go visiting any theatres when she was nearing her due date.

She was wishing now that she'd come by car, as it was after ten and she was tired, plus she'd been hit by a sudden wave of sickness that seemed to come out of nowhere, and she felt a little panicky about the likelihood of her throwing up at any moment. She was definitely not looking forward to the tram journey back to Allerton. But she had to save what precious petrol she had, though she wondered how long it would be before she'd have to give up driving; Nelly had already hinted at it, and she'd ignored her.

She shakily kissed her mother and father goodbye, nodded to her sister and then left the house, peering up the street to see Joan standing on Olive's doorstep waving. As she waved back the first wailing notes of the siren shattered the stillness of the spring night.

'Monica! Mon, for God's sake, get back here now!' Joan yelled, covering the few yards quickly and grabbing her friend's arm. 'You can't go home now, not in this! There won't be any trams, and you can't walk all that way!'

'But what about Mam and Dad . . . ?'

Joan was pulling at her arm. 'Your da, like the rest of the men, will be out any minute now, going to their posts. Your mam and Eileen will be under the stairs, as usual – you know what they're like – so just you come back with me, Mon, please? Look at you, I've never seen you so green in the face. And you can barely keep your eyes open. Are you feeling sick? You've got to think of the baby now.'

'But, Joan, I . . . we can't! The ambulances . . . I . . . we'll both be needed.'

Joan nodded grimly but continued to pull Monica towards Olive's house. She knew what this baby meant to Monica, and she remembered the dreadful exhaustion and sickness all too well; she wasn't going to let her friend try to walk home in a raid, or drive an ambulance. Feeling the way Monica did, she'd be no use to anyone. Joan herself would go out, but the roads were in such a state that she was afraid her friend would suffer a miscarriage, being thrown around in the way they often were as they tried to avoid bomb craters, falling masonry, blazing gas mains, other emergency vehicles, and people fleeing in terror from their devastated homes. The chances of that happening, especially if she wasn't fit to drive, feeling as sick as she looked, were too high for Joan's liking.

Once she'd got Monica safely in the shelter with Olive and the two elderly gentlemen lodgers, Joan decided that she would go back for Nelly and Eileen. There was room in their shelter, which was safer than under Nelly's stairs, and Monica wouldn't have to worry about them. There was enough for all of them to worry about, knowing their husbands and fathers were out there in the hell of the bombing raids.

Monica was relieved when her mother and sister arrived and settled themselves; she just wished Joan wasn't going back out there.

'Anything going on yet, Mam?' she asked Nelly who, as usual, had brought her knitting, while Eileen had brought the letter she was writing to Harold.

'The batteries have opened up on the dock estate, and I could hear the first wave of them coming in over the river, heading for the docks, as usual,' Nelly replied soberly.

'God help them in Bootle and Anfield, then,' Olive added.

No one said it but everyone was thinking, *and God help us in Everton, too.*

As the hours wore on, and midnight came and went, the bombing continued on until three o'clock, the shelter shaking and vibrating from explosions that seemed too close for comfort. Each time, Olive and Nelly looked at one another in fear and anxiety, thinking of Frederick and Arthur and their homes, whilst Monica began to fret that she wasn't out with Joan doing what she could to help. Her sickness had passed long ago and she was furious with herself that she hadn't just swallowed it down and gone out with Joan.

'I feel so useless just sitting here!' she protested. 'In fact, I think it's actually worse than being out in it. Then you just don't have time to think about anything! You just have to get from A to B as safely as you can.' She was thinking that there would be badly injured people out there, praying for someone to come and help them, longing to hear the sound of an ambulance bell over the surrounding bedlam. What was she doing? Sitting here, shaking like a scared rabbit, and doing nothing to help when she was perfectly capable of doing so.

'Well, you're not going out there, Monica, and that's that!' Nelly said grimly. 'It's bad enough that we've all got to sit here just waiting, without us having more worry piled on our shoulders. You've not just got yourself to think about now.'

'I know that, Mam, and I know it can be dangerous in the early days, but morning sickness is normal any time of the day, and . . . and I'm needed!'

'Yes, and your baby needs you, too, in these first months of its life!'

Monica gave up, just wishing the raid would end. Everyone was worn out, they'd had no sleep, and they would all go to their work in the morning, no matter what state the city was in. It had become a matter of principle now.

The 'All Clear' sounded half an hour later and they all slowly got to their feet, collecting up what they had brought with them and hoping against hope that their homes were still standing, when suddenly there was a terrific explosion that threw them all to the ground. Monica and Eileen screamed aloud in fright as they were flung against the metal base of a bunk. Olive clutched Nelly's arm tightly, her eyes wide with fear, and the two gentlemen were visibly shaken. Only the wicker crib, pushed to the back of a bunk, which held the sleeping Jamie McDonald seemed not to have moved at all.

'Oh my God! What the hell was that? Did they sound the "All Clear" too soon?' The questions tumbled from Monica's lips.

Olive tried to calm herself. 'Whatever it was, it seemed very close. But it was probably at the docks.'

Nelly nodded, pulling herself together but expecting the worst. 'Yes, very likely the docks. It just sounds closer than it really is.'

'Mam, that was one horrendous explosion!' Monica cried, thinking of her father, Frederick and Joan, all still out there.

'Yes, the whole street could have gone, Mam!' Eileen added, tears of fright in her eyes.

Nelly was wondering if Everton itself had gone, but she shook her head firmly. 'Now just stop that, Eileen! That kind of speculation isn't going to help anyone!'

'I think we should stay in here for another half an hour, don't you, Mrs Garswood?' Mr Compton suggested. 'Perhaps they did sound the "All Clear" too soon. Maybe we should wait for it to go again to be sure.'

Olive nodded her agreement, and as she did so another huge explosion rocked the building. 'What the hell are they playing at? Sounding the "All Clear" when obviously it's not!' she demanded, as she got to her feet, terrified for the safety of her husband and daughter, and oblivious to Eileen Savage's sobs of fear.

Monica sat down on the bunk again, rubbing her shin,

which had been bruised by her fall during the first explosion. Obviously, someone had made a mistake – it happened, even though it shouldn't. But maybe it was just a straggler dropping the last of his load, although that first explosion had been too big for it to be a couple of incendiary bombs. They were getting to recognise the type of bomb now – and that had been unlike anything she'd experienced before.

Fifteen minutes later, after yet another explosion, Arthur Savage appeared, his face black with soot and grime, the whites of his eyes standing out strangely. His warden's tin hat was pulled low over his forehead and he looked exhausted.

'Oh, thank God, Arthur! What the hell is going on?' Nelly cried, clasping his arm.

'I've just run down to explain it all, Nell, luv. I knew you'd all be getting in a state after hearing the "All Clear". It's the ammunition ship the *Malakand*, she's berthed at the Number Two Huskisson Dock. A barrage balloon was shot down and fell on her deck, and she's caught fire. There are over a thousand tons of high-explosive bombs in her hold, as well as other munitions. There's nothing that can be done to save any of it, or the ship, so the explosions you can hear are the munitions blowing up. They're going to have to let her blow herself out, but there's no cause for alarm, it's not bombs dropping.'

'Oh, Arthur! Thank you so much for coming here to tell us, otherwise we'd have been terrified for the rest of the night,' Olive cried, relieved.

'And what about the others?' Nelly queried.

He managed a grin, his teeth white against his dirty cheeks. 'As far as I know, everyone is safe. I last saw your Joan driving like a maniac down York Terrace, with the bell going full pelt, followed by a fire engine. Frederick's been with me most of the night, Olive, and both houses are still standing, although I think there will be some damage to ours, luv. Next door's roof has been blown off.'

Although very relieved, Nelly gave a thought to her neighbour. 'Poor Florrie! She's only just got straight after the last raid – and she's got her sister and her four kids living with her now, after they were bombed out in the last one. So, it's all right for us all to go back home now?'

Arthur nodded. 'Although I think Monica should stay with you, Olive.' He turned to his elder daughter. 'You look done in, luv, and I know you, you'll insist on helping your mam clean up and then be off to work. I really do think you should consider staying in Mersey View with us for the rest of the week, rather than go back to that empty house in Allerton. We'll no doubt be a while yet, Olive, and so will Joan,' he finished, before turning to leave. Even though it was now nearly four o'clock in the morning, there was still plenty to do. The city, for the third night running, was once again in flames.

'Will you all stop treating me like a sick child?' Monica demanded. She was tired and hungry and thirsty, but Joan would be in a worse state, and it would be hours yet before she got home. 'I'm not staying with you all week, Mam. If there are more raids then it's my duty to do what I can to help. Rick wouldn't want me to be doing nothing except sitting in a damn shelter for hours on end. Oh, I suppose we're going to have to put up with this for days until that ship blows itself up!' she cried as another explosion shook the shelter. 'Pass Jamie over to me, Mam. I'll take him back into the house.'

Nelly picked up the wicker crib from the bunk, marvelling at how Joan's son had managed to sleep through the entire raid and the continuing demise of the *Malakand*.

Chapter Eighteen

—————

By Thursday, after almost a week of continuous bombard-ment, the citizens of Liverpool had begun to wonder just how much more they and their battered city could take. Warehouses, factories, business premises, hospitals, tenement buildings and private houses had been bombed repeatedly and indiscriminately. Huge fires raged the length of the docks, from those at Bootle in the north end of the city to those in the Dingle, eight miles to the south. Public and civic buildings had been destroyed or suffered heavy damage, rendering them unusable. The museum and library, the technical college, the Rotunda Theatre, Lewis's department store, the Bluecoat School, all had been targeted. St Luke's Church at the top of Bold Street was a burnt-out ruin. Even the magnificent but unfinished Anglican cathedral had been damaged. Everyone was exhausted, but grimly determined to try to carry on as normal – and still the ammunition ship continued to blaze and its cargo to explode.

Despite her best intentions to return to her home in

Allerton after work, Monica was forced to go to Nelly's house that night when the raid began much earlier. She'd not long finished at the salon when she realised that going back to Garthdale Road was not an option. She would have to go to her mother's house, and as quickly as possible.

'Mam, you can forbid me to go out until you're blue in the face, but I'm going! I'm not going to sit in that damn shelter for hours and hours until *they* get fed up and go home! I'm going out in the ambulance with Joan – they'll be glad of every pair of hands. Even our Eileen is on the fire-watching rota now,' she reminded her harassed mother. Her sister was one of the dozens of teenage girls and lads who did the vital job of dousing as many incendiary bombs as possible, tracking their descent, and using water from the hand-operated stirrup pumps to try to stop the flames taking hold and spreading. As well as the damage they caused, the incendiaries also acted as beacons for the bombers that circled endlessly overhead.

'Well, on your own head be it, then!' Nelly retorted as she gathered up what she could carry. She was very thankful now that there was room in Olive's shelter, for she certainly didn't relish sitting huddled under the stairs by herself, with both Arthur and Eileen out. She hadn't really expected her elder daughter to come tonight. Monica seldom took much notice of her these days; she mostly did as she pleased.

Joan was on her way out of Olive's empty house when Monica arrived. 'I didn't expect you to be here tonight. I thought you said you were going home?'

'I was, but I didn't have the time. Are they all safely in the shelter?' she queried.

Joan nodded. 'Are you absolutely certain you want to be out tonight?'

'Yes! Even if I can't drive, I can at least help in some way. I'm used to dealing with casualties now. I've already sent word to my own station, telling them why I can't come,' she replied as they ran down the street.

As they reached the bottom of York Terrace buildings were already alight around them, and the figures of wardens, firemen and fire-watchers could be clearly seen moving between the flames. 'Here we go again!' Joan muttered grimly as they both ran into the drill hall that was being utilised as a headquarters for the volunteer services.

'Anything for me to do, Mr Yardley?' Monica asked as she recognised the warden in charge. He lived halfway down Northumberland Terrace.

'Don't ask daft bloody questions, Monica Savage! You can drive, can't you?'

'I can,' she replied, smiling at his use of her maiden name.

'Then get the keys off the desk and go out with Joan, there's been a direct hit on one of the hospitals – Mossley Hill, I think. We don't know how bad it is, but do whatever they tell you to do; someone will have emergency plans for the evacuation of patients to another hospital.'

She forgot all about herself and her condition as she doggedly followed Joan's ambulance down the main road, both vehicles instinctively swerving to avoid the hazards and obstacles that were becoming more and more frequent. All she could concentrate on was getting to her destination as quickly as possible, all thoughts and fears for her own safety and that of her family and friends forgotten. Joan, too, had gritted her teeth and pushed everything from her mind as the small fleet of ambulances hurtled down the main road. When she thought at all it was to wonder how long tonight's carnage would go on for.

'I just wish she hadn't gone, Olive,' Nelly confided quietly to her friend and neighbour as they sat in the shelter, once again waiting out the raid. There was plenty of room now, she mused. Frederick, Arthur, Joan, Monica and Eileen were all out doing what they could to help. Just the two gentlemen lodgers and Jamie were their companions – and the baby was fast asleep.

'I know, Nelly, luv, but I'm sure she'll be fine. She's a healthy young woman.'

'I know, I can only hope and pray that she stays that way, Olive. I tell you what, though, I'm beginning to think that your Lily had the right idea, even though I certainly didn't approve at the time. She, David and Bella are a damn sight safer than we are.' She lowered her voice. 'How much more can we take of this? Another night and it will have gone on continuously for a whole week! It's never been as bad before.'

Olive nodded slowly; Frederick had told her that he'd heard there were now over fifty thousand people homeless in the city, with the Council desperately trying to find any kind of accommodation for them. Families had been bombed out two, three and even four times now. The city was in ruins, and still each night the bombers came back.

'I think they're determined to completely destroy the docks and bomb us into giving up,' Olive muttered darkly. 'But by

God we won't, Nelly! If London can stand it then so can we. I told Frederick—'

Nelly never heard what Olive was going to say, for the roaring in her ears was so great that she cried out as she was flung to the floor. Trickles of soil came down from the roof of the shelter, coating them in dust and dirt. When she regained her senses, she saw that Olive had flung herself bodily over Jamie's crib and the child was wailing. Her ears were still ringing as she pulled herself to her feet. Mr Compton was frozen rigid with terror, while Mr Whitworth was on all fours on the floor, attempting to get up.

'My God! Olive! That's got to have been a direct hit on the street. Are you all right? Is everyone all right?'

Olive nodded as she rocked her grandson in her arms to try to calm him down.

'Thank God for this shelter, even though I hate it! I wonder whose house it was, Nelly?'

'Or houses, Olive. That was too close by half. I just hope those girls and the men are all right. This is the worst we've had it so far.'

They fell silent as their thoughts turned to their families, and whether or not they still had somewhere to call home. Had they just joined the ranks of the tens of thousands who now had nothing, except their lives and the clothes they stood up in?

When streaks of daylight filtered through the clouds and the first rays of the May sunlight sparkled on the grey turgid waters of the river, the 'All Clear' finally sounded.

The two women stood up, Olive still holding the now

sleeping baby, and they looked at each other with trepidation in their eyes.

'Well, we'd better go and see what's facing us,' Nelly said, biting her lip. She had this horrible feeling that she couldn't rid herself of; she was fearful that the entire street would be in ruins, for there had been many more explosions, although none as bad as that first one.

Olive nodded grimly. 'Well, Nelly, we've been through bad times before, so we'll cope, together, we always do.'

'Somehow we will, Olive, even if it means we have to camp here in this shelter permanently – God forbid!'

As she went up the steps and pushed open the door of the shelter Nelly was surprised to feel the warm rays of the sun on her cheeks – it wasn't what she had anticipated at all. Behind her she heard Olive let out a slow sigh of relief as the fact registered that her house was still standing, albeit with a partly damaged roof. Debris was scattered all over the yard, part of one of the yard walls had collapsed, and the sunlight sparkled on the sea of broken glass from the windows. Despite them having been taped up, every window in the house had been blown out. 'Oh, Nelly! Thank God! I don't care how much mess there is, we've still got a roof over our heads.'

Nelly had rushed to the yard door, now sagging on its broken hinges, and, pushing it aside, looked out. Then she gasped in horror as she took in a scene of massive destruction. Only Olive's house was left standing in the entire street. Where her own home had been there was now just a huge crater, surrounded by rubble and bits of furniture and rags that had once been soft furnishings. The feeling of dread she hadn't been able to dismiss these past hours had been proved correct. Mersey View had gone. There was nothing left.

Olive was still holding the baby but she moved him into the crook of her left arm as she put the other around Nelly's shoulders, utterly horrified. 'Oh, dear God! I . . . I . . . never expected . . . this!'

Nelly could only shake her head in disbelief.

Olive fought to pull herself together. 'Don't you worry, Nelly, luv. There's plenty of room for you, Arthur and Eileen in our house.'

Nelly's hand went to her throat as if she were choking. 'I . . . we . . . we've lost . . . everything, Olive!'

'I know, luv, and so has everyone in the street, but you're still in one piece – we all are, and so will the others be, too, please God.' It wasn't much in the way of comfort, but what else was there to say? It would be hours yet before they would know for certain if the rest of their families had survived the night, but in the meantime she would get them all back inside, and hopefully be able to make a pot of tea while they waited. That was if the gas and water mains weren't fractured and her crockery wasn't in bits on the kitchen floor.

It was full daylight, with the sunlight valiantly trying to penetrate the clouds of smoke that still billowed into the spring air, as the two girls walked slowly home. They were both exhausted, their faces grey with fatigue and shock, their eyes ringed with dark circles and dull with anxiety, weighed down by the memories of the horrors they had lived through these last hours. Thankfully, Monica thought, they had seen both Frederick and her own dad when the two men had returned to the station.

'You look done in, the pair of you. Get yourselves home now, you've done enough,' Arthur Savage had urged.

'Aye, both your mams will be worried sick about you,' Frederick had added.

'What about our Eileen? Has anyone seen her?' Monica had asked, thinking for the first time in hours about her sister who had been fire-watching.

'I sent her home over an hour ago, it was obvious that the worst was over then,' Arthur had informed her, remembering how utterly haggard his younger daughter had looked. She was only eighteen, for God's sake, he'd thought bitterly. She shouldn't have been out, facing the sights and horrors they'd all had to endure, she was too young.

Monica turned to her friend now, grateful for the sensation of the gentle spring breeze on her face. 'All I'll have time for is to get a wash, a cup of tea and a bite to eat before I get off to work.'

Joan turned to look at her friend. 'Mon, you need to get some sleep, you really do! Surely everyone will understand if you don't go in until this afternoon, after the night everyone's had.'

Monica shook her head; tempting though the thought was, she knew it was impossible. 'No, I've got customers booked in. I can't let them down, Joan. They'll have been up all night, too, and will have to work – and they've probably been looking forward to a new hairdo as a bit of a treat. It would just be selfish of me to let them down.'

'Let's just hope the factory's still standing, then. Not much else is. The whole city is like a wasteland!' Joan finished, staring ahead at what seemed like miles and miles of utter destruction. 'It's a miracle neither of us came to any harm, Mon. It all looks so much worse in daylight. I've never seen so many craters in the roads, they're almost unusable.'

'It's pretty bad, I have to admit,' Monica replied as they stepped over coils of electricity and telephone cables that snaked across the street.

To their right, workmen were frantically trying to shut off a damaged water main, and the members of a fire crew were still damping down the embers of a building, which made their journey slower and more cautious.

When they finally reached the corner of Northumberland Terrace and turned into Mersey View, they both stopped dead, utterly appalled.

Monica clutched Joan's arm tightly. 'Oh no! Oh, dear God, Joan!'

Joan swallowed hard, unable to believe her eyes, but her mind registered the fact that Olive's house still stood, because nothing else did. 'It . . . it must have been a direct hit, Mon, and a bloody big bomb – or bombs!'

'Yes, thank God Mam was in the shelter and not under the . . .' Her voice broke as she thought of what would have happened to her mother if she'd not been in Olive's air-raid shelter.

'We just have to keep counting the blessings we're left with. We know your mam and Eileen and your dad are all safe, Mon. I know that Jamie, Mam and Frederick are, too.'

Monica managed to nod. 'Oh, poor, poor Mam. She's lost *everything*, Joan! All those years of scrimping and saving to get a decent home together, and now . . . it's all gone.'

'She's not on her own, Mon, we've seen enough tonight to

know that. And everyone in the entire street has lost every-thing.'

On top of all that, Joan knew they'd have to go and try to find somewhere else to live. They'd need to get themselves essential clothes and new ration books and other documents, whilst trying to cope with the reality of losing their homes and possessions, trailing through the shattered streets to official buildings that might not even still be there. The world was such a cruel place, now, she thought bitterly.

Monica was trying to pull herself together, to think rationally. 'Well, yes, they are all safe, thank God, and they can come and live with me. At least I've got a home, and there is certainly enough room. We haven't heard whether that part of the city has suffered heavy bombing, have we? I can help them with clothes and things – they'll have to sort out the ration books and other stuff, though.'

Joan squeezed her arm. 'Your mam's lucky, Mon, luckier than most.'

Monica looked at her friend with a glint of scepticism in her eyes. 'That's of course if she'll come and live with me. She's lived here in Mersey View all her life.'

'I can't see that she's got much choice about it now, Mon. Mersey View has gone. I know Mam will have already offered to take them in, but she'll be better off with you, and then Mam can take in someone else, maybe Ethel and Harry Newbridge. Well, come on, we'd better go and see how they all are.'

Monica slipped her arm through Joan's, thinking that at times like this, good friends were beyond price. With Joan's help and support she'd get through the days and months ahead.

And then she would be responsible for another life, just as Joan was, and she'd find the strength to deal with that, too.

She felt far older than her twenty-one years and, as ever, wondered where Rick was and what he was doing – and most of all, whether he was safe and well.

Chapter Nineteen

———◈✦◈———

The heat of summer had been very oppressive, Lily thought, and it had taken its toll on both David and herself, although Bella seemed to be able to cope with it very well. They had stayed in the city, although many residents had headed for the small towns and fishing villages on the Estoril coast and the Algarve, or north and inland along the Douro River to the mountains to escape the heat. Over the summer weeks, the heat at midday had shimmered in a mirage-like haze over the narrow streets and houses in the old part of the city where they lived.

At least now that September had come it was getting slightly cooler, and she was thankful for that. She still didn't really think of Lisbon as 'home', and she couldn't feel entirely at ease with so many foreign spies in the city – particularly those who so obviously belonged to the detested Gestapo – but most native Lisboans and Portuguese were very friendly, and so they managed. She adjusted her sunglasses and tilted the large brim of her hat further down over her forehead as she alighted from the tram at the edge of the Praça do Comércio, the huge elegant square which fronted the ocean and was cooled by a welcome breeze.

The news from home throughout the summer hadn't been good. What they'd been able to glean was from the newspapers and the wireless – and the 'grapevine' at the Opera House. A letter had arrived from Olive at last, in early August, heavily censored. Lily still couldn't get over the fact that entire streets had disappeared all over her native city. Buildings and whole areas she'd known and loved had gone forever. It seemed incredible to her that the city centre was now a vast bomb site, with only the statue of Queen Victoria on her pedestal in Queen's Square still standing, its stone features surveying the miles and miles of devastation that surrounded it, for not another building was left standing. Olive had written that the 'May Blitz', as they now called it, and which had gone on for an entire week, had been hell on earth but that, thankfully, they had all survived – even if Mersey View hadn't.

Monica had taken her family to live with her in Allerton, something Olive gathered wasn't pleasing Nelly at all, though Eileen was delighted with her lovely new bedroom and the fact that there was the luxury of an indoor bathroom, as well as gardens front and back, not just a yard – and it was in a much nicer neighbourhood, too. Monica had had to give up work when she was six months into her pregnancy, and that wasn't helping things much, Olive had written. Two women in one kitchen didn't go well, particularly two as strong-willed and opinionated as those two, even though Monica was inclined to give Nelly free rein of late. Nelly was fervently hoping that the arrival of Monica's baby wouldn't coincide with Eileen's wedding to Harold Stevens, although that was unlikely, since the wedding was set for September and the child wasn't due until early November. But apparently, it was something she often spoke to Olive about. She made the long and wearisome journey to see her old friend and neighbour at least three times a week, on the days when she wasn't compelled to stand for hours in queues for the rationed food and household items. Nelly was missing her beloved neighbourhood, Lily surmised.

She pushed these thoughts to the back of her mind as she walked on across the square and towards the wide boulevard where the Opera House was situated. She turned into a side street and entered the building by the back entrance. It was so much cooler inside, she thought, as she walked down the long corridors that seemed to be in semi-darkness after the brilliant sunlight outside. Like most theatres she knew, backstage was a labyrinth of corridors and small rooms that always smelled musty – the gilding and the velvet upholstery, the crystal lighting and flowers, were all reserved for the stage and front of house. People paid small fortunes for tickets to the opera these days – in fact, for any kind of entertainment. The thought brought a frown to her forehead, as she wondered if Bella had had any news yet? For the past two months her adopted niece had been a permanent member of the opera chorus, but two weeks ago she had been singled out, with two other girls, to audition for the position of understudy to Lucia Renata for the forthcoming production of *La Bohème*. The previous understudy had left in high dudgeon after a row with the famous soprano.

She and David had been delighted that Bella had been

picked out, but she had sat the girl down and told her not to get her hopes up too high.

'You are the youngest of the three, Bella. The other two are well into their twenties,' she'd impressed upon the girl. No one had ever heard of a girl as young as Bella even being considered before.

'I know, Aunt Lily, and I'm aware they have far more experience than I have, so I will try not to be too disappointed if I am not chosen. But I can act better than they can, I know it, and my time will come.'

Lily had smiled. 'I've told you that often enough, haven't I, Bella? One day, it will be your turn to step out on that stage as "La Diva"!'

Bella had smiled back and Lily had felt a little relieved, but she still hoped against hope that Bella would be selected. After all, the girl had more than a wonderful voice – and granted, the other two hopefuls sang wonderfully, too – but Bella was young, beautiful, had been studying drama, and had great 'stage presence'. That was something that couldn't be taught – something that the other two didn't have. If by chance she did get the role, it wouldn't go down very well with the unsuccessful candidates, but because Bella had such a lovely nature, Lily was sure the rest of the chorus would be happy for her.

'*Bom dia*, Elena,' Lily greeted the wardrobe mistress, who was engaged in studying a wad of detailed notes regarding the costumes for the forthcoming production. She gestured towards the lists. 'I see there will be plenty for us to do.'

The woman nodded. 'Never is there time enough,' she agreed, her command of English far better than Lily's

Portuguese. 'There is news though, of the auditions . . .'

Lily stopped in the act of taking off her flower-trimmed light straw hat. 'You have heard? Bella?' She held her breath.

Elena smiled, revealing very white teeth. 'You will be happy, Lily. It is good.'

'Oh! She got it? She really got it?' Lily cried in astonishment.

Elena nodded. 'Even though she is very, very young, she is so very gifted, Lily. Never have I seen one so young who have so much . . . talent. And neither has Manuel dos Santos, he told me so himself.'

He was the director of the Opera House and his word was law, Lily knew that well. The excitement was now beginning to overwhelm her, and her eyes were sparkling with happiness. If the great Manuel dos Santos had such faith in Bella, then . . . oh, everything she and David had hoped and dreamed was coming true. All their sacrifices had been worth it. The very first time she and David had heard Bella sing, they'd both been certain she was destined for greatness. Lily had watched from the darkened wings of the Empire in Liverpool – together with Ben Stoker, the manager – as on an equally darkened stage the fifteen-year-old Bella, believing herself to be alone and unobserved, had unselfconsciously sung and acted out the '*Habanera*' from the opera *Carmen*. The girl had watched performances from the same wings by a touring opera company, just two weeks before.

They'd taken Bella to be coached by David Frances, the best in the city, which was how she had first met her future husband. He'd been in agreement that a talent like Bella's should never be wasted, and so Bella's classical training had begun; Lily and David had been married a short time later.

They'd learned from the girl that her deceased mother, Isabella, had been a famous *Fado* singer in Lisbon, before she'd had Bella. It was a genre of music that was at the heart of Portuguese culture and not easy to master at all. Isabella had passed down her musical talents to her daughter, but Bella had chosen her own path – opera was both Bella's passion and a discipline more widely enjoyed outside Portugal.

Before Lily could say another word to her companion, Bella herself burst into the room, her cheeks flushed and her dark eyes sparkling.

'Oh, Aunt Lily! Senhora Pereira! I am to be understudy! I am so happy!'

Lily hugged her tightly. 'I told you, Bella! I told you! It is the next step in your career! Oh, Uncle David will be so delighted, and you must write at once to Olive and Joan!'

Elena Pereira hugged the girl too and, speaking in Portuguese, wished her every success and the hope that she might get the opportunity to step in for Lucia Renata at some stage in the proceedings.

A little frown creased Bella's forehead at the mention of the Italian soprano who would be the leading lady, playing the role of the beautiful, young but already dying Mimì in the opera.

Lily noticed at once and understood. 'What's the matter, Bella? What has she said to you?'

Bella shrugged. 'Maestro dos Santos took me to see her, Aunt Lily, and although she was polite and wished me well, I could tell she did not really mean it. I could tell that she did not like me. In fact, I think . . . I think she really despises me and does not like it that I am to be her understudy!'

Lily tutted. 'Typical! Sit there!' she commanded, gently pushing the girl down in a chair set in front of a large mirror. It was obvious to Lily that the woman was fiercely jealous. 'Now, what do you see?'

Bella was confused. 'I . . . see . . . me, Aunt Lily, that is all.'

Lily shot a glance at Elena Pereira, who nodded. She'd come to know Lily well in the time she'd worked with her, and knew her ambitions for the girl who, to all intents and purposes, Lily thought of as her own daughter.

'Well, we see a beautiful young girl of eighteen who can light up a stage when she walks out on it, and who has one of the most magnificent voices ever to be heard in this opera house, and who has such a pleasant, undemanding nature that she is much liked by everyone. Never mind if *that* one likes you or not, she doesn't matter, Bella, you do! Her star is fading fast, yours is rising – and rising so brightly and so quickly that she will be nothing more than a memory very soon.'

Bella looked trustingly up at her. Her Aunt Lily had never failed her yet, so she must believe what she said. The happiness and excitement started to bubble up again inside her, dispelling the doubts. She would make them all so proud of her, one day – and maybe it would be sooner than she had hoped.

Lily smiled back at Bella through the mirror, but she had a determined look in her eyes. Lucia Renata's days were numbered, she was getting old, losing what looks she had once had, and her temper was legendary; she had few friends, and no wonder. 'Well, lady,' Lily vowed silently to herself as she placed her hands on Bella's shoulders, 'one wrong word to Bella, one screaming tantrum targeted at her, one malicious act, and you'll be finished instantly. I'll make damn certain of that – and then Bella will have her day!' As Bella gazed back at her aunt in the mirror Lily was glad to see the confidence return to the girl's eyes.

Bella's letter had arrived that morning, so her wonderful news was now spreading to her Liverpool family.

Monica had made the journey to Olive's house to see Joan – against Nelly's advice, of course. 'I don't know why you keep traipsing up there when you should be resting,' she'd remarked sharply.

'You should talk, Mam! You're never away from the place!' Monica had replied just as acidly.

'I miss everyone,' Nelly had replied defensively, and Monica had let it go at that, knowing it was the truth.

Now, she was confronted by Joan swathed in a large rubberised apron, her sleeves rolled up above her elbows and her hair confined under a turban. It was wash day, Monica realised, thinking she was a fool not to have remembered that everyone who still had a roof over their head and piped water did the big wash on Mondays. Nelly, of course, now had far more modern amenities than a copper boiler in a wash house in the yard, so she was not restricted to a Monday, as Joan and Olive were.

'Can you take a bit of a break from all this?' Monica asked, waving her hand in the direction of the washing line strung across the yard. The 'dolly' tub and washboard were propped up next to the boiler and the heavy mangle, utilised to get as much water as possible out of the washing by compressing it between two big wooden rollers, by turning a handle.

Joan grinned and pushed a stray tendril of hair back under

her turban. 'I'll just finish putting this lot through the mangle and quickly peg it out. You go in and put the kettle on. Mam's busy upstairs, stripping beds. By the way, we've had a letter from Bella in the morning post – Mam will tell you all about it.'

Monica went into the kitchen where she found Olive gathering up a pile of sheets in her arms, ready to take outside. 'Good morning, Mrs Garswood, I was told to come in and make a pot of tea. Joan says you've had a letter this morning from Bella?'

Olive smiled. 'We have, and it's really great news, Monica. I'll just take these out to our Joan and then you can read it. I know your mam likes to hear all the little details Bella and our Lily manage to put into their letters.'

Monica nodded as the older woman disappeared through the back door. As she waited for the kettle to boil Monica sat down at the kitchen table and placed her hands in the small of her back. It always seemed to ache these days, but she was getting rather bored being at home and doing very little. She still had two months to go, and Joan was always telling her to get as much rest as she could, because when Master or Miss Eustace arrived she'd get precious little for months and months, if not years. Jamie was teething, so she knew all about lack of sleep.

She looked around Olive's kitchen – it was damn hard work keeping an old house like this up to scratch. After the May Blitz, Olive had had to do a massive clean-up, as well as having all the windows replaced and the hole in the roof repaired. And, in addition to Joan and baby Jamie, Olive had the two gentlemen lodgers and both Ethel and Harry Newbridge living with herself and Frederick, until such time as they could find premises suitable for their business. And, of course, they also had Charlie when he was home on leave, which she assumed would be within the next week or so. Eileen's fiancé, Harold, was due home, too – the all-important wedding was looming ominously.

She made the tea and poured it out as soon as Olive and Joan reappeared, and Olive handed her the letter from her apron pocket. Monica read it quickly but took enough care to remember nearly everything to impart to Nelly later.

She looked up and smiled. 'Well, that certainly is good news. Lily and David must be delighted; they've both worked so hard for Bella.'

Olive sipped her tea thoughtfully. 'They have, and I'm glad for them, too, even though I've not agreed with all the travelling our Lily has insisted on doing. Dragging them first to London, then back here, and then to Lisbon of all places!'

'Well, we all know you thought she was mad, Mam, and so did I, but it's obviously paid off,' Joan replied, grinning at her mother across the table before turning to Monica. 'Will Bella get the chance to take this Lucia Renata's place, do you think, or will she just have to hang around and be ready and hope for the worst?'

'I don't honestly know, Joan. I suppose she will have to hope the woman is sick, or gets tired and wants a night off. I should imagine it's pretty demanding, having to perform every night. A bit hard on the voice.'

Olive nodded but looked thoughtful. 'I think we'll find that she does get to sing, even if it's only for one night – if our Lily's got anything to do with it,' she added before refilling her cup. Her sister was a force of nature. She turned to Monica. 'So how are you doing, luv?'

'Getting fed up, I can tell you, and not just because of all the waiting. Like Mam, I'm sick to death of this damn wedding. Honestly, I know I made a fuss, but you'd think our Eileen was the only girl ever to get married – and Mam still hasn't really forgiven Dad for giving his permission. She still thinks they're far too young, and I have to say I agree with her!'

'Some would say we were both too young as well, Mon,' Joan said quietly.

Olive sighed; Joan was right. But somehow both she and Monica had seemed far more mature than Eileen when they had got married. She knew full well what Monica meant, though, for Nelly was virtually at her wits' end with the palaver over all the arrangements. It was difficult enough in wartime to organise any kind of event, with all the uncertainties and shortages, never mind a fancy wedding. Nelly had protested that she'd be very glad when it was all over. Although, as the new Mrs Stevens would continue to live with herself and Monica, it wouldn't be a bed of roses even after the wedding was done and dusted.

'Has it been decided yet just where Harold's mother is going to stay?' Olive asked, knowing it was proving to be a bone of contention between Nelly and her younger daughter, and there had been many letters between Birmingham and Liverpool over the past weeks. Mrs Stevens had dismissed every option presented to her thus far, and without a hint of gratitude for the trouble Nelly and Monica had been going to in order to accommodate her.

'Well, I'm adamant that she's not staying with us after how

rude she's been! We haven't got the room, and in my condition I'm not giving up my bedroom and sleeping on a camp bed. I've told our Eileen that if that woman won't stay in the accommodation we can find for her – and that's proving hard enough, with the city in ruins – then it will mean Eileen sleeping on a camp bed in the sitting room, and I don't care if she is the bride!'

'I just hope Harold gets home in time. He's on the same convoy as our Charlie, and we never know exactly when to expect him home. You know how dangerous the convoys are. And just how slow,' Joan added.

Monica looked horrified. 'Oh, for God's sake, Joan, don't say that! I don't think I could stand the drama if that happened – and neither could Mam! Can you just imagine it? Our Eileen would be worse than this Renata woman Lily writes about.'

Olive nodded. 'It would be the straw that broke the camel's back, if that happened, Joan. Poor Nelly's nerves are on edge as it is.'

Monica refilled her cup. 'And she's already taken a dislike to Harold's mam, and she's never even met her!'

'Well, from what she's told me, the woman sounds like a bit of a pain in the neck, what with all the demands she's making about needing the right bed, and what kind of food she'll be given, and how quiet the neighbourhood is. She's not being very amenable, considering it's wartime. It really doesn't help either Nelly or Eileen,' Olive concluded, and both girls nodded their agreement.

Monica had, up to now, been fairly indifferent about her sister's future mother-in-law, but she was beginning to see

Olive's point of view. She was very thankful she had such a treasure as Nancy Eustace, who never interfered or made demands. Thinking of Nancy made her feel anxious about Rick – again. Where exactly was he now? she wondered. She knew he was in North Africa, but beyond that . . . nothing. All she could do was pray that he was safe and would come home one day, so they could start to live their lives together again.

Chapter Twenty

In the end Monica decided to go to stay with Nancy and Claude, leaving room in her own house to accommodate Harold's mother. She didn't want to impose any more burdens on her own mother, and it felt as if she'd be best making room in the house for their new guest.

Neither she nor Nelly liked the woman from the moment she arrived. Violet Stevens greeted them with a pinched face as she looked them all up and down, before scrutinising Monica's house and declaring, 'I suppose this will have to do.' The cheek of the woman! Although Monica did at least try to be pleasant and welcoming.

Nelly was just about civil. 'Just who does she think she is, Monica? All the complaints out of her about the journey – what did she expect, for God's sake? A private train like royalty? And as for all the poking about in your bedroom, feeling the quality of the curtains and the blackout blinds, checking whether the mattress was soft enough for her and the bedspread and eiderdown warm – I ask you! I bet she's never had such a comfortable – downright luxurious – bedroom in her entire life. Our Eileen said from what she's gathered they live in a fairly small terraced house. Oh, in a respectable area, but still, just a terraced house. Nothing like this – and she has the nerve to turn her nose up.'

Monica had sighed. This didn't bode at all well for the future, she thought. She certainly didn't envy her sister – but then after she was married Eileen would still be living here, she wouldn't be going to Birmingham, so maybe things would work out just fine. She hoped so; living through a war was bad enough, without having to exist under the same roof as a mother-in-law like Violet Stevens.

Eileen had continued to refuse to wear Monica's wedding dress, but both Nelly and Monica assured her that the powder-blue two-piece costume she had bought was lovely.

'It's very smart, and the hat is a perfect match,' Monica reassured her as she helped her sister dress on the morning of the wedding. She'd done Eileen's hair and was now placing the small pale-blue confection of net, feathers and stiffened grosgrain over her sister's carefully set hair. 'The bag and shoes have come up very well, don't you think?' she commented.

Eileen glanced down at the plain court shoes that had been dyed to match her outfit. They weren't new, and neither was her bag, but Olive had suggested dyeing them and giving them a new lease of life, and they did now look, well . . . nearly new. 'I still don't know if the flowers look right?' she fretted.

Monica sighed. Eileen was working herself up into a state of nerves. 'Now just stop that! You know how hard it was to get flowers at all, the summer blooms are finished now. And Dad paid a small fortune for those few cream rosebuds,' she reminded the bride as she eyed the bouquet sitting on the window ledge. 'Thankfully, smilax is still plentiful and fairly cheap,' she added, though privately she thought there was far too much of the trailing greenery. With so few flowers available, and knowing just how much those roses had cost, she would have opted for less smilax so the blooms could be seen to better advantage.

The wedding was to be held at All Hallows, the local parish church of Allerton. But that had caused another upset, as Nelly had wanted to go back to Everton, to St George's, where Monica had been married and which by some miracle was still standing amidst the surrounding dereliction. On this Monica had sided with her sister. They would need at least two cars to get there, and that was virtually impossible now that petrol was so short, and it was much too far to walk. The only alternative would have been the bus or the tram, and she had supported her sister's opposition to that option, even though Nelly had stated that the tram had been good enough for Arthur and herself.

'Mam, that was years and years ago! I'm just not going on a tram; what will Harold's mother think – and say?' Eileen had protested.

Nelly had glared back and muttered that she couldn't care less what Harold's mother thought.

Monica smiled at her sister's reflection in the dressing-table mirror – *her* dressing-table mirror. 'Right, I think you look gorgeous, and I'm sure Harold will be delighted with you. And don't forget that we've all begged and cajoled and pleaded to be able to put on a decent buffet afterwards. Everything will be just great!'

Eileen smiled at her sister's words, but at the mention of the buffet, the smile faded. Mrs Stevens had written that she assumed, despite the 'difficulties' of the present times, there would be a good hot meal at a decent hotel or some similar venue. Nelly had been almost incandescent, Monica remembered, and so she decided not to pursue that subject any further now.

Even though the church was only around the corner, Monica had decided she could spare some of her precious petrol and drive her sister there. Everyone else would have to walk but, with what Monica considered an act of supreme generosity, Nancy, her own mother-in-law, had suggested that they take both Nelly and Mrs Stevens in their car; her two daughters would be happy enough to walk from Monica's house.

That, at least, should make the woman happy, Monica thought, as she handed her sister her bouquet. Harold was lucky to be staying with Charlie at Olive's house, and so had avoided all this last-minute angst; she just hoped her sister would not dwell on the differences between her wedding at St George's and her own. She had had a proper, suitably decorated wedding car, a fabulous lace dress and veil, gorgeous flowers, and her bridesmaids had looked splendid, too. Today there would be no Bella to sing the beautiful solo '*Panis Angelicus*', either. If Eileen started to think about all that then it would definitely mar her day. But as everyone had impressed upon her – there was a war on!

'Now, you just sit here and wait for Dad to come up for you. I think Nancy and Claude have arrived,' Monica urged, hearing voices coming from the hall below.

'Monica, were you . . . well, were you a bit nervous about what would happen . . . on your wedding night?' Eileen asked timidly, suddenly overcome with nerves.

Monica turned back and took her hands. 'It's very normal to be nervous, but you don't need to be. It's all very natural, and even if it's a bit awkward at first, it soon won't be, because you love each other. I loved Rick desperately, I still do, and I know you love Harold just as much; so there is nothing to be afraid of, or nervous about. It will all be just wonderful, Eileen, I promise!' She bent and kissed her sister on the cheek. She wondered how long it had been since she'd done that, but today she wanted her to be happy.

'Well, I thought it all went off very well – considering,' Joan announced as Nelly and Arthur bade farewell to the last guests, and they left the Community Hall where the reception had taken place. 'Your Eileen actually looks happy for once, too,' she continued.

'I think she's had a few sherries,' Monica informed her friend. 'She was a bit apprehensive about the wedding night – I told her not to be.'

'I should think not! Aren't she and Harold going to share your lovely bedroom until he goes back to sea? Then I presume you'll go back home?'

'Too right I will, although Nancy's spare room is very comfortable, and she insists on bringing me tea in bed each morning. I feel quite spoilt.'

'When is she going home?' Joan asked, beginning to tidy up the dirty plates and indicating Mrs Stevens with a jerk of her head.

'Soon, I should think, especially if Mam has got anything to do with it. She can't stand her!'

Joan grimaced as she took in the small, stout figure in the rather drab russet-coloured dress and hat. She was looking decidedly disapproving about everything. 'Well, at least your Eileen isn't going to Birmingham.'

'Not yet, but I suppose in time she will. After all, it's his home town.'

'If I were her, I'd string it out for as long as possible. At least she gets on fairly well with your mam, and now she's a married woman they should have more in common.'

It was Monica's turn to pull a face. 'I wouldn't bank on that too much, Joan. Now she's a married woman I think our Eileen will find out she's got a mind and will of her own when it comes to decisions about the way things are done. I know I did; but then I'm so lucky with Nancy and Claude.'

Nelly hadn't expected Harold's mother to do much to help with the clearing up, so she wasn't disappointed when she remained firmly seated. She was sure, though, the woman couldn't find fault with the service or the reception. Of course, it hadn't been like Monica's wedding, but there was a war on.

'I expect you're relieved all the fuss is over now, Mrs Stevens, I know I am,' she said, going over to where Harold's mother was sitting. 'But I have to say it was a very nice service, the vicar spoke beautifully, and we'd managed to acquire an organist.' Now that it was all over, Nelly was trying to be conciliatory.

'I thought the choice of hymns could have been better, I always think that "Amazing Grace" is more suited to a funeral,'

Harold's mother replied, delving into her large handbag for her handkerchief.

'Really?' Nelly replied, biting her tongue. She was not going to be baited. Monica had reminded her that Violet Stevens would be back on a train to Birmingham the day after tomorrow, so she would try to keep the peace until then. 'I really hope you have enjoyed your stay here in Liverpool. I thought you might have stayed a little longer, until Harold goes back to sea?' she queried. The woman was so possessive, she'd have expected her to remain in Liverpool until the convoy sailed.

Violet Stevens dabbed at her nose. 'Oh, no! I couldn't possibly stay on here in Monica's house. I would feel most uncomfortable, I mean with Eileen and Harold there.'

Nelly was rather taken aback. 'Didn't you start off with your in-laws, then? Arthur and I stayed with my mam until we got a place of our own, everyone did then, things were still hard after the Great War. Of course, Monica and Rick are actually *buying* their house. She wanted to make you very welcome and, if I might add, comfortable? I mean she's actually given up her bedroom for you – and in her condition, too.'

Violet Stevens sniffed. 'Oh, she has, but I still wouldn't feel comfortable. I know it won't be long before Harold brings Eileen down to live with me. He's always been such a good, caring son – and even more so, since his father died. Quite honestly, I was very surprised, not to say taken aback, that he has considered marrying so young.'

Nelly nodded. 'I agree with you there; if I'd have had my way, Arthur would have refused to give his consent until Eileen was twenty-one, but she's a good girl and I know she'll make a good wife. We've done our best to get them both off to a good start, but married life is not easy, and I'm grateful that at least she'll be here with me while Harold's away. You have no idea what it's been like up here, the bombing was terrifying – and the convoys are so dangerous! My friend Olive's boy, Charlie, sails with the merchant fleet, and we worry so much.'

'Don't you think I know how that feels! My poor Harold away for weeks, months on end, and facing such hardships and dangers!' She dabbed her eyes. 'Please God, I'll soon have him . . . them both . . . back at home with me, where he belongs.'

Nelly's eyes hardened. 'I think it should be Harold's decision where he lives, when and if this war is ever over, after he and Eileen have discussed it, of course.'

'It is *not*! There will be no discussion! I *need* him with me! How am I meant to manage on my own, and me a widow?' came the curt reply.

'There are plenty of women who are widows, and there will be plenty more before this war is over! They manage because they have to. Young Joan McDonald over there is a widow, and she's only twenty, but you don't find her carrying on about it. Your Harold's first responsibility now is to his wife and any children they may have. Not to you. You must know that.'

The other woman's mouth was set in a hard, tight line. 'His responsibility is to me! His father would turn in his grave if he thought that Harold would desert me, not look after me in my advancing years.'

Nelly folded her arms and glared down at Violet Stevens. Oh, she saw it all now, she thought. 'Oh, so that's the real reason you don't approve of this marriage? You want him and our Eileen to look after you, wait on you hand and foot, put up with your airs and graces. Well, I can tell you, Violet Stevens, in my opinion mothers should not demand their children be at their beck and call. And in fact, if you made fewer demands and expected less from others, you might actually end up with a lot more!'

It was Monica who came to the rescue as, hearing raised voices, she quickly hurried out of the kitchen. She put her arm around Nelly's waist. 'Come on, Mam, I think we can leave the rest of this until tomorrow. Let's all get off home now. We're exhausted, and Claude and Nancy are waiting to run you and Mrs Stevens back.'

Neither woman replied, but silence was better than argument, Monica thought. It had probably been a bit of an ordeal for them both today, but at least it was over now.

Bella stared at herself in the long mirror in Senhora Pereira's sewing room, and smiled. Never had she thought this day would come, and even though the costume for Mimì was far from glamorous, since the poor girl was supposed to be a poverty-stricken, dying waif, its simplicity suited her, and she knew she looked good.

The wardrobe mistress smiled back at her. 'You look very much the part, Bella. Much more so than many a Mimì I've seen in the past. You *are* young and beautiful, and so slim that you look as if you might be dying. Not as so many others, who look as if they have eaten like queens all their lives. Have they told you yet when you will be called upon to appear?'

Bella shook her head. 'No, not yet, but I hope they will tell me soon. Senhorita Renata must get tired; she will surely have a night's rest in a week or two?'

Elena Pereira shrugged, thinking not if the woman saw Bella in that costume, she wouldn't. She had already been asked to let out the seams in the prima donna's dress once. 'I think it will benefit from just an inch off here, Bella,' she advised, pulling the fabric around Bella's waist a little tighter. It was such a pleasure to dress a girl like Bella, so lovely, and at the very beginning of what she was certain would be a fantastic career. It was a long time since Portugal had produced such a soprano. She smiled. 'Before you take it off, child, go and show your Aunt Lily how you look as Mimì, but don't be long. That dress needs to be finished.'

Bella flashed a grateful smile at her and carefully lifted up the long skirt of dark-grey taffeta, before going to find Lily.

To her surprise and disappointment Lily's workroom was empty. She was in a dilemma. Senhora Pereira would be waiting, and Bella didn't know where Lily was, or how long she would be, but she didn't want to go wandering through the corridors looking for her. She would wait for just a few minutes more, then she would have to return. She was just trying on the fancy little bonnet that the leading tenor, Rodolfo, buys for Mimì, and which Lily had obviously been working on, when she heard a tapping on the door, and frowned. Lily wouldn't knock, and neither would any other member of the wardroom department, but she went to open the door.

It was a young man she had never seen before – he was tall, very handsome, and with very blue eyes. He raised his hat courteously, so she smiled at him. 'Sir, can I be of help?' she asked in Portuguese.

'I am afraid I do not speak much of your language yet, Senhorita. But I have an appointment with Senhor Manuel dos Santos.'

Bella smiled at him again. He was obviously a foreigner, judging by his strong accent, but he was pleasant. 'I think you must be lost, then. This is the wardrobe department.'

'Ah, you speak very good English. You must be part of the opera production?'

'I am Annabella Ferreira Silva, I am Lucia Renata's understudy,' she answered proudly. Oh, that sounded so wonderful! And it obviously impressed him, for he reached out, took her hand and kissed it.

'I am honoured indeed,' he murmured.

Bella felt herself blushing, no man had ever kissed her hand before. Was this the sort of treatment she could expect from now on?

'If perhaps you could direct me to Senhor dos Santos's office, please, and then maybe later I could be permitted to meet you again? When you are next free, of course.'

Bella was even more confused now. Was he asking her out, or did he mean he would wait until she had finished here, to speak to her again? 'Oh, I don't know. I . . . I'm not sure. I . . . I don't even know your name . . .'

He smiled at her again and she felt her heart flutter.

'I apologise, you must think I have no manners at all. I am Mr Paul Keller, and I have only recently come to Lisbon, a truly beautiful city.'

Before he got any further, Bella was surprised and a little relieved to see Lily appear in the corridor behind the young man.

'Can I help you?' Lily asked.

The man turned abruptly, a fixed smile still on his face.

'Aunt Lily, Mr Keller got lost, he has an appointment with Maestro dos Santos but was asking me the way . . . and, er . . . talking to me . . .'

Lily's eyes hardened as she scrutinised the man more closely. She'd seen his type before in the city hotels. These men would find some excuse to talk to a young, vulnerable woman, lying about being lost or needing directions, and then they would seduce them for their own pleasure – or use them and later cast them aside when they'd had their fun. Mr Keller's accent, his demeanour and the tale he'd spun Bella about being lost, told Lily exactly what kind of man he was. How dare he! How bloody dare he! she fumed inwardly.

He was still half smiling, but the smile didn't reach his eyes, and his expression had altered slightly.

'Was he really, Bella? Well, then, *Herr Keller*, I suggest you go and keep your appointment and do not trouble my niece again. We do not wish to have anything to do with the likes of *you*! I bid you good afternoon!' She pushed past him and closed the door firmly in his face, before turning to her niece. 'Bella, did you not realise that he is, in all probability, a German spy? *Mr* Keller, my foot! With that colouring and that accent, he's most likely one of the Gestapo! You know Lisbon is full of them!'

Bella was near to tears, she'd suspected nothing. Yes, he was foreign, yes, he had blond hair and very blue eyes, but she'd thought him Dutch or Belgian – and she'd liked him, and that confused her. He was the same as those terrible men who supported Herr Hitler, who had been responsible for dropping bombs on her, her family, her city, causing so much fear and death. 'Oh, Aunt Lily, I am so, so sorry! I . . . I . . . did not think . . .'

Lily put her arms around her. 'Of course you didn't, Bella, luv. Some of them are so very plausible, but they are also arrogant and cruel and will have no respect for you, no matter what they say. You must have nothing to do with them. Now that your star is rising, there will be many more of them coming here and flattering you – showering you with gifts, too – but they are *evil*, Bella, I promise you!'

Bella began to sob. 'Oh, I didn't think. I didn't know.'

Lily stroked her hair. 'Hush, Bella, of course you didn't know, you are still so very young. But don't worry, you have Uncle David and me to look out for you,' she soothed.

Now that her niece's career was progressing, they would most certainly have to be on their guard, for there would be others like Herr Keller. Lily felt a little stab of fear. She and David, too, were foreigners, and she'd heard whispers that if these Nazis were crossed, people could just disappear. Bella, at least, could claim Portugal as her homeland, and hopefully she would soon become too famous for anyone to threaten her safety or well-being. But first, Lily would have to make sure Bella achieved that position.

Chapter Twenty-One

———◆·◈·◆———

Almost as if to reinforce her determination for Bella's success, Lily had a serious run-in with Lucia Renata the next day. The soprano had sent her maid to ask Senhora Pereira if the repairs to her costume would be ready for that evening's performance, as she wished to try it on now, but it was Lily whom the maid found in the wardrobe mistress's room, finishing off that very task.

'You will come to her, Senhorita Frances, please? You will explain everything to her, she is getting very . . .'

Lily could see the girl was already flustered; she had probably spent the day so far being run off her feet by *that* one. She smiled and got to her feet, the dress over her arm. 'I will come now, Anna.'

The maid smiled back gratefully and followed Lily along the corridor to Senhorita Renata's dressing room.

Lily glanced quickly around the stuffy and untidy room, before holding out the repaired costume. 'It is ready, Senhorita, and we have done our best. But I must tell you that the material is now so fragile that we will not be able to repair it again.' Lily's sweeping gaze had caught sight of an open box of expensive chocolates amongst the other detritus strewn thoughtlessly across the diva's dressing table. If the woman wasn't so careless with everything she owned, she might not constantly split the seams of her dresses, she thought.

The woman stood up – she wasn't quite as tall as Lily. Her dark hair had obviously been dyed black and, in Lily's opinion, her make-up was far too heavy for 'off stage'.

'Then you must make me a new one! Am I not the great Lucia Renata? Do I need to keep having to wear such things! I will not have the patched-up clothes! What am I, a poor beggar woman?' she demanded, her temper rising.

Lily said nothing, but she knew what Manuel dos Santos's reaction would be to spending money on new costumes so early in the production. Lucia Renata had only been wearing this one for two weeks. An opera house like this needed constant maintenance and upkeep, and the box office receipts only just about covered the expenses and outgoings.

'Well, Senhora Frances?' the woman demanded hotly.

Lily took a deep breath. It was perhaps time someone spoke to this wretched self-centred diva plainly. 'It is far from "patched up", Senhorita, the stitching is perfect, but in all honesty – and, I might add, for the sake of authenticity – if the costume looks a little "shabby" then it will hardly be noticed or commented on, because the character Mimì is a poor soul stricken with poverty and tuberculosis, and would indeed have been dressed as such.'

It had been the wrong thing to say, Lily instantly realised that. The woman's face flushed bright red and her double chin wobbled as anger coursed through her.

'You think that I . . . I do not know that this is so? I have played this role so many times, over so many years, and in so many opera houses, that I know it! It . . . it almost . . . bores me!' She threw her hands in the air in a gesture of supreme annoyance.

Despite the signs of an impending tantrum Lily made a serious error of judgement. She seized the opportunity she thought was being presented to her. 'Then perhaps, Senhorita, I may suggest that you take an evening or two to rest? It must get rather tedious singing the same role, over and over, even for such a *grande dame* of the opera as you undoubtedly are,' she suggested, her voice as conciliatory as she could possibly make it, though speaking through gritted teeth.

She had hoped her suggestion would be received with at least civility. What she hadn't expected was the sheer explosion of wrath her words conjured up. Clutching the embroidered silk kimono to her ample figure with one hand, the soprano advanced on Lily and threw the offending dress at her, then wagged her finger an inch or so from Lily's face. 'I will have a new one! And, oh, I see now what your little game is, Senhora Frances! Do not think to fool me! You want me to rest, do you? You have no care for my health! You do not wish me to perform tonight or any other night! I will be *resting* while your niece will take my place! Oh, no! No! Never! I will never "rest" so that stupid, simpering . . . *child* can take my place!' Lucia Renata began to pace the room like a caged animal while the young maid shrank back against the wall, hoping to become invisible. Lily stood as still and as white as a statue, but inside she was fuming.

215

'You may think she can sing and act, and she may think so, too, but I, the greatest soprano of these times, know she cannot! She will *never*, *never* be as I am! She has not the talent, the experience or the personality – and certainly not the voice! *Pah!* Go away from me and do not come back with your devious plans! Tell Senhora Pereira I will have a new costume – and by tomorrow. And you will know that I will never, *never* let that girl take my place!'

She turned away and threw a small china vase hard against the wall, where it smashed into fragments.

Lily compressed her lips tightly, to stop herself from shouting at the woman, and gathered the dress in her arms as she turned towards the door. Never in all her long years in the business had she been spoken to like that. And how dare she say Bella had no talent, when it was obvious to all that Lucia Renata's day was over. That outburst had shown Lily just how jealous and afraid the woman was of Bella. 'Well! I'll teach you not to cast such slurs on my niece!' she muttered furiously to herself as she walked back down the corridor. 'We've not travelled so far, and sacrificed so much, to have it all destroyed by such as . . . *you!* Bella has way more talent than you *and* a kind heart, and she works harder than anyone. She'll succeed because of this, I'll make certain of that. And if karma has anything to do with it, your career will be over, and in a few months no one will even remember you. It will be my young, beautiful Bella people will pay to see and hear, not you!' The words were just a whisper, but never had Lily meant anything quite so much in her entire life. She'd never liked Lucia Renata, but now she positively loathed her. Well, the diva would get her comeuppance eventually, so for now Lily would have to bite her tongue, bide her time and wait.

'Lily, what has happened?' Elena Pereira cried as Lily entered the room and threw the dress down on the work table.

'She . . . that . . . woman! She wants a new one, she demands a new one – and by tomorrow! I tell you, Elena, how I held my tongue I don't know! And she has sworn that Bella will never take her place! She intends never to miss a performance! Not once in my career have I had to put up with behaviour like that.'

The older woman shook her head and her dark eyes hardened as she picked up the discarded costume and examined it. 'There is nothing wrong with it. The director will not allow a new one, so soon; does she think this company is so very wealthy that new costumes must be provided every few weeks, just because she can't take care of anything? I will speak to him, Lily. Do not upset yourself. You are the best, most able assistant I have ever had. Sit down and have a rest, then when I get back we will have a glass of vinho verde together. Do not let her upset you.'

Lily nodded her thanks as she sat down, still slightly shaking with temper. Already there was a plan forming in her mind, but one she could not put into action for a week or two yet.

Olive was completely unaware of the developments in Lisbon, for the postal system was still dreadfully disrupted, but she lived in hope of news arriving soon. That morning, Joan had insisted on going to the shops and standing in the queues – she could take Jamie in his pram, the weather was still mild for late September.

Olive was alone and was drying the breakfast dishes when

she was startled by a very loud noise and then a crunching sound from the yard. She rushed to the back door, tea towel in hand, and peered out. Frederick, with Harry Newbridge's help, had cleared the yard of rubble and had started to rebuild the part of the wall that had been demolished the night the street had received a direct hit. As she took in the scene before her she uttered a cry, and a hand went to her throat, dropping the tea towel, for amidst the half-rebuilt wall – now collapsed – was Monica's small green car, the bonnet scattered with broken bricks. The windscreen was shattered but the girl was attempting to climb out of the car.

Olive ran across the yard and caught her arm. 'Monica! Monica! Are you all right, luv? What . . . what happened?'

There were small scratches on the girl's face, which had started to bleed, and she was shaking, tears coursing down her cheeks. She shook her head, unable to speak.

'Oh, luv! Come on inside and let me get those scratches bathed, and then we'll get some hot sweet tea down you. What's wrong? What's happened? Is it your mam?'

Still Monica could only shake her head, but she managed to get out one word, 'Rick!' and drew from her pocket a crumpled telegram.

Olive's heart plummeted like a stone down a well as she guided the girl towards the kitchen and sat her down at the table. 'Oh, Monica, luv! What . . . what is it?' she asked, although she feared the worst.

Monica pushed the now grubby envelope towards her, dropped her head in her hands and began to sob heart-brokenly. She'd been at home on her own when it had arrived, earlier that morning. Both Eileen and her dad were at work,

218

and Nelly had gone to the local shops, chasing a rumour that the butcher had some sausages. Her hands had been shaking so much that she'd hardly been able to read it, but it was there in brutal black and white. Rick was dead. He had been killed in action in Libya, in the push towards Tobruk, his tank suffering a direct hit from a division of Rommel's Panzerkorps.

She hadn't been able to take it in at that first moment. She had looked around her familiar kitchen as if it was a totally alien place. Where was she? In seconds her life had fallen apart! It couldn't be true! It couldn't, she'd told herself, over and over again, until just one clear thought had penetrated her befogged mind. She had to go, to leave here! She wouldn't, *couldn't* stay here alone! Joan! Joan was the only one who would know how she was feeling at this minute. Joan had known just what it was like! Without another thought, and with tears pouring down her cheeks, she'd grabbed her keys and the telegram, and slammed the back door behind her.

She'd driven most of the way half blinded by tears, twice having to swerve violently to avoid hitting another vehicle, and when she'd finally reached Mersey View what little control she'd managed to hang on to had deserted her, and she'd run straight into the yard wall. But all she felt was relief that she'd got here at last.

As she took the girl in her arms, tears started in Olive's eyes as she remembered the day they'd got the news that Jim McDonald had been killed. She could understand why the girl had come here; it was Joan she needed now. 'Monica, luv, your mam . . . ?' she queried, wondering why Nelly had let the girl drive here in such a state.

Monica's throat felt as if it had closed over. 'Shops . . .

all . . . out,' she stammered. 'Couldn't . . .'

'No, of course you couldn't stay there alone, luv! Now try to take deep breaths, and I'll make some tea. Joan won't be long now; she's gone to the shops, too.'

Monica's sobs subsided a little as she sat at Olive's kitchen table, something she'd done so many times in her life. The pain was giving way to a numbness; a feeling that this wasn't really happening to her. 'I . . . I never thought he'd . . . I always thought he'd be all right.'

'It's something we all think, luv,' Olive soothed, praying that the shock wouldn't bring Monica into labour, and that Joan really wouldn't be long now. Someone had to get word to Nelly – and what about his parents? Had they received a telegram, too, or did the army just send notification to the next of kin – Rick's wife, Monica. Jim McDonald had been different, he'd had no family other than Joan.

Monica couldn't hold the cup steady, and her sobs had increased. Olive was relieved when Joan appeared in the doorway, carrying a struggling Jamie, a hemp shopping bag over one arm, her eyes wide with horror, having seen the wreckage of Monica's car.

'Dear God! Mam! What's happened? Is she hurt?'

Olive shook her head and took the baby from Joan. 'Oh, Joan! It . . . it's Rick.'

Joan's dark eyes widened and she paled, shaking her head, memories of the day she, too, had received a telegram flooding into her mind. 'Oh, God! No! Not Rick, too?' Her voice was harsh with grief.

Olive nodded. 'Killed in action, in North Africa. She was on her own, poor lass, they were all out, so she drove here.

She's lucky to have got here without being killed, she's that upset. It's you she needs now, Joan. I'll feed this child and then I'll get the tram to Allerton. Nelly won't know, and she'll worry where Monica is, and then there's Nancy . . .'

Joan just nodded, before she sat down beside her devastated friend and took her in her arms. Oh, she knew only too well how Monica was feeling; she'd gone through this herself, and not so long ago that the pain and anguish had had time to wear off. She knew what it was like to have to go through the hopeless, dreary weeks and months, bowed down by grief, until the baby was due. But she knew, too, just how much comfort and hope Monica's baby would bring. She didn't think she would have had the strength to go on but for Jamie. There were dark days ahead for Monica, but she'd be there with her, every step of the way.

As she got ready to leave, Olive knew the tasks that lay ahead of her were hard. She would have to tell Nelly the dreadful news, and she was aware that she might well have to accompany her friend to see Rick's parents. Poor Claude, she mused. His only son, a fine young man he'd worked so hard to build up the businesses for. At least, in time, they would have a grandchild to comfort them. She would write to Lily and her family with the news. Lily had always liked Monica, and had thoroughly approved of Rick Eustace as her choice of husband, often remarking that they would go far in life, those two. Any dreams Monica and Rick might have had were gone forever now, she thought bitterly. War was the greatest evil to ever befall mankind. So many young, innocent lives wasted – just like last time. She dabbed at her eyes as she reached for her hat. It was going to be a long and traumatic day.

* * *

It had been exactly as Olive feared, she thought, as she sat on the tram that evening, a sleeping Jamie held in her arms, with Nelly beside her, still quietly weeping. She felt drained of emotion, utterly exhausted.

Nelly had taken it far worse than even Nancy had, blaming herself for being out so long, waiting for damn sausages which in the end hadn't materialised. Nancy had barely said a word but had put her arms around a weeping Nelly while she gently patted Claude's arm. He'd had to sit down very suddenly, every ounce of colour drained from his face, so it had been Nancy who had made the tea and had taken the brandy decanter from the sideboard and added a generous tot to everyone's cup. She'd said she would tell Ruth and Beverley of their brother's death when they arrived home from work.

It had been Nancy who had urged Olive to return home to Mersey View and to keep Monica there with Joan, if she thought it wise. Obviously, Nelly had objected, saying her place was at home with them now, and she knew Arthur and Eileen would be just as devastated as she was – they needed to be together as a family. Quietly, before Olive and Nelly left, Nancy had urged Olive to do what she thought was best for Monica right now. Later, they would all have to start picking up the pieces of their broken lives.

Olive was grateful that both Arthur and Eileen were at home when they arrived back in Allerton. Arthur would know how to soothe Nelly, who was nearly hysterical with grief, and Eileen would hopefully be able to provide her mam with some comfort, too. She was determined that Monica wasn't coming back here tonight. Surely they couldn't expect her to come home now on the bus or tram? Maybe tomorrow – and perhaps Joan would come with her. To her great relief Arthur expressed the same opinion, telling Nelly that Monica would benefit from Joan's company and a night's rest – which she wouldn't get here, unless both his wife and younger daughter tried to pull themselves together. It was a terrible shock for everyone, but at this time Monica must come first, and at that Nelly had agreed.

As Olive made her way on the tram back to Mersey View, a sleeping Jamie in her arms, her heart ached for the family's pain, and all the terrible harm this war had wrought for so many.

Chapter Twenty-Two

Monica felt as though she hadn't slept at all, in spite of Joan's attempts at comforting and trying to calm her sobs. The heavy dullness that had pervaded her spirit was threatening to drag her down into a terrifying darkness where there was no hope, no spark of light. Now, the cuts and bruises she'd sustained when crashing her car were beginning to make themselves felt. It was as if she had been kicked all over, and her head hurt where she had banged it hard against the windscreen. Even the car was gone now, she mused miserably. Rick's lovely, shiny-green sporty little car that had given her such a sense of freedom was now a ruin, half embedded in Olive's yard wall. Damaged, she imagined, beyond repair. She really didn't care about it now, except that it had been Rick's, and so many memories were attached to it.

As if to remind her of its presence the baby began to kick.

'Oh, don't start now, poppet, your mam needs some rest and is just too upset,' she groaned.

Immediately, Joan sat up in the bed beside her. 'What's

wrong, Mon? Are you in pain? Is it the baby?'

'No, Joan. The baby's just reminding me it's here, but right now I only want to sleep . . . well, to try to block out the pain.'

'Then let me prop another pillow at your side. I know it can be damn uncomfortable when the baby starts moving around,' Joan said, thinking that hopefully her friend had two more months yet before the birth. By then, maybe Monica would be feeling stronger, less bowed down with grief. She didn't hold out much hope, though, remembering how slow her own recovery had been. She still missed Jim so much, and knew she always would do, but she couldn't say that to Monica – not yet, anyway.

After a sleepless night, Monica went home the following morning, accompanied by Joan and the baby. Joan was insisting that she stay at least until the end of the week, for privately she knew Nelly always meant well, but there were times when she could be tactless and insensitive, even with her own daughter. She knew her friend still needed her by her side.

Most of the time Monica didn't know where she was, or who was with her; she'd even forgotten all about the war that had changed her life and robbed her of the person she loved most in the world. Joan was wonderful and so patient with her, she often thought, in those terrible days that followed. She was the only one in the house who treated her in a semi-normal way. Her mother, father and sister crept around, either in silence or speaking with lowered voices, as if it were her and not Rick who had died.

But gradually, as the shortening days of September merged with those of October, and the leaves on the trees in Calderstones Park and along Mather Avenue turned gold, orange, red and then brown, before fluttering to the ground, things gradually began to take on a semblance of normality. Joan returned home, once she saw that her friend was beginning to find the strength to try to come to terms with her loss. She knew it wouldn't be easy – it certainly hadn't been for her – but it was necessary for the baby's sake. And eventually, some of Monica's pain and grief and loss would fade. It would never go away, but it would ease.

One evening at the beginning of November, Monica idly picked up her father's discarded newspaper and surprised herself; instead of folding it up and putting it aside, she found she was reading the war news. Sadly, as she read, she realised there would be many, many more girls and women like herself now. The British forces were pushing further and further forward, heading towards the Egyptian border and the Nazi and Italian strongholds. With the aid of New Zealand reinforcements, they had finally broken the siege of Tobruk that had lasted for thirty-four weeks, though with heavy losses.

Raids on Liverpool had thankfully dwindled to a spasmodic few, never as heavy as those of the May Blitz, so she didn't fear going into labour and having to sit in the shelter in the garden – and, mercifully, both Charlie Copperfield and Harold Stevens had survived the dangers of the convoys so far. She sighed as she folded the paper – so much misery and still there didn't seem to be an end in sight. What kind of a world was this to bring a child into? And a child that it would be her responsibility to feed, clothe, educate, nurture and love the way Rick would have wanted.

Despite feeling the weight of facing that burden alone, she was praying her baby wouldn't be late. She just wanted it all to be over now. She was comforted by the knowledge that Olive had been helping her mam to get over the traumatic turn Nelly's life had taken: losing first her home and everything she'd ever cherished, and then a son-in-law of whom she had been so fond and proud.

When Joan called next, she said as much to her friend. 'I know Mam hasn't found it easy to cope with everything, Joan, but I don't know what she would have done without your mam. She's been a real rock.'

Joan nodded. 'I don't know how we all would have coped without her. Oh, I know she had a lot to put up with in her life, even before the war, but she's strong – and like everyone else, she's had to learn to live with situations none of us ever dreamed we'd have to face. Especially not you or me, Monica.'

'Will we ever accept it all, come to terms with the fact that we're both war widows, Joan?'

'Eventually I suppose. We'll just have to. At least we've still got the rest of our families to help us.'

Monica winced as she shifted her position in the chair to ease her back. 'No letter from Lily, I take it?'

'No, it's been ages, and Mam did write about Rick. I know that for a fact. And I know that Lily would have written straight back, so I presume that either she never got Mam's letter, or Lily's reply is stuck in a post office somewhere. Oh, wouldn't it be great, Mon, not to have to face another miserable winter without enough coal for even one decent fire in the house? And no Christmas treats to look forward to, and no new clothes, either! Not that we're going anywhere to wear anything new, but it would be nice to be able to get something different instead of altering all our old stuff. I'd love to be able to buy Jamie a really lovely romper suit for his first birthday. But,' she smiled, 'I'm so grateful your mam's knitting him some new clothes. She's making a pair of leggings, a matinee coat and a hat out of that pale-blue wool jumper and cardigan I unpicked. Mam's hopeless at knitting.' Joan peered at her friend – she was doing her best to cheer Monica up with her chatter, since neither of them really wanted to listen to the wireless. It was just too depressing.

'I wish Lily were here, Joan. She and Bella were great at sewing. Our Eileen is already moaning that she wished she could get something nice for Christmas, in case Harold's home. I ask you? She's never satisfied, she had that new costume for her wedding and . . . Ouch!' she clutched the cushion at her back more tightly.

'What?' Joan demanded, getting to her feet immediately, vivid memories of Jamie's birth beginning to resurface.

'A pain. A sharp pain and . . . oh . . . Joan, I . . . I've wet myself! God, isn't that awful? A grown woman wetting herself!'

'No, Mon, you haven't "wet yourself". Your waters have broken. Baby is on its way! Don't worry, it'll likely be a while yet. You just sit there while I go and get your mam. I can get Nancy, too, if you like. How do we get hold of the midwife, do you know?'

Monica felt a sense of rising panic. As much as she'd hoped and prayed for this moment, now it was actually here she was terrified of what lay ahead. 'There's a number on the pad by the phone in the hall – and, Joan, keep our Eileen away from me! I can do without her wailing and panicking! Mam will be bad enough.'

'No, she won't, Mon, she'll be great. You'll see.'

Joan was proved right. Nelly didn't panic at all, but calmly sent Eileen around to Nancy's house to be with Rick's two sisters. Then she telephoned first the midwife, followed by Nancy Eustace. Monica's mother-in-law said that it was very good of both Monica and Nelly to ask her to be present at the birth, but she was certain that the midwife would be happier if she stayed with Claude and the girls. The fewer people under her feet the better, was bound to be her motto, and Nancy was worried about Claude of late; he'd taken Rick's death very badly, and she didn't want him fretting about how things were progressing in Garthdale Road. If Nelly would be so kind as to phone and let her know when it was all over, then they would both be delighted to come to the house and bring Eileen back with them. Nelly was right; it was no place for a young girl like Eileen, even if she was a married woman, for as they both knew well, all those hours of labour were not a pleasant experience.

As the evening wore on and Nurse Nolan, the midwife, arrived, Monica would have heartily agreed. Never had she experienced such agony. The pains tore at her until she feared she would pass out. The sheets and her nightdress were soaked with sweat, and at times she was sure she was going to die. Joan and Nelly took it in turns to wipe her forehead with flannels wrung out in cold water, while Nurse Nolan tied one of the old towels to the bedpost for her to cling to and attempt to drag herself up as the contractions got worse, urging her not to 'push' just yet.

'How can I possibly not do so when the urge is over-whelming?' she pleaded with Joan.

She was certain that Joan hadn't had to go through all this. But was that just her memory playing tricks?

'I . . . I can't stand this much longer, Joan!' she cried through gritted teeth. 'I'll die!'

'Of course you won't die – and you can bear it, Mon, you'll see that you *can*. This is what they don't tell you about having a baby. And even if they did, I don't think anyone would believe it. No one can understand the agony and the sheer bloody hard work until they've experienced it. I know I didn't! But it is worth it, Mon, It really, really is!'

An hour later, Monica finally believed her friend as she sank back, utterly exhausted, against the sweat-stained pillowcase, and looked up at a smiling Nurse Nolan. The midwife tenderly handed her a little bundle, wrapped up in a towel.

'There, Mrs Eustace. You have a perfect, beautiful daughter. It was worth it, don't you agree? I think you'd go through all that again – and willingly, too – for such a little miracle.' The stout, genial woman, who had delivered more babies than she cared to remember, beamed at the new mother.

Monica looked down into the little screwed-up face and cradled her baby's head, with its fine down of blonde hair. She felt a huge surge of relief and happiness wash over her; she hadn't been so happy for months, not since . . . but she wasn't going to think like that now. She had to be positive. Oh, he'd be so proud and pleased. She really did think the baby looked like him, even though she obviously wasn't very happy about being thrust out into the world in such a traumatic way and was making that fact known. 'Oh, she's beautiful!' she whispered.

Joan smiled down at her. 'They all are – and I must say, she's certainly got a good pair of lungs! What a noise from such a small scrap! You must be exhausted. I was worn out after having Jamie.'

'I could sleep for a month,' Monica agreed, tracing the outline of the soft little cheek with a finger. Exhaustion was washing over her, and she was desperately trying to keep her eyes open.

'What have you finally decided to call her?' Nelly asked, smiling at the sight of her first granddaughter, and looking across at Joan. There had been a lot of suggestions, and some of them far too fanciful in her opinion, mainly those from Eileen, Ruth and Beverley. Young girls seemed to have feathers for brains these days.

'Richenda Jane,' Monica replied, without hesitation, for she'd finally made up her mind, two weeks ago.

Joan smiled. 'I like that. It's appropriate and unusual.'

'Plain Jane would have been more suitable. She'll have trouble with Richenda when she goes to school, you mark my words, Monica,' Nelly prophesied, although still smiling.

'No, she won't, Mam, because I'll make sure she goes to a decent school that doesn't stand for any kind of name-calling or bullying,' Monica replied, while Joan gently took the baby from her friend and began to rock her in her arms; what Monica needed now was rest.

Joan knew that in the years ahead Monica would make sure little Richenda Jane Eustace had the best she could afford. But trust Nelly Savage to make some comment about the child!

She was certain Nancy wouldn't be so tactless, and she prayed that in some way his new granddaughter would help Claude to get over his son's death.

Chapter Twenty-Three

⬥━━⬥⬥⬥⬥━━⬥

Lily frowned as she left the *confeiteiro* with her purchase. The carefully wrapped box was nestled inside a smart carrier bag, suitably embellished with the name of the establishment in gold lettering. To her the weather was still warm, but many people were now wearing jackets and lightweight coats. It was increasingly cloudy, and the air felt heavy, as if the grey skies were pressing uncomfortably down on the city. Then she smiled to herself – whatever the weather, it was certainly much better than November at home. She hadn't heard from Olive for months now, so she had no idea if her letters had gone astray – as, obviously, her sister's had – but she read the newspapers avidly and knew of the Allied campaign in North Africa and prayed that Rick Eustace would come through these battles without injury. She was so very fond of Monica.

As she walked towards the tram stop at the edge of the square, she smiled again as she patted the carrier bag containing the box of very fancy chocolates she'd just purchased. They'd cost her a quarter of a week's wages, but she hadn't begrudged the expense at all. No, it was time to make sure Bella stepped into the limelight, even if just for one night, and to give Lucia Renata a tiny taste of her own medicine. There had been no new costume for the prima donna, despite her threats to break her contract, for Senhor Manuel dos Santos was just as fed up with her tantrums as everyone else. Lily suspected that he was biding his time, waiting for the right opportunity to nudge the diva into retirement. Well, Lily's intended prank should help move things along a little faster, ensuring Bella became the hit she was always destined to be.

She would put her plan into action this very afternoon, she thought, as the tram took her through the avenues and boulevards of smart Lisbon, heading towards the Opera House. She'd told no one – not even David, as he would surely tell her she was being childish, and especially not Bella, as the girl was so naive she might give the game away. No, it was one of the oldest tricks in the book, but seldom used these days, because there was very little opportunity; most people – especially film and stage stars – did not gorge themselves on expensive chocolates like Senhorita Renata did. These days, fashionable people tended to copy that dreadful woman Wallace Simpson – or the Duchess of Windsor, as she was now called – in striving to be painfully thin. Lily would be free this afternoon, for there was nothing out of the ordinary that would demand either Lily or Elena Pereira's urgent attention. There would be plenty of time for what she had to do, which would be a delicate and fiddly task, and then she'd place the box in a prominent position in the star's dressing room. The woman would be taking her afternoon nap, something she really did need these days; she was beginning to look haggard.

Making sure that she would not be disturbed, Lily placed the box down on the work table and carefully slid the ribbon from around it, opening the lid. Removing the sheet of gold corrugated paper, she had to admit that the chocolates looked very, very tempting – and all the more so since such treats were way beyond her means. Besides, she would feel so guilty eating such expensive sweets when Olive and her family were suffering such awful shortages back home. From her handbag she carefully withdrew the thin glass syringe she had purchased earlier from the *farmácia*, where no awkward questions had been asked. That was one of the things Lily liked about Lisbon: if you went into a shop to buy something, no one wanted chapter and verse as to why, or what it was for. They considered it to be none of their business – which was a big improvement on Ethel Newbridge, who'd had the corner shop in Mersey View.

She worked slowly, carefully and diligently. There must be no obvious sign that the chocolates had been tampered with in any way, but it was a very fiddly process. First she pierced each sweet with a needle – on the underside, where the hole had little chance of being detected – and then she drew a tiny amount of the liquid she had prepared earlier that morning up into the glass syringe, and then slowly released it, drop by drop, into the hole. Just enough laxative that, even if the prima donna ate the entire box of delicacies, she would come to no harm. But equally, enough to be sure of having the desired effect, were she to eat only a few. And knowing the woman's habits so well, Lily was confident she would just go on eating the chocolates, putting the first rumblings of indisposition down to an upset stomach, or nerves. But she'd eventually be so desperate for the loo that she wouldn't make it on to the stage. And Bella would have her long-awaited chance.

When she'd finished, she put all the tools she'd used in her handbag and slid the ribbon back in place, before adding a gift card which read:

To the most beautiful and magnificent soprano in the world
With sincere admiration and affection from an ardent
admirer

'Lily Frances, you are the most devious but determined woman in this entire city – and that's saying something!' she said to herself as she put the box inside a brown paper bag and made for the door.

Still, the Lucia Renatas of this world shouldn't abuse their talent, position and good fortune. They should be grateful for the years of success, fame and wealth they'd already had. And it was just for one night, after all – one night when Bella would have her turn to establish herself.

Thankfully, as she'd guessed, Lucia Renata was not in her dressing room, and Lily was equally glad that Anna, the young maid, was also absent. But that didn't cause her to linger. Pushing aside an assortment of fancy glass bottles, Lily placed the box at the front of the dressing table where the tempting chocolates could easily be seen, making sure the gift card was clearly visible. Gifts were quite often left at the stage door for the stars and then usually passed on to their dressers or maids, or to someone who would see they got to the intended recipient. No one had seen her come into the room and as she opened the door a crack, she made sure the corridor outside was empty.

The deed was done.

It was the evening both she and David had long anticipated, to say nothing of Bella.

'Oh, Aunt Lily! How can it be? Never, never did I think that she would . . . oh, I am so nervous, what if I . . . I . . . *can't* sing? What if I make such a fool of myself?'

Bella had cried when the news came through that Senhorita Renata was unable to perform this evening and that, as understudy, Bella should prepare to take over. Whispered accounts of the prima donna coming out of her dressing room in full costume, only for her to suddenly clutch her growling stomach, eyes wide with panic, before she had to bolt to the lavatory, had spread like wildfire throughout the theatre. The official reason for her absence was, of course, more dignified – and Senhorita Renata would be fine in no time – but for this evening the stage would have to be Bella's.

Lily caught the girl by the shoulders and shook her hard, gazing steadily into the big, dark eyes that were wide with fright. Bella's hair had already been dressed, her make-up applied, and she was clutching the thin, worn shawl of her costume tightly around her. 'Bella! Stop this! Stop this! You will be wonderful, I promise you! Senhor dos Santos knows exactly what he is doing, and he personally picked you out as understudy – it is your time now, Bella! Think of all the long years of study, all the months of waiting and hoping and having to put up with *her* and her moods and her spiteful remarks! It is what you have dreamed of for years, Bella. It is why you suffered all the terrors of the bombing in London and Liverpool, why we all made the dangerous journey here to Lisbon! You can do it! You *must* do it, Bella!'

Elena Pereira had added her encouragement, stating effusively in Portuguese that Bella had a voice like an angel, that she was young, talented, beautiful and would bring to the role of Mimì a sweetness and sincerity that people would remember long after tonight's performance was over.

Lily had managed to get word to David through one of the young stage runners whose mother lived in the same street and who was a cleaner at the Opera House. He arrived, ten minutes before the curtain was due to go up, rather flustered and flushed by his rapid journey.

Lily quickly took his arm. 'Oh, David! Isn't it a miracle! Now everyone will see just how talented Bella is. Everything we have worked for, sacrificed for, schemed for . . .'

'I know, Lily, dearest. But it was a bit of a rush to get here in time—'

'Don't worry about that, David. We just have time to find a place in the wings, although I expect everyone else will be trying their best to see or hear her. We've all had quite enough of Senhorita Renata.' She guided him down the narrow, dark corridors towards the stage and the orchestra pit where they could hear the musicians tuning up. 'Elena Pereira has already gone on ahead, so hopefully we'll get a decent spot.'

'Just what is wrong with our famous prima donna?' he asked, out of curiosity, for Lily had told him privately that she thought the woman would never in a million years allow Bella to perform in her place. 'Must be something serious, I presume?'

'Not at all, she'll be fine. The result of greed and gluttony, that's my personal diagnosis. You know the way she just stuffs herself – it's disgusting! But the official version is she's had these symptoms – particularly the cramps – in the past. In Milan a few years ago, before the war, they took her to hospital, but then the symptoms just magically went away. I think it's just a tale to save the woman's blushes. If only it were true, then Bella might have a much longer run in the role.'

This production still had another month to run, and if everything went well tonight there was a chance Bella could have everyone at her feet, begging her to replace the old diva. Oh, wouldn't Lily have such great news to tell Olive when she wrote again! Bella had finally got her chance.

Bella had certainly made the role her own, Lily thought, at the end of the evening's performance.

Tito Schipa, the great Italian tenor who had sung the lead role of Rodolfo, presented his Mimì to the audience, and then Senhor dos Santos led the beaming and deliriously happy eighteen-year-old girl out to take encore after encore. Almost to a man, the audience was on its feet, clapping, shouting, cheering and throwing flowers – they simply wouldn't let her go. Lily was aware that they had all come to see Lucia Renata and that many would have been disappointed – initially, but not now, for Bella had surpassed herself.

Oh, it was so much more splendid than she could ever have imagined, Lily thought, brushing away the tears on her cheeks with the back of her hand and smiling up at David, who was nodding and grinning. 'Oh, David, they love her! They just *love* her!'

'They loved her from the very first notes she sang, Lily. And her acting was superb. I think for everyone watching she was a huge improvement on the previous Mimì – she was just the epitome of that lovely, young, tragic French girl. I think they all realised, Lily, just as we did, that she is very special – young as she is. She is going to be the next truly great soprano.'

Lily could only nod her agreement. She was so proud of Bella that she could hardly swallow, and David's words brought tears to her eyes once again. She had seen other performances of *La Bohème* in the past, but as soon as she heard the opening phrase of Bella's first aria, '*Sì, mi chiamano Mimì*' – 'Yes, they call me Mimì' – rise over the hushed audience, the tears had started to trickle slowly down her cheeks and she'd become lost, completely captivated by the girl's performance, as had everyone else in the theatre, from the backstage staff to those who had paid for a very expensive private box. Everyone in the building had forgotten about Lucia Renata, and by morning, everyone in Lisbon would know that a wonderful new star of the world of opera had taken her place. Bella's name would become familiar across the whole of Portugal, and then . . . who knew? Here and now, only she and David knew the girl's story. With her mother dead, and abandoned by her father, she'd travelled by ship from Lisbon to Liverpool, alone and with no money, at the tender age of twelve. She'd been cared for firstly by Olive and then by Lily herself, who had saved Bella from cruel and serious bullying in her first job as an apprentice seamstress, and then been utterly astounded to hear her sing. One day, the whole world would know Bella's story and the obstacles she'd overcome to achieve success.

Lily clung to David's arm, overwhelmed by the momentum of the evening, and he patted her hand. Bella had been their protégée but they loved her, too, and would never begrudge anything they'd done to give her the chance she so richly deserved – and in front of an audience of her own people, too.

The cast began to leave the front of the stage, and they were soon surrounded by people exclaiming how wonderful Bella had been. Finally, Bella and Senhor dos Santos appeared. Bella was almost breathless with excitement, and half hidden by the armfuls of flowers she was clutching, which she instantly pressed into Lily's arms.

'Oh, Aunt Lily! Uncle David! It was so . . . I can't find the words!' Bella cried, hugging Lily to the detriment of the floral offerings, while the director looked on, smiling ecstatically.

'Senhora Frances, was she not *maravilhosa*? Everyone loved her! Were we not right to *know* how great she will soon become?' enthused Senhor dos Santos.

Lily smiled back at him. He'd had faith in her niece, too; he'd recognised how talented she was, even though she was so young. He could have chosen an older girl as understudy but, no, it had been Bella. 'Senhor dos Santos, she was indeed *maravilhosa*.'

He reached out, took Lily's hand and kissed it. 'I thank you, Senhora Frances, for bringing me such a treasure, one I thought I would never see. You have brought to me a beautiful *Portuguese* soprano; that is something I did not think I would ever see in my lifetime. I warn you, I will not let her go, we must have new contracts, contracts that will keep her here safe in Portugal.'

'And Lucia Renata?' David enquired.

'Senhorita Renata will go back to Italy when she is well. Even before tonight, I fear she has exhausted herself with so many . . . how you say . . . consecutive performances? It is not good for the health in a lady of her age and it is especially not good for the voice. And after her absence tonight, she is unable to fulfil the terms of her contract, as I have already pointed out to her agent, Senhor Rossellini.'

Lily nodded but her expression had changed slightly. 'I am so glad that there will be new contracts; it will make life so much more secure for us, but it will also be worrying for us. Bella is so young and, as you know, this city is filled with people of all nations, some of whom are not what they seem – it will be up to us to make sure she is safe and protected.'

He bent closer, frowning, and lowered his voice. 'I understand, but do not fear. I, too, will take her safety and protection very seriously. I will give strict orders to those of my staff in charge of such things. My car and driver will be at your disposal, and maybe you should also think of changing your *casa* and . . .' His voice dropped to a whisper. 'I am not the greatest admirer of His Excellency António de Oliveira Salazar but for the sake of my theatre I . . .' He spread his hands in a gesture they both knew well. 'You understand?'

Both Lily and David nodded. They were thankful that he only tolerated the regime of Salazar and the foreigners who had made his country their temporary home. And they were relieved that he, too, would look after Bella.

'Oh, Maestro dos Santos, how I wish this terrible war was over,' Lily stated, fervently.

He smiled again at the little trio. 'But then you might be tempted to take my wonderful Annabella Ferreira Silva away from Lisbon, away from Portugal, back to London perhaps?'

Lily smiled back. 'I suppose we might . . . eventually. But not for quite a while, I promise.'

Chapter Twenty-Four

———◆◄►◆———

Joan had decided that she was going to make Jamie's first birthday and Christmas as special as possible, war or no war. Nelly had finished the matching set of pale-blue leggings, matinee coat and hat she'd been knitting for him, in plenty of time for his birthday. Olive had managed to get him his first pair of shoes from somewhere, as he was attempting to walk now, though she flatly refused to tell Joan how much she'd paid for them or just where she'd bought them. He was Olive and Frederick's first grandchild and he'd have the best they could afford, she'd stated. They hoped, of course, that one day Charlie would return home for good and, in due course, marry, so Jamie wouldn't be their only grandchild. They were all coming to believe that the little Barcelos rooster was indeed bringing him luck.

Christmas was on all their minds as they sat in Olive's kitchen that Sunday afternoon in early December. Monica had brought the baby down in the travelling crib Nancy had acquired second-hand, while Claude had insisted on driving her to Olive's house, informing her he'd return at teatime. He knew how much she appreciated these visits to Joan and how much good they did her. He only wished Joan lived closer.

He just wished something . . . *anything* would help him to overcome how depressed and unhappy he felt. Never in his life had he thought he would miss anyone quite so much as he missed his son, but he was trying desperately hard to get on with life, even if there seemed to be little purpose now.

They sat around Olive's table, its surface covered with bits and pieces and odds and ends. Richenda was asleep in her crib and little Jamie was being kept amused by a handful of pipe cleaners Nelly had given him to play with. Joan had been saving as much as she could in the way of gold and silver foil from the gentlemen lodgers' cigarette packets, which, together with the pipe cleaners, she would use to make decorations for the Christmas tree they hoped to get nearer the time. St John's Market – Liverpool's largest – had been razed to the ground, as had so many other buildings in the May Blitz, so it would have to come from one of the smaller ones.

'I don't suppose we'll be able to get a very big tree, and you won't be able to stand it in the parlour window, Mam – not this year, or my laddo here will have it over on its side in minutes,' Joan reminded her mother.

She, her mother, Nelly, Eileen and even Monica were trying to do their best to make Christmas special this year, for the last two had been disastrous what with the bombing raids and their personal loss and grief. And now Monica had another worry, one she'd already confided to Joan. Claude Eustace was no longer a well man; he just didn't appear to be making any attempt to get over the loss of Rick. He showed no interest at all in his businesses, not like he always used to, and didn't even show much interest in baby Richenda.

'It's just not like him at all, Joan,' she observed now. 'He was always so full of drive and enthusiasm for any ideas us girls might have. Now Nancy says she can barely get him to eat.'

Joan shook her head. 'It must be hard for him, Monica. With Rick gone, there's no one to give meaning to his work – Ruth and Beverley aren't in the least bit interested in running the salons. There are no men left to pass the businesses on to.'

Monica frowned as she fiddled with a pipe cleaner that Joan had tinted red with some old cochineal food dye she'd found at the back of a shelf in Olive's larder. 'So what? Women can run businesses – and successfully, too. Yes, Claude oversaw everything. But, well, it was the salon manageresses who ran the businesses. Oh, I know that most women have been conscripted for war work now, but why does everyone assume we can't be as successful as a man in any other capacity?'

'I don't assume anything of the kind! But I suppose it's because we're sort of . . . conditioned to still think like that. "A woman's place is in the home" and all that,' Joan reminded her.

'But not when there's a war on. Then the men are damn grateful to us for stepping into their shoes – although I sincerely hope they don't drag us off to some factory, making shells or such like. I've heard from some of my customers, who've heard it from friends, that the stuff they use to fill shells turns your hair green! Well, even with my experience, I wouldn't know what to do with hair like that! You daren't put bleach or tint anywhere near it; I suppose all you can do is cover it up until it grows out.'

Joan grimaced. 'If it's doing that to your hair, what the hell is it doing to your lungs? Oh, for heaven's sake, Jamie McDonald, give that to Mammy now or you'll be poking your brains out! Mam, take that thing off him; he's intent on shoving it up his nose! Give him that big pompom Nelly made to use the spare bits of wool up.' It was one of the few toys the child had, she thought sadly.

Olive removed the offending pipe cleaner and handed over the multi-coloured ball before her grandson could begin to protest. 'It certainly won't do anyone's lungs much good, I'm sure of that,' Olive replied as she eyed up a silver bell made of cardboard and covered with silver paper. 'Does this look a bit oddly shaped to you?'

Both girls inspected it and came to the conclusion that if they put it high enough up on the tree its deformities wouldn't be noticed.

Monica sighed. 'I wonder, will we ever have a decent Christmas again? The year Bella made the decorations, the tree looked wonderful – she had a talent for stuff like that.'

Olive nodded. 'She did – and I've kept most of them, too. I do so wish I'd get a letter from our Lily soon. I *know* she will have written, probably half a dozen letters by now, just as I have, but maybe one will get through in time for Christmas. I do miss them, you know, even though our Lily and I don't always see eye to eye.'

'Neither do our Eileen and me, but then she tends not to get on with anyone these days. I don't think marriage is turning out quite as she expected it to. She's even started to mutter about going to Birmingham for Christmas, not in Mam's hearing, though. She keeps saying that Harold feels it's a bit off, like, to leave Mrs Stevens on her own down there, as there's very little chance he will get home. In fact, he's not been home for Christmas since the war began.'

'Then it's unlikely our Charlie will, either,' Olive added. Like Monica, she wondered if things would ever get back to something approaching normal. 'Oh, it just goes on and on, but I suppose we have to keep our spirits up, no use letting everything get you down.'

'I'm getting anxious for Nancy. She doesn't complain, but I know she's worried sick about Claude.'

'Isn't there *something* we could do to try to cheer him up?' Olive asked. Claude Eustace was the same age as her Frederick, and these days her husband had to work far harder and put in more hours than he used to do – there was nothing to be done about that, with so many young men and boys away. At least Claude didn't have to work *that* hard. 'Do you think he'd like to go for a drink with Frederick and your dad, Monica? At least you can still get *something* to drink, even though spirits are definitely off.'

Monica shrugged. 'He might. I'll try and persuade him, although he's never been one for having a night out with the lads.'

'It might just be the answer. But if not, then try and persuade him and Nancy to come here one evening. Oh, I know this place isn't what they're used to but, well, I might just be able to manage a drop of decent whisky for them.'

Joan's eyes widened. 'Where did you get that from, Mam?'

Olive smiled conspiratorially. 'You've to say nothing, Joan, do you understand me?'

Joan and Monica exchanged glances of suspicion, before both nodding their agreement.

'Our Charlie. He's a good lad, and so is your Eileen's Harold, Monica. The first thing they do when they get ashore in Canada is make for the grocery shops – or "markets", as they call them over there. Officially, they're not supposed to but, well . . . your mam and I have done quite well so far, Monica. In fact, Christmas won't be too bad this year. We've both been saving tins of ham and salmon and peaches and pears and evaporated milk and even corned beef. And something called "Spam" – which I think is some sort of meat. Charlie says it's such a pity they just have to stick to stuff that will keep. Anything fresh won't last the journey home – or if it did, it would have to be eaten right away. I always reimburse him. I won't have him out of pocket, but it's a great help, I can tell you.'

The two girls looked at each other in amazement. 'Well, what a pair of dark horses! You'll be opening up on the black market next!' Joan grinned. 'Is that where the drink is coming from, too?'

Olive nodded. 'I will not be having anything to do with the black market, it's all strictly for us! And, yes, I've two half-bottles of scotch, one of brandy – that's for medicinal purposes – and two full bottles of sherry. Decent stuff at that, too. None of your Empire rubbish!'

'For God's sake, don't let that get out, Mam! You'll have what's left of the neighbourhood descending on you, particularly Mo Clancy. I bet he can't get anything like all that!'

'I'll certainly mention both ideas to Claude on the way back home,' Monica said firmly. 'And if he's not keen, I'll enlist Nancy's help. We've got to try something!' Then she got to her feet as two tiny fists began to wave in the air over the rim of the crib. 'Here we go, madam is awake, and no doubt hungry. You'll have to carry on without me for a bit – Claude isn't coming until tea time.'

True to her word, on their way home Monica told her father-in-law about both invitations. But even though she described them as brightly and cheerfully as she could, she wasn't surprised when he showed little enthusiasm.

'I was never one for propping up a bar with the lads, Monica, luv,' he replied, staring grimly ahead at the darkened road.

'I know that, but it might just cheer you up a bit. Maybe Nancy would like to get out for an evening as well. You haven't been anywhere for ages.'

He nodded. 'I . . . I'll speak to her about it this evening, Monica, but . . . but I really haven't got much in common with either your father or Joan's stepfather – and quite frankly, the two old gentlemen can be bores.'

'Oh, I know that! But, well, I'm sure you men could find something to talk about . . . even if it's only war news.'

'I don't think any of us want to hear that kind of news – it's just dragging on and on,' he replied morosely.

She sighed and nodded as they turned into Garthdale Road. Maybe Nancy could persuade him, but she doubted it.

To everyone's surprise Claude had finally agreed. It was exactly 'that kind of news' that had decided him, for the following morning on the wireless they'd all heard about the Japanese attack on the American naval base at Pearl Harbor in Hawaii. The Americans had been completely unprepared; only twelve days before, they'd been absolutely assured by the Japanese Prime Minister that there was nothing to fear.

That Sunday, Japanese planes had destroyed five US battle-ships, fourteen other smaller ships, and two hundred aircraft. Two thousand four hundred people were dead and now, absolutely outraged by the attacks on its territory, America had finally entered the war.

'There'll be no more shilly-shallying,' Frederick announced on Tuesday evening, as he ushered Claude, Nancy, both girls and the baby into the parlour.

'No, there won't,' Claude agreed. 'This should certainly change things from now on. Before we know it, there'll be GIs streaming off troopships here in Liverpool, just like there was last time,' he added.

Nelly glanced at Olive, then Nancy. 'Well, let's hope they don't bring us as many problems as they did before,' she remarked, rather acidly.

Olive poured all the ladies a small glass of sherry. 'It's a terrible tragedy for all those who've lost husbands, sons, fathers and brothers – and we do feel for them, we *really* do, we know what it's like – but let's hope that, like last time, it will prove to be the beginning of the end. Maybe, after all, we can look forward to peace and getting back to normal. And then our Lily and her little family can come home. And we can pick up the threads of our lives.'

'Hitler's troops are already starting to realise how the bitter winter will affect them on the Russian front. Let's just hope

251

he's overstretched himself, like Napoleon did. And with the same result – utter defeat,' Arthur added.

Claude took a deep breath and then a sip of the whisky Olive had poured for him. 'And the campaign in North Africa is now going well, so here's to the downfall of all those evil men who have tried to eradicate our world, our countries and our way of life – to say nothing of our young men. Our brave young men like Jim McDonald and Richard Eustace – our Rick!'

All four women sipped their drinks but were fighting back the tears. Hope, however, had entered their hearts.

Chapter Twenty-Five

—◦◦❉◦◦—

Christmas that year was different for everyone. The entry of America into the war had brought a glimpse of light at the end of the tunnel. It was just a tiny ray of hope – the belief that the tide might be on the turn, at last – but hope all the same. People who felt that they and their embattled nation had struggled on, alone and desperate, for so many dark years now felt that those days were possibly coming to an end. It could be witnessed in people's attitudes, the smiles, the cheerful words, and the determination that things were now going to get better. That shortages and sacrifices could, and would, be borne with fortitude – for, thank God, there was now the prospect of an end to them.

Early the following year, the arrival of the American forces would put heart into the people. Troops would be cheered as they disembarked from the ships that arrived in Liverpool, cheerfully looking forward to their onward journeys to the south of England, but shocked at the utter devastation that met their eyes, with city after city in ruins.

Monica had insisted that Claude, Nancy and the girls come to her for their Christmas dinner. In answer to Nancy's protests that it would all be too much for her, she'd replied that her mother and father had been invited to Olive's house, and Eileen had insisted on going to Birmingham – her sister had not softened towards her mother-in-law but felt she'd be letting Harold down if she didn't go. So unless they came, Monica would be on her own – except for Richenda, of course, and she was too young to know what was going on, although her eyes followed the coloured tree lights as they flashed on and off and she gurgled happily. Nancy had had no argument against that; in fact, she was rather relieved, as Claude's health had not improved. It needed something like this to cheer him up.

When Olive first announced her plans for Christmas, there was something of a joint conference in her kitchen.

'Are you quite sure, Olive, luv?' Nelly queried. Monica would have a house full, but then so would Olive, for there were the elderly gentlemen lodgers, Joan and Jamie and Olive and Frederick, as well as herself and Arthur. It was taken for granted that neither Charlie nor Harold would be home.

'Yes, I'm certain, Nelly. You know I'd have asked Monica, too, but I think it's a good thing that she's going to be kept busy organising Christmas in her own home. It will take her mind off . . . off being without Rick.'

Both Nelly and Joan nodded their agreement, thinking of Rick Eustace and Jim McDonald, but Joan spoke first.

'I know what it was like for me, the first time . . . but I think, Mam, if you don't mind, when all the fuss of the day is over, I'll leave Jamie with you and slip down to see her. She'll really feel it when they've all gone home. It's worse when you're alone and the house is so quiet.'

Olive nodded her agreement. 'You know my laddo will be fine with me and Frederick, and we'd be happy to have him, but why not take him too, luv? You'll miss him terribly if you don't. It's Christmas, and he'll be so worn out with all the excitement that he'll be no trouble – why don't you stay overnight with Monica, Joan? She's got room, and there'll be no trams or buses running on Christmas Night. You'll have a job getting home, and I'm not having you walking. It's too far, and there will be too many people hanging about; the pubs will be emptying out, and the streets are far from safe these days. And that way, Nelly and Arthur can stay here overnight, they can have your room.'

Joan smiled at her. 'Thanks, Mam. I know she'll appreciate it.' She grimaced. 'We can cry into our sherry together.'

'Aye, there will be many who will be feeling like that, Joan,' Nelly agreed.

'Right then, let's get the arrangements sorted out,' Joan said firmly, before the mood of melancholy deepened.

'I think we're all agreed that we'll pool our resources? We've got enough food between us to go around, and it would be selfish of us not to share it,' Nelly proposed.

'Oh, I know all the traditional things will be off – like Christmas pudding and mince pies. We might possibly get a chicken, but no turkey or goose – unless you know someone out in the country and we don't – but we've got ham and salmon instead, and tinned fruit and evaporated milk for pudding, thanks to our Charlie,' Olive put in.

'At least that's better than trying to make a pudding with

the only rubbish that's available,' Joan agreed. 'Madelaine from the factory salon was telling me that her mam had tried to make one with just flour, milk, diced carrots and parsnips, and some old currents she had left but which were stale. She said it tasted like sawdust and made everyone feel ill! And don't forget there are the biscuits; Jamie's just about old enough to be able to suck a finger of shortbread. Our Charlie brought that big tin, on his last trip home, so everyone will be able to have a few each. What a treat!'

'There are plenty of spuds and carrots, sprouts, turnips and parsnips ready now on the allotment,' Arthur added.

Both he and Frederick grew as much as they could on the small piece of land they'd cleared in a sheltered corner of the bomb site that was all that remained of Mersey View now.

Nelly's forehead creased in a frown. 'Do you think we should give a few bits and pieces to Ethel?' she asked. The former shopkeeper and her husband had managed to find themselves a couple of rooms to rent in a house in York Terrace that had been damaged but was more than habitable. There had even been some talk about Ethel using the front room as a shop, but what with all the shortages and the excessive paperwork involved in starting up a business, she was wondering if it was worth it.

'No, I don't, Nelly! She'd probably sell it; you know what she's like,' Olive replied firmly. 'All right, she was good enough at putting things on the slate, but that was how her business worked. People couldn't afford to pay their grocery bills in a lump sum – there'd be little enough left of their wages after forking out for the rent. I had the pair of them here for nearly two months after they were bombed out; she paid me a token rent but she never offered to share anything.'

Times had been bad after the May Blitz, and she'd offered the couple a home, but she'd been very glad when the Newbridges had moved out. The house had felt dreadfully overcrowded, and she hadn't got on well with Ethel at all. The woman was too forceful in her opinions for Olive's liking, and she was not prepared to give and take, as people had to do if they were to survive the crowded conditions they had to live in.

Joan nodded. 'I agree with Mam. I don't suppose you begrudge sharing with Monica and Nancy, though, do you, Mrs Savage?'

'Not at all. Nancy has offered to give our Monica what she's got – not that it's much – and also as many coupons as she can spare. Needless to say, our Eileen has taken her ration books down to Birmingham with her. I hope she manages – she isn't known in the shops down there, and won't be considered for anything they might have that's a bit . . . extra, like. And you can bet that auld one won't part with much. Eileen insisted on taking down some of the tins Harold had brought home. I don't suppose I minded that, really – I can imagine what kind of a Christmas she'll be having there!' Nelly finished scathingly. She hadn't wanted her younger daughter to go at all. The trains were still so terribly unreliable, she wasn't familiar with the neighbourhood where Violet Stevens lived, and she was sure the woman would play on Eileen something shocking. What was worse was that her daughter was determined to stay on.

'Well, it's her choice, Nelly,' Olive replied, although she agreed with her neighbour.

'I think she's mad,' Joan put in, before rescuing the jumper Nelly was knitting, and which had been put down on a chair, from the hands of her small son. 'All that way on God knows how many freezing-cold trains, then having to lug her cases to this Solihull place on public transport. And then having that old misery to put up with. I bet there won't even be a cup of tea waiting for her when she arrives – she'll be expected to make it herself! She'd have been better off staying here. She gets on well with Ruth and Beverley Eustace, doesn't she?'

'For reasons beyond me she actually does, but she felt she couldn't let Harold down. She says she needs to be there to look after his mother, at least until the war is over,' Nelly replied, carefully picking up the dropped stitches, the result of Jamie's attentions to her handiwork.

'Good God! Does she intend to stay there that long?' Joan asked, astonished. It was the first she'd heard of this, and she wondered why Monica hadn't told her.

Nelly pursed her lips tightly, and it was Arthur who answered for her.

'So she says, Joan – and, in a way, I can understand. The woman is getting on, and she is on her own and not in the best of health. Oh, I know she's got more in the way of material things than Nelly and me, but well, with her only lad away, surely she's entitled to some affection and help from her daughter-in-law. Apparently, there's plenty of room.'

Nelly shot him a furious glance, before returning to her task.

'Well, I suppose if you look at it like that, then it's her choice, Mrs Savage. But don't let it put the damper on your Christmas. You've got your gorgeous granddaughter this year, don't forget,' Joan urged, smiling at Nelly.

* * *

The day had gone very well, Monica thought, as she saw her in-laws into their car on Christmas Night. The baby was now asleep in her crib; her routine hadn't been interrupted a great deal, although she'd been spoilt by her aunts and grandmother. She'd been so busy preparing, cooking, serving and then clearing away that she'd hardly had time to think about Rick. Everyone had said that it was a meal fit for the King himself – and, of course, they'd listened to his speech on the wireless. She'd thought he'd sounded tired, but then the Royal Family were as stressed and worried as everyone else – and subject to the same shortages, too, although she doubted they would have had tinned ham for their lunch. The ladies had sherry before their meal, and to toast the King and Queen, and Claude had said the whisky was an excellent blend and that Charlie had developed very good taste. He'd insisted on driving to Olive's in the late winter afternoon and bringing Joan and Jamie back with him. Monica was very grateful for his offer, for she didn't like the idea of Joan having to make her way here in the blackout, and with very little in the way of public transport.

Joan was unpacking her overnight things and settling Jamie in the cot beside the bed Monica had made up for her; the little boy had already been fast asleep when he'd arrived and Claude had carried him in from the car. She'd busied herself clearing the cups and plates and had reset the coffee table with two clean glasses and the rest of the sherry, having arranged the last of the shortbread biscuits on a plate with a fancy doily she'd cut from a square of red crêpe paper.

She glanced around the room, checking it was tidy, and

thinking how warm and comfortable it looked in the glow of the fire and the one table lamp which cast its light away from the crib where her daughter slept peacefully. She turned and caught sight of herself in the mirror over the fireplace. Her hand automatically went to her hair, to pat it in place, before she bit her lip. Appearances were so deceptive, she thought. To a stranger this would be a scene of perfect domestic bliss. A beautiful baby, asleep and content. Crystal glasses on the low table, sparkling in the firelight. Bone china and the luxury of biscuits and the remains of a bottle of pale sherry, the decorated Christmas tree, the sprigs of holly behind the mirror and decorating the picture frames – every comfort, in fact, and yet it was all so false and superficial. And she felt as if she had barely left her girlhood behind.

She felt the tears slowly begin to prick her eyes, and then Joan was beside her, her dark eyes brimming with unshed tears – tears she, too, had held back all day. 'It would be perfect, wouldn't it, Mon, if only we had them both here with us and knew that they would always be here?'

Monica nodded, brushing away the tears with the back of her hand. 'I think they have to be the saddest words in the English language, Joan. "If only."'

'They are. Oh, let's try not to dissolve into hysterics, Mon. Let's try to be grateful for what we have. It's not much, compared to what we'd hoped and dreamed we would have in the future, but . . .'

'If you say "there's a war on", Joan McDonald, I will strangle you with my bare hands! I swear I will!' Monica hissed between clenched teeth.

'I was going to say it's better than a lot of people have got!

We've both got good homes, there will be jobs when we need them, and we've family who will look after the children – and we've got Jamie and Richenda Jane. They are our greatest blessings, Monica, the greatest gifts that Jim and Rick could give us, and we . . . we'll never, ever forget them or what they sacrificed.'

Monica nodded slowly and then squared her shoulders. Joan was right; they would both do everything they possibly could for their children. It was all they could do now – invest in their children, the next generation, and hopefully raise them in a world without the scourge of war. She poured the two glasses of sherry and they both sat down, silently staring into the flames, remembering other years, other events and so many bitter-sweet memories. It was then that Monica swore to herself that she would never marry again, for there could be no one who would compare to Rick. She'd resolved she would work, and work hard, to continue the businesses Claude had built for his son, and she would do that for her daughter. She knew that Joan was thinking along the very same lines.

'Would you ever think about remarrying, Joan?' she asked quietly, finishing her sherry.

'I don't know, but I don't think so, Mon. There's no one out there who could compare with Jim, and I'll not settle for second best.'

'I feel the same. We'll go on together, Joan, as we always have – looking out for each other. We have to look forward now, this war has got to end at some stage, and then we can look at something we can do together, both of us.'

Joan looked quizzical as she finished her drink. 'I don't know what, Mon. You're professionally trained, I'm not.'

'Oh, we'll find something, Joan. We *will*! We haven't gone through everything together, only to give up on all our hopes and dreams.'

Joan managed a smile. 'I like your optimism, Mon. We have to get through the rest of this damn war yet, before we can think about any kind of future.'

Monica reached over, took her friend's hand and squeezed it. 'We'll manage. We have so far – and it's been pretty awful, at times.'

'Is there any more sherry in that bottle?' Joan asked.

'Just about a glass each.'

'Well, given what this year's been like, it wasn't a bad Christmas, was it?' Joan remarked as Monica emptied the bottle.

'Better than I'd imagined. I must say, most of the credit has to go to your Charlie and our Eileen's Harold. They both deserve to come through this safely, if it's just for the food they brought – it certainly lifted everyone's spirits,' Monica said.

'It did,' Joan agreed, before she frowned. 'Although we still haven't heard from Lily. I wonder what they've been doing for Christmas? I bet they've had all kinds of fancy foods. There's no rationing there, and the weather's bound to be better.'

'Let's hope we hear soon – it's been months and months now.'

Joan managed a smile. 'Knowing Aunty Lil, if good food was available then they would've eaten well today.'

Monica nodded. 'Thanks, Joan, for coming to stay tonight. I really appreciate it.'

'What are friends for? And besides, I don't think I could have got through the day without you, either. And if I'd have stayed at home, I'd have had to suffer your mam and mine—'

'And all the old men, too! No, much better to spend it together,' Monica interrupted.

Chapter Twenty-Six

———————

Joan was right, had she but known it. There was plenty of luxury at Lily's house for Christmas. This year, Bella was insisting that they keep the customs of her native Portugal and, in the run-up to the celebrations, she planned to invite Manuel dos Santos to join them.

At the director's insistence they had moved from the cramped little *casa* in the Alfama district last month, somewhat to Bella's regret. Lily, however, had fallen in love with this traditional villa in the elegant Campo de Ourique area of the city as soon as she'd set eyes on it.

'I worry about your safety, up there in the old town. It is a small house, with easy access to anyone, and some of the residents are not trustworthy,' Manuel had confided to David after he had found the Villa Rosa for them. 'It will be much better to move out – and to a bigger house, too.'

David had been cautious, wondering if they could afford it. But when the figures had been mentioned for Bella's new contract, he'd been astonished.

Lily had been utterly delighted with her new home. 'Well, thank God we can now at least afford to rent a decent house in a decent area, and with that lovely, peaceful little Jardim da Parada at the end of the street. It's such a tranquil, exotic little square – and it never seems to be crowded.'

'But we have no need to go to the park, Aunt Lily, we will have our own *jardim!*' Bella had added, just as delighted and astonished as her aunt that they could now afford to live in such a beautiful place.

Lily had soon found that she loved her private garden and spent as much time as she could relaxing in the shade of the exotic jacaranda trees, surrounded by a riot of hibiscus and other tropical plants and palms that she could never have grown at home, even if she had had a garden. Whenever Bella had to go to the Opera House, they all went. True to his promise, Manuel always sent his car; a luxury compared to the rackety wooden trams they had previously used.

Her garden was the perfect place to write her letters, Lily thought, although there had been no news from Olive for months and months, which disturbed her. She knew that America had entered the war and was anxious to know how this had affected things back home, but so far there had been no word.

'Aunt Lily, I have something to ask you,' Bella announced hesitantly, one afternoon. She seated herself beside Lily at the wrought-iron table and matching chairs, set beside the small fountain of water in the shade of a huge old jacaranda that was covered in a haze of purple flowers. It was getting late, and they would soon be going to the theatre, but Lily had a large jug of iced lemonade on the table.

'What is it, Bella?' she asked, feeling a little drowsy. It wasn't particularly warm, it being December, and she wore a long-sleeved pale-blue wool crêpe dress with a matching jacket. Sometimes, of late, she tended to flag a little at this time of day. Unlike most people here, she never took a siesta; she had not been brought up with the custom, and tended to just doze, even in the fierce heat of summer afternoons.

'I think we should ask Maestro dos Santos to share Christmas with us. He has been so good, so kind to us, and I would really love to have all the old customs, Aunt Lily, for this is my first Christmas back in Portugal. Oh, I don't think I will have much time in the years ahead of me, but just for this year? It is so special to me!'

Lily was now more alert and she poured them both a glass of lemonade. 'And you think he will enjoy spending Christmas with us? Perhaps he has family or has already made plans, Bella?'

Bella shook her head, her dark curls falling over her cheeks; her well-cut cream wool dress revealed a slim but shapely young figure. 'No, I have asked him. He has no wife, she is dead, and his family do not live in Lisbon. They live in the far north of the country, in the vineyards of the Douro, by the border with Spain. It is quite sad, Aunt Lily, but he feels he has no friends, no one he wishes to be with.'

Lily nodded, she could understand that. 'He is a very busy man, Bella. I imagine he has many acquaintances but few real friends. Invite him, by all means, but he may not accept.' She pondered the prospect – she didn't object, and it would do Bella's career no harm. And besides, there were things she would like to discuss with him but had wondered when she would get the right opportunity. This might just be it.

'I hope he decides to join us, Aunt Lily. I thought he could come with us to the *Missa do Galo* at the Cathedral, and then back here for salted cod, potatoes and green vegetables. I know Senhora Andrade who cooks for us would be happy to make and serve the meal – it's our traditional one, and she will be familiar with it.' Bella knew that her aunt viewed the cook, housekeeper and gardener who came with the villa as luxuries she'd never even dreamed of. 'Oh, it will all be just as it used to be, Aunt Lily, when I was a little girl!'

Lily smiled at her; it all sounded rather unusual. In Liverpool, salted cod was popular as a Sunday morning breakfast, but you had to soak it for two whole days to make it edible, otherwise you could virtually sole your shoes with it, but for Christmas . . . ? Well, hopefully, Bella would only want to follow these customs for this first year in her homeland, for she certainly didn't fancy salted fish as a festive lunch each year.

When Bella issued the invitation to him, after that evening's performance, to her delight Manuel dos Santos accepted gladly.

'This is so kind of you, Bella – and, of course, your aunt and uncle. It will make me very happy to share the feast with you all,' he replied, bowing politely to Lily and David. Turning to Bella, he smiled broadly; she had all the delighted anticipation of a child shining in her dark eyes.

The Opera House would, of course, be closed over the holiday. He usually spent that time trying to recover his energy and sort out any problems he had not yet had time to address, but it would be pleasant to be with people whose company he really enjoyed. There were not many he could say that about, these days, and in this city.

Now that he had accepted, Lily flung herself whole-heartedly into the arrangements and preparations with Bella and the cook and housekeeper. It appeared that Christmas Eve, and not Christmas Day, was the centre of the feast, although children put out a *sapatino* – a shoe – overnight for the Christ child to fill, and Bella had insisted on buying the best *berço* – crib – she could find. To her surprise Lily found that Senhora Andrade's recipes for the traditional dishes sounded very appetising indeed, for she didn't propose sticking rigidly to the ingredients.

David suggested that they buy some bottles of good wine, and a bottle of champagne. 'After all, we have plenty to celebrate, Lily. Bella's remarkable success, and our new house and way of life, if not the end of the war.'

'Lord, David! Can we afford champagne? I know we're better off now, but still, maybe it's a bit too showy?' Lily remarked, though she fully intended to buy a couple of smart new cocktail dresses for herself and Bella for the occasion. There were some really good dress shops in Lisbon.

Both Lily and David agreed that the Mass at the Cathedral had been very touching and, judging by the number of people who greeted Manuel dos Santos, she began to realise that he was an important man in Lisbon society. The service had had an almost mystical element to it: the candles, the incense, the flowers and the music. It had reminded Lily of Monica's wedding – except, of course, tonight Bella did not sing. The weather was very clement for the time of year, she thought, as they drove back through the streets. No frost, no sleet, no snow, no fierce biting winds. When they finally arrived back at the Villa Rosa, the house and the gardens were ablaze with light, and the people Lily was now coming to think of as her 'staff' were waiting to wish them all *Feliz Natal*.

As they took their glasses of wine into the dining room, Lily almost gasped aloud with delight at the sight of the dining table. A beautifully embroidered cloth covered it, and huge banks of gorgeous flowers were set down the length of the table, the light catching the crystal glasses and the silver cutlery. She'd never experienced anything like this in her life before. Both her 'ladies' had done her proud, and she determined to reward them handsomely. She was also very pleased to see that Manuel dos Santos was looking at the room with approval and admiration.

As he'd got to know them better, the director had gradually become more acquainted with both Lily and Bella's background, and he was aware of how hard they'd worked to achieve their goals. 'Senhora Frances, this is . . . magnificent! I congratulate you!'

Lily actually blushed. 'Thank you! But it is the hard work of my ladies. And please, can you call me Lily? Senhora Frances sounds too formal now.'

'I will be delighted, Lily, and er . . . David, I envy you such a wife and stepdaughter.'

David nodded his thanks and agreement as he held out his wife's chair for her and their guest gallantly held out Bella's.

As the food was served the director glanced around surreptitiously. He admired Lily very much, and he couldn't help feeling a little envious of David. Lily was a beautiful, elegant woman, with exquisite taste, who more than knew her own mind and was prepared to fight for Bella's career, no matter what the cost. He admired her courage and determination in overcoming the dangers she had faced in order to get Bella and David to the safety of a neutral country. And most of all, he admired the way she had brought Bella up. Although still very young, Bella was one of the kindest, most thoughtful, talented and beautiful girls he'd ever met – and he'd met many aspiring young opera stars. Often, young women with such talent were spoilt, cruel, with all the arrogance of youth, beauty and money, but not this girl. He wondered, would time and success change her? He hoped not.

After the dessert was finished and the coffee was served, Lily signalled that David should pour the bottle of very expensive Dom Perignon they had purchased.

'I think we should celebrate this evening, Manuel. And there is something I would like to discuss with you.'

He looked closely at her over the rim of the crystal flute. Ah, so it seemed there was a reason behind this evening's enjoyment. But he also had something he wished to discuss with her, and he already had a slight inkling of what Lily had in mind. 'And what is that, Lily? Perhaps in our minds we think the same things?'

Lily put down her glass carefully. She had been watching what she'd drunk so far this evening. 'Perhaps . . . Manuel?'

'Bella needs an agent, Lily, we have all realised that. And after I informed Senhor Rossellini, when he enquired about filling this potential role, that his services would not under any circumstances be required . . .' He let the sentence trail off, interested to hear what Lily had in mind.

Lily relaxed a little – enough to take a small sip of her drink – before choosing her words carefully. 'I would like to hear what you think of me becoming Bella's agent? No one knows her better.' She smiled across at Bella, who was looking a little mystified.

'No one does know her better, and I would say that both you and David have cared for and nurtured her very well—'

'And will continue to do so,' Lily interjected quickly.

He nodded. 'It is not an easy position.'

'I am aware of that, and I am aware that I have no experience as an agent, but I can be hard-headed when needs be. I was born and grew up in an area of Liverpool where you had to be tough to survive. I worked my way up in the theatre – not an easy thing to do for someone with no training or background – I know how the business works, and I can learn, Manuel, you can be assured of that. Neither David nor I will ever let Bella down, we will always do what we think is best for her. We know what a treasure she is; we know what talent she has. We want the very best for her and will accept nothing less.'

He nodded slowly. She was right in everything she'd said, and he trusted her. He just hoped she would be tough enough in what could be a cut-throat world, and one almost exclusively dominated by men – ruthless men. He turned to Bella, who had been sitting listening in apprehensive silence, knowing her future depended upon her aunt.

'Well, Bella? It is your career, your life, what do you think?'

Bella looked down and studied her empty dessert plate. 'I am happy to trust Aunt Lily and Uncle David. Always I have been happy to trust them.' She looked up and smiled shyly at the older man. 'And look at where I am now, Maestro. When I went to Liverpool, I had nothing. They . . . they took me in, they have done *everything* for me. Why should I want someone like Senhor Rossellini for an agent?'

'Why indeed, Bella? Well, if you are happy, that is all that matters to me.' He turned to Lily. 'When we open again after the holiday, I shall expect you in my office so we can discuss the contract for *Madama Butterfly*, our next production and one for which, I'm sure you will all agree, Bella is entirely suited.' He smiled at Lily. 'Butterfly – or Cio-Cio-San – the fifteen-year-old girl who is taken advantage of by Lieutenant Pinkerton of the United States Navy, who then deserts her, only to return, as she had hoped, but bringing his American wife with him. Then, to add to her sorrows, they take her child away with them and so, unable to face the disgrace and the enmity of her family, the poor girl kills herself. A story I'm sure you're as familiar with as I am.'

Lily took a rather deep gulp of her drink. 'I've always wondered why so many operas are depressing and tragic.'

He laughed. 'I believe that is the very nature of them, Lily.'

'Well, at least Bella's story won't end like that, Manuel. Not if I've got anything to do with it. Hopefully, she will find only success and happiness,' Lily pronounced firmly, thinking suddenly of Billy Copperfield, Bella's father, and of how he had deserted both Bella's mother and her own sister, Olive. In life, things were often not so very far from fiction.

She shivered, wondering if one day Billy Copperfield would

crawl out of whatever place he'd been hiding in all these years? Well, he'd get short shrift from her if he did!

She could barely believe how far she and Bella had come in these last few years. In her wildest dreams she could never have imagined that she would become the agent of one of the most promising young opera stars of this era.

Chapter Twenty-Seven

May,
1942

Lily's fears that Bella's natural father would appear were unfounded, but with the advent of the increasingly warmer days of spring, it was a previously unknown relative who made his presence felt in their lives.

Puccini's *Madama Butterfly* was a complete sell-out for its entire season, and Bella was becoming an established and well-known soprano. Her confidence had grown greatly, Lily thought, as she watched her niece adjust the awkward black and rather heavy wig of a Japanese lady to a more comfortable position. Oh, Bella still swore she was always a complete bag of nerves before going onstage, but Lily suspected that, with each performance, it was becoming less and less true.

'This is giving me a headache already, Aunt Lily, it is the one thing I hate about this role; the make-up and the costumes are horrible and uncomfortable,' she said, frowning at her image in the dressing-table mirror. She meant it. She thought she looked terrible, and the make-up required for the role took hours – and all this while the nerves in her stomach danced even more manically.

Lily was now responsible for supervising the dressers, whereas she had used to dress Bella herself. 'Never mind, Bella, the discomfort will fade once you're onstage and immerse yourself in the role. And then perhaps after the performance you would like to go somewhere for supper and a glass of wine?'

Bella smiled at Lily's reflection in the mirror. 'I would – as long as the place we choose isn't full of foreign spies.'

'There are fewer and fewer of them in the city of late, Bella. I've heard on the grapevine they are being recalled, because the war is not going well for either Hitler or Mussolini, particularly since the Americans have made their presence felt. I wonder . . .'

Whatever Lily was about to say was cut short by the appearance of the theatre director, accompanied by a tall, dark-haired, middle-aged man in immaculate evening clothes. Neither Lily nor Bella had seen him before. Lily looked enquiringly at Manuel dos Santos, for he never allowed anyone to go backstage before a performance – and particularly not into Bella's dressing room. His rules were rigidly enforced, and even David seldom ventured to see his niece before she went out onstage.

'Senhora Frances, Bella . . . this is Senhor Luis Ferreira Silva, a patron of the Opera House and an important man in Lisbon society.' He turned slightly towards his guest. The man was smiling at both women, apparently charmed to be in their presence. 'And, Bella, I believe he is your uncle?'

Lily had to stop herself from uttering the surprised cry that came to her lips as she looked quickly at Bella. He must be one of Bella's mother's brothers, she surmised.

Bella, too, was fighting to control her voice and her emotions. She had never hated anyone in her life before – not even the woman and the girls who had bullied her mercilessly when she'd been an apprentice seamstress, and made her life hell. Nor had she *hated* Billy Copperfield, her father. He'd hurt and disappointed her so often, but it wasn't in her nature to hate anyone – except this man who stood before her with an arrogant, ingratiating smile on his handsome face, his hand extended in greeting.

'I am very pleased to meet you at last, Annabella. We did not know where to look for you until now, but we have found you at last!'

Bella was on her feet, her dark eyes flashing with anger, her hands tightly clenched into fists, all colour drained from her face. Everyone in the room was taken aback, and it seemed to Lily that waves of pure fury emanated from the girl. Neither she nor Manuel had ever seen Bella like this before.

'How dare you! How dare you come here to me now, with your false smiles and your lies! You did not *want* to look for me! You wanted nothing to do with me or my *mãe* – my mother! To you we did not even exist! You threw her out, you abandoned us, and you did nothing to help – not even when she was dying!'

Luis Ferreira Silva took a step backwards in the face of this outburst. 'Annabella, you have to understand the circum-stances! Ours is an old and a proud family, one of the foremost in *Lisboa*, and what Isabella did was . . . unimaginable . . . unforgivable! You do not understand. For years we had to suffer the shame, the slights and the distain of our peers. She shamed us all, Annabella, going off with a common seaman who would not even marry her! She was content to live in sin with him, brazenly, openly! He who would not even recognise you as his child! He who would not give you the doubtful benefit of his name! You still have her name – *our* name!'

'I *choose* to use her name. He did give me his name! My name is Copperfield, but . . . what he did to her is nothing, *nothing* to what you did to her and to me! You left her to die in poverty, an abandoned woman, helpless, unable to look after her child. And that is your excuse? Pride! Pride!'

Bella began to pace the room, her hands clasped tightly together. 'I was twelve years of age, *Uncle Luis*, and I had no one; no father or mother, no family, no one to turn to for help, and no money. All I had was an address and my baptismal certificate.'

He tried again to explain. 'Annabella, I am sorry, but I cannot turn back the clock . . . these things you say . . . these events—'

'Nor do I wish you to turn back the clock!' she shot back, quick as a flash.

'Please try to understand how great was the shame and the trauma? It killed your grandparents, Annabella!'

'So, even they did not really care for her? Their own daughter! All you thought and still think about is how you all felt! You didn't care about how she felt, she didn't matter. How could you all do that to her? You are wicked! She told me that everyone disapproved of her, even before she met my father, because she had become a *Fado* singer. That is the life she wanted, and that is the gift she left to me – my voice. And, it is only because of my voice, and the position I now hold in the world of opera, that you are here now! All my life you have ignored me, despised me – but not now!' She pointed her index finger at him and stamped her foot smartly on the floor. 'Oh, no! *Uncle Luis!* Now, you decide I am fit to become part of this family. I am famous enough, I have the prestige now, but I have decided I do not wish to become part of you. You are not my family!'

She turned to Lily, reached out and took her hand. 'This is my Aunt Lily, she and Uncle David brought me up, and they mean more to me than you ever will. They have done so much to further my career, and Lily is now my agent. I have a sister, Joan, and a brother, too, and a stepmama. They are my family, and I do not care what you or anyone else in "society" thinks! Now, go away and do not come back! Ever! You are *not* my uncle! I want nothing to do with you or your family!' With that, she turned her back on him.

As all this had been conducted in Portuguese, Lily had had a hard time understanding. But she realised that now, after years of silence, Isabella's brother Luis and his family had finally decided to acknowledge Bella – but as the girl had said, only because she was now famous and on her way to becoming a wealthy young woman.

She squeezed Bella's hand, for she could see that her niece's dark eyes were full of tears and that she was shaking with the force of her emotions. 'I think, Senhor Ferreira Silva, that you should leave – now! You have upset my niece a great deal – and that is not good, to say the least. Not before a performance which, in itself, is demanding and draining for a girl so young.' And whose libretto had strong echoes of Bella's own life, she thought, glaring at the man. She considered him arrogant in the extreme.

Luis Ferreira Silva compressed his lips tightly. He hadn't expected this reaction at all. He'd fully expected the girl to be happy, grateful even, at the news that she would now be welcomed into such an exalted family. He hadn't anticipated such a strong-minded, confident young woman – but in that, he had to admit, she did take after his long-dead sister. Nor had he expected to have to confront this woman whom Annabella called 'Aunt Lily'. She, too, was clearly strong-willed and confident; he imagined she was very capable of managing his niece's business affairs, and men like Manuel dos Santos. He almost admired her; she was a very elegant and glamorous woman in her floor-length black velvet evening dress, accessorised with long evening gloves, a pearl necklace and earrings. Not a single blonde hair was out of place.

Manuel dos Santos was trying to digest all this. He vaguely remembered some old scandal concerning Luis's family, but it was more than twenty years ago. He now realised that it fitted perfectly with Bella's age. Lily was right, of course. Bella was upset and would need time to calm down before going onstage.

He gently placed a hand on Luis's arm. 'I think it is best that we leave Annabella now, she is upset. The *teatro* is fully booked, and to even think of cancelling . . .' He threw his hands expressively in the air.

'I understand, Manuel, but despite everything, remember that she is my niece. I will do what is best for her – whether she wishes it or not.' He bowed politely and formally to both Lily and Bella, before turning to leave.

Lily sat Bella down in front of the dressing table and placed her hands on her shoulders. The girl was still shaking. 'Take deep breaths, Bella, luv. You must calm down, there is not much time left . . .'

Bella nodded. Her anger was fading now, leaving her exhausted. 'I know, Aunt Lily, but why? Why did he have to come now? Why did he have to remind me? And then . . . all the lies! They don't want me; all they want is to be able to say I am their niece! They didn't want my mother! She used to cry softly when she thought I was asleep. He . . . papa . . . had gone to sea, and we never had enough money, sometimes I didn't even have shoes, so I couldn't go to school. And now . . .'

Lily gathered her into her arms. 'Hush, Bella, hush! You have a family who love you very much now. Wipe your face and let me retouch your make-up,' she coaxed gently.

She could cheerfully murder that man for coming here tonight and upsetting Bella like this. And the girl was right, they didn't want her, it was just to assuage their damn pride, boost their prestige and massage their egos. She would have something to say to Manuel for bringing him in here. After all his years in the theatre, surely he should have known better? Mentally she shrugged as she reapplied the heavy white make-up to Bella's face. Obviously, Manuel dos Santos was in awe of Bella's Uncle Luis, and had been hoping to ingratiate himself. Well, it hadn't worked, and she didn't care! She wasn't going to stand for Luis Ferreira Silva trying to use his influence with Bella. That's just what she was here for: to protect the girl, both professionally and personally.

'There, as good as new,' she said, smiling at Bella and giving her a hug.

Bella managed a weak smile. 'Aunt Lily, when will we be able to go home to Liverpool? I know, if I am to succeed on the stage, I won't be able to live there all the time, but I miss everyone so much. Even to return for a short time would make me so happy.'

Lily nodded. 'As soon as we possibly can, Bella, I promise. This war surely can't go on for much longer, and then . . . then we'll go home.'

When it was finally over, she wondered, would Bella still want to go back? Or would she have settled down, and become happy again, with her career and what was becoming a privileged lifestyle in this country? Of course, when the war was over, the world would be Bella's oyster, and she would be able to travel anywhere. The countries of Europe would eventually rebuild – and then there was America. Canada. Even Australia. Bella was only nineteen; her whole life was ahead of her.

When David called to escort Bella to the stage, Lily began to tidy up everything on the dressing table. Maybe later tonight, when the performance was over and she'd got Bella to bed – they'd give dining out a miss tonight – she would write to Olive. Again. She had no idea of how things were progressing back home, for correspondence between them had virtually stopped.

From now on, she vowed, she'd take more interest in the war news. There were times when both she and David were homesick, so she did understand why poor Bella wanted to go home, and particularly now. She, too, missed her family and friends. But in the end, the progress of the war remained out of their hands – they would just have to wait and see.

Chapter Twenty-Eight

—————•◦♦◦•—————

June,
1944

Ll everyone seemed to do these days was *wait, endlessly wait!* Olive thought, as she pegged out the washing that dismal June morning. She was even wondering if it was wise to peg it out at all, it certainly looked like rain. 'Flaming June,' she muttered to herself, 'it's more like January.'

It was depressing, but life just went on despite the continuing shortages and hardships and the terrible losses. It was five years now since their lives had all changed when the war had started, but these last few days there had been rumours that an invasion was imminent – though no one knew anything definite. People were conditioned now to heed the warning posters that declared 'Careless Talk Costs Lives'.

Looking around, she felt a wave of depression wash over her, and not just because of the weather. Hers was the only house still standing on what was just a large bomb site, and

Frederick and Arthur's sad little allotment did nothing to help dispel her mood. Growing anything that could be classed as a 'flower' was unheard of – food was the priority, and so much more important. Joan had been called up for war work. Every day, she undertook the long journey out to Speke, in the south of the city, to the munitions factory, and Olive missed her company. Joan never complained, and she was very well paid, but it was dirty and dangerous work. Olive knew that her daughter hated it, and that she hated the time she was forced to spend away from Jamie, who would be four this December, and was becoming more of a handful.

She sighed, straightening up and pressing her hands into the small of her back to ease the stiffness. Her grandson was yet another child growing up having lost his father, and never knowing anything so far except conflict, shortages and spasmodic air raids. But then, of course, Monica's daughter was in the same boat. Nelly and Nancy between them looked after their granddaughter, Richenda, while Monica worked in the factory salon. She had also taken on overseeing the smooth running of the other two factory salons Claude had established. One was in Kirkby and one in Speke, which made life difficult for her, being at opposite ends of the city from each other, but at least she could drive, which really did help, otherwise she'd barely have any time at home with her daughter.

Claude's health had deteriorated so much that his doctor had advised him to sell up and retire to one of the North Wales coastal resorts, something Nancy absolutely refused to agree to – not while Monica needed her help, she stated emphatically, whenever the subject was mentioned. He could take things much easier now that their daughter-in-law was looking after all the salons. Claude could rest at home, see to the back garden which he – like everyone else – had turned over to vegetables. They even had a few chickens to provide much-needed eggs – and Nancy had already earmarked one creature for Christmas lunch. She had insisted that Claude give Monica the full use of his car, as hers had long since gone for scrap, and the doctor had recommended he did not drive. So, Olive supposed, all in all, they were managing, but life seemed to be one long, depressing struggle.

The quarrelsome tones of the postman interrupted Olive's deliberations. 'I wonder if it's 'ardly worth my while draggin' up 'ere, Mrs G, what with there bein' no one else livin' 'ere!'

'I know what you mean, Stanley, but thanks, anyway. And I suppose all you've got for me are bills? That's all we ever get these days,' Olive remarked, holding her hand out for the mail.

'No. There's a foreign one, so it seems like your sister 'as managed to get one through, even if it looks as if it's been around the globe at least twice.'

Olive almost snatched the letter from him. Lily! Oh, thank God! Lily, at last! She'd almost given up hope of ever hearing from her sister again. It was nearly two years since she'd last had a letter.

She bade the postman good morning, tucked the letter into her apron pocket, and took the clothes basket back into the kitchen. She'd make herself a cup of tea and then sit down and read about what Lily had been up to all this time. Oh, she certainly hoped Lily had some good news to report; she definitely needed something to cheer her up on this grey, miserable June morning.

She'd settled Jamie at the kitchen table with the brightly-coloured plastic puzzle game Charlie had brought the child from Canada on his last trip, which the little boy found fascinating, and then she read slowly, savouring every detail – Lily had always been good at the details. Oh, in parts, she could almost feel the warmth of the Portuguese sun and taste the delights of foods she'd not had for over five years now. She marvelled at their being able to go out without coats and umbrellas and the damn ubiquitous gas mask. Just the thought of sitting and having coffee in a pleasant square where there were trees and flowers, and the buildings were all still in one piece! It must be heaven.

'I see you've made a brave decision, Olive!' Nelly interrupted her thoughts as she bustled into the kitchen and placed a small parcel wrapped in newspaper on the table.

'What? Oh, you mean the washing? Well, yes. What's this you've brought, Nelly?' she asked, automatically pouring her old friend and neighbour a cup of tea. It was a fair way from Allerton on the tram.

'Just a few bits of shoulder end of lamb I got from Taylor's butchers; it might do in a pie with some spuds. You've more mouths to feed than I have.'

'Thanks, Nell, it's good of you to share. I've had a letter from our Lily – at last! It was written last year, would you believe? And she says she's written me dozens of letters. God knows what's happened to them!'

'Maybe they'll all turn up at once,' Nelly suggested, feeling a thrill of excitement herself, for Lily was bound to have plenty to say.

'I won't hold my breath!'

'Well? What's been happening, I'm on pins!'

Olive grinned at her across the table. 'Plenty of news, I'll say that, and all of it good – for Bella, at least. And our Lily and David don't seem to have a bad life, either.'

Nelly sipped her tea. Her eyes widened in surprise and astonishment as Olive revealed all the news. When her friend had finished, Nelly shook her head in wonder. 'You mean your Lily is managing Bella's whole career now? Organising contracts and meeting important people?'

'I expect David advises her, too – and this Manuel dos Santos bloke.'

'I can't get over it, Olive! Your Lily living in a big fancy house, and with a cook and housekeeper! Those were the kind of jobs the likes of us thought ourselves lucky if we could get. But Lily in charge of the household . . . and mixing with all those posh people, even if they are foreign – I don't suppose she speaks the language all that well. And Bella! Well, we always knew she had a beautiful voice, but to think she's on her way to becoming a star of the opera! It's a world above anything we've known. Oh, I have to say it, Olive, your Lily certainly knew what she was doing when she insisted they all up sticks and move to Portugal.'

Olive nodded. 'I thought she was mad. Stark, staring mad. But I have to agree with you, Nelly. She's done the best she could for Bella – even going so far as to virtually get rid of that Italian woman. I was a bit mortified about that, Nelly; I didn't think she'd go *that* far! I mean it was a bit drastic . . .'

'But typical of your Lily. She'll not let anything or anyone stand in her way. I've always thought she was a force of nature, was your Lily.'

Olive nodded. 'I tend to agree with you, Nell.'

'And it's certainly brightened up the day,' Nelly finished.

The two friends smiled at each other. Lily's news had brought some much-needed sunshine into their lives.

The war news had brought sunshine into Lily's life, too, for while Olive and Nelly had been sitting discussing Lily's letter, unaware of events happening in Europe, the Allied forces had landed in Normandy and were now sweeping inland towards Paris, pushing the enemy back towards the borders of their own country, and liberating the occupied nations.

Lily was sitting reading the newspaper in the shade of the big jacaranda tree while the strong June sunlight made shifting patterns through its leafy branches on the tiled patio below. Oh, thank God! she thought. Thank God! The invasion had begun, and it looked as if it was going to be the success everyone had prayed for. How soon would she – they – all be able to go home? When she had promised Bella they'd return, one day – that evening when Luis Ferreira Silva had imposed himself upon them – she'd had no real hope of it being any time soon. Granted, two years had passed, but now, now she could offer Bella that hope, and they could all look forward to travelling when the war was over.

She looked out over the garden, with its beds of vibrant-hued flowers, and inhaled the sweet scent of the deep-pink roses that festooned the pergola outside the dining-room window. She narrowed her eyes, thinking of Bella's Uncle Luis. Thankfully, he had never approached his niece again. Yes, they'd seen him at performances in the Opera House, and occasionally at receptions and in high-class restaurants, but he'd had the sense to realise he would be unwelcome in their company. He had restricted himself to a polite bow or a raised hand in greeting – from a distance – and that's how things suited her. She wondered if Bella even thought about him at all these days, her life was so busy.

She had to agree that her niece had become more mature of late. She occasionally went out with a group of friends, suitably chaperoned by Lily or David, as was the custom here, to fashionable restaurants and seafood bars on the coast, or to the cinema or the occasional dance in Lisbon – but only when she had a night off, of course. Lily felt that, at her age, Bella should have other interests and other friends; she should not totally immerse herself in the world of opera. The girl was very happy to give her understudy a little time in the limelight – unlike many other operatic divas – and, quite often, Bella had her own ideas. Lately, she was beginning to speak her mind more, which Lily viewed as no bad thing. Bella had turned twenty-one after Christmas, and it was only right that she express her views. Lily had always believed in more freedom for women and girls.

She looked quickly towards the house, hearing raised voices, which disconcerted her. She was about to get up when, to her surprise, Bella herself came running across the lawn.

'Bella! Bella, luv! What's wrong? What is it? Is it Uncle David?'

Tears were streaming down the girl's cheeks. She shook her head so violently that her mass of dark curls escaped from the pretty floral bandeau keeping them in check, and which matched her light cotton summer dress.

'No! No, Uncle David is all right! Oh, Aunt Lily, I won't

do it! I just won't do it! They . . . they can both fall on their knees at my feet and beg, but I . . . I *won't! I refuse!*

Lily was totally confused but the girl was obviously very upset. 'Do what, Bella? Please, please don't upset yourself like this. Whatever it is can be sorted out, I'm sure. Now sit down next to me, calm down and tell me everything,' she urged, for she'd not seen the girl like this in years.

'It is Uncle Luis! It is all his idea! All his doing, but I won't agree! He is here now, with Maestro dos Santos, and they are talking . . . to . . .'

Lily was on her feet. 'Oh, is he indeed! Well, dry your eyes, Bella! He won't be here long!' She patted Bella's hand. 'What exactly is it that's "all his idea"?' she asked, thinking it would be better to know what all this was about before she took matters in hand.

Bella had calmed down a little. 'Maestro . . . he . . . he says that Uncle Luis has obtained for me the most wonderful, the most prestigious opportunity of my career! One I cannot refuse, but I will! I will refuse, Aunt Lily!'

Lily's eyes narrowed. This sounded like more of the insufferable man's desire to boost his own position in society, to say nothing of his ego. 'Which is?'

'If Maestro dos Santos will agree – and he does – a special performance of *Turandot*, a grand gala performance, with me in the role of the Princess Turandot, for – *especially* for – President Salazar!' Bella's sobs increased, though they were fuelled mainly by outrage and anger.

Lily's eyes widened in surprise. It was certainly quite an achievement that Luis had pulled off. For Bella to perform as the beautiful but cruel Princess in Puccini's last opera, staged for the President and his wife and entourage, would be viewed as a great honour and opportunity. No wonder Manuel had jumped at the idea, even though he was aware of Bella's views on her uncle – and despite the expense that would be involved.

She bent forward and gently drew the girl to her feet. As she did so, she caught sight of David emerging from the house, accompanied by two men, and crossing the lawn towards herself and Bella. Bella trusted her implicitly, she had never been given any reason not to, and now Lily was torn – as, no doubt, Luis Ferreira Silva knew she would be – between upholding that trust and turning down this undreamed-of opportunity for the girl. 'Leave it to me, Bella. There is no reason for you to get so upset, this will be sorted out.'

She nodded in response to the greeting of both men and caught the anxiety in her husband's eyes and the concern on his face. She held tightly to Bella's hand – she could feel the girl still trembling slightly.

'As you can see, Bella is very upset. She has no wish to do this, no wish to perform at any special gala,' she began firmly.

'My dear Senhora Frances, I wish to impress upon you that I, too, only have Annabella's career at heart, and I do not understand why she is so upset. It has not been easy; it has taken many months to achieve this, but—'

'I am not your *dear* Mrs Frances! And we will keep this discussion on a strictly business level,' Lily snapped.

He held up his hands in a gesture of mock surprise at her response. 'I apologise sincerely! I do wish the best for her.'

'That may or may not be true, but it will also be of great benefit to you, and that is something Bella does not want. She does not wish to be *used* by unscrupulous people! As you know full well, she has no desire to have anything to do with your family. That is why she is upset that you have assumed that you can arrange things for her, without thought or consideration for her feelings on the matter – any matter – and without a word of consultation! It is arrogant in the extreme.'

Before Luis Ferreira Silva could reply, the director, who had been following closely, broke in. 'Senhora Frances, Lily, please listen, I beg you. It will be a special night. The *teatro* will open for this one performance, and I will ensure it is as magnificent as I can possibly make it. The audience will be by invitation only – the British Ambassador is sure to attend – and it is for the *Presidente*! Surely, surely you must understand how . . . how great an opportunity, how great an honour it will be for Bella – the news of it, and the photographs, will be in all the newspapers and will go around the world!'

'No! No, Maestro! I don't care! I will not do it!' Bella cried, dry-eyed now and glaring up at her uncle.

'Bella, think! Think! Reconsider, please?' He glanced around frantically at Luis and David for help. Lily, he knew, was implacable. He met David's unflinching and hostile gaze but Luis wasn't going to back down – not now, after all he'd done, and before this slip of a girl, no matter how stubborn she was.

'You have all read the news, and it is good! I have it on good authority that our President is very relieved that soon the Allies will have driven the German forces out of France; Paris will again belong to the French, and their General de Gaulle can go home. Soon you, too, will be able to go back to Britain, Bella – sadly, the country you now call home – and you will also be able to travel the world. If it is reported that you have entertained President Salazar himself, and that the people of Portugal have taken you to their hearts – a young and greatly gifted girl – to all you will be a shining star for the future, the bright light of youth and talent in a world emerging from such terrible darkness, a figure of hope—'

'I think we get the picture, without further poetry, Luis!' Lily cut in, for she could see indecision in Bella's eyes.

'I speak nothing but the truth, Senhora Frances. You must see it.'

'It's not my decision to make,' she replied curtly.

Manuel, too, tried again. He couldn't have put it better than Luis had done, but he'd certainly try. 'Bella, your uncle is right. It will be the greatest night of your career, possibly your life! You know the people love you, why should you not perform for *el Presidente*?' He reached out and took her hand, causing Lily's eyebrows to rise as she scrutinised the man more closely. 'Bella, please, do this for me, please? It will make for me, too, a huge difference, the prestige, the importance . . .'

And the future revenue of his theatre, too, Lily thought cynically, although in her heart she knew that it was the greatest opportunity Bella would have in her life. Who knew, it might even one day lead to her performing in London before the King and Queen? In her opinion, they were of far, far greater importance than Salazar. She could see the girl was weakening, but she shook her head. 'You must think about all that has been said here, Bella, and then make up your mind. When we agreed that I would be your agent, I told you that I can and will advise you but that every big decision must, in the end, be yours, and yours alone. This is just such a decision. It is too important to dismiss out of hand.'

Seeing that the situation was changing, Luis decided to leave any further coaxing to Manuel.

'Will you do it to please me, Bella? Not for one anyone else – for you know I have a great affection for you, and would never willingly do anything at all to upset or harm you,' the director pleaded, still holding her hand.

So, that's the way things were shaping up, Lily thought. She'd made a serious error in missing the signs of this. He was falling in love with the girl – and why not? Bella was beautiful, talented and possessed of a sweet nature. And from what Lily knew, his wife was long dead. Whenever she had invited him for after-show suppers, or to join them for lunch, he really enjoyed himself. Now she realised why. She herself had married late, and she'd been very happy, so why not Manuel dos Santos? He would guide Bella's career, he knew the business well, and by the time he was getting on in years her niece would be a mature woman, well able to look after herself and her business affairs. It wouldn't be a bad match. Well, only time would tell if Bella felt anything for him, other than the affection of a friend, colleague or mentor. She must never be pressured into a relationship she didn't want. And as for this presidential performance, everything now depended on Bella's decision.

Slowly, Bella nodded, and all three men let out a sigh of relief.

Lily managed a tight smile. She hated Bella being upset, and this *had* upset her, but it had been the girl's own decision – and maybe it would show her things that she had never imagined existed. It would certainly be a grand occasion for the girl, even if some of that glory would also fall on her Uncle Luis. The poor child would be a bag of nerves on the night, for Lily supposed that President António Salazar must command some degree of respect in Lisbon society – although, if some people were to be believed, not a great deal.

'I think that now Bella should be allowed to go and rest,' Lily stated, removing Bella's hand from the older man's tender grasp. 'And you and I, Manuel, should look at the paperwork for this one, special performance.'

Bella's fee would not be cheap. Lily would make sure they paid handsomely for the privilege of her performance. She turned to her husband. 'David, darling. Would you please show Senhor Ferreira Silva out?'

He smiled back at her, thinking she'd handled all that tactfully but with authority. He never ceased to wonder at the talents he had never suspected when he first met and fell in love with the feisty Liverpool woman from the streets of Everton.

Lily, however, was not quite so sanguine, thinking that the sooner the Allies got to Berlin the better – after this Gala Performance, it would become increasingly hard to keep Luis Ferreira Silva away from Bella. She knew that Bella's feelings towards her mother's family would never change, and she could foresee nothing but friction and difficulty from that quarter.

Chapter Twenty-Nine

February,
1945

Bella had never had such a magnificent dress in her life as the one made for her presentation to the President after the performance of *Turandot*. It was a production that had taken far, far longer to organise than had been anticipated. Manuel dos Santos had insisted on going to extraordinary lengths to refurbish the theatre, and had even had new costumes made for the entire cast. Materials such as paints and gilding, crystal lights, heavy brocades and velvets were difficult to obtain, with many items having to be imported. But finally, Bella's big night had arrived.

Lily was profoundly thankful that at least, after this evening, everyone would be able to relax; as the weeks had passed, nerves were becoming more and more frayed. She was also thankful that Bella had put huge reserves of energy and concentration into her forthcoming performance, for it was a role that was new to her. As Manuel's nerves and temper became more and more strained, with the hold-ups and delays, the continual presence of Uncle Luis at the theatre had tested everyone's patience still further. At first, when he'd appeared backstage, Bella had felt the anger rise in her. But of late, she'd just ignored him, eventually understanding him for what he was: a pompous, arrogant, self-centred and insensitive man who probably did not even enjoy opera but felt it was required of him to attend, because it was the 'done thing' and she was – by blood, if not by choice – his niece.

'You must insist that he leave us all alone, Maestro. We have important things to do, he is becoming a nuisance, and he upsets everyone, not just Bella, by interfering in things he knows little about!' Lily had stipulated fiercely. And so, as tactfully as he could, Manuel dos Santos had succeeded in effectively banning Luis from the theatre for the next month.

However, Lily had been observing, with increasing interest and a little unease, the bond that seemed to be growing between her niece and the director. At times, it quite amused her to see how Bella took the upper hand when a situation became serious, managing to turn it into something lighter. On one occasion, Manuel had been fit to explode when the curtain accidentally fell halfway across the stage in the middle of a scene they were rehearsing. Bella instantly defused the situation by continuing to sing while daintily wrapping the end of the curtain around herself as though it were a skirt, and making everyone laugh in the process. Her niece was certainly growing up.

She herself had taken the girl to the best *costureira* in

Lisbon. For this occasion there was to be no expense spared, no going into a shop and buying whatever presented itself. No, that would never do, and so Bella had been meticulously measured, then chosen fabrics and trimmings and styles. Accessories, too, had been discussed in detail. Sometimes it bemused Bella, she admitted to Lily. That she who had made her own clothes for most of her life, and had at one time been training to be a seamstress, was now having the best that Lisbon could offer. Of course Lily was having a dress made, too, but that was nothing compared to Bella's – for she would not outshine her niece on this occasion, she had vowed to David. Later that evening, Manuel had called to discuss details of the staging with Lily, and she took the opportunity to mention the costumier's bills in David's presence, as the perennial subject of the cost of the Gala Performance arose. This was one bill that she and David would have to foot themselves, but David said nothing, merely helping himself to a large glass of whisky.

As Manuel and Lily had continued their discussions, David had tuned in to the wireless, calling out to them both when the news came through that the RAF and the American Airforce had increased their bombardment of Berlin, which, on top of the success of the Allied offensive in the Ardennes the previous month, was bringing the end to the conflict in Europe even closer.

'I do not envy the citizens of Berlin and Dresden, Manuel,' David had said, pressing a glass into Manuel's hands and helping himself to another, for he felt they both needed fortitude in the face of all that was happening in the world. 'In fact, I feel only pity for them – it is the most terrible thing you can imagine, having to sit for hours listening to destruction going on all around you, not knowing if you or your home will survive the night.'

Manuel dos Santos had pushed his own worries to the back of his mind as he sipped his drink. Thankfully, he had never had to experience anything like that. 'But you have told me of the terrible damage they did to all your cities, David, especially Liverpool and London, so are you not glad that it is their turn to suffer?'

David had shaken his head. 'No. Two wrongs do not make a right, Manuel. And it is not the soldiers who suffer in the Blitz, but innocent civilians: the old and infirm, women and children, even babies. But, please God, it will end soon; it has gone on too long, and there are too many dead, injured and displaced,' he replied, thinking of Jim McDonald, Rick Eustace, and the thousands of young men like them, as well as the utter devastation of cities such as Liverpool, London, Coventry and now Dresden and Berlin. 'But we must think about other things, Manuel. We must toast Bella and, I suppose, be thankful for Luis Ferreira Silva's ambitions.'

Manuel had smiled and raised his glass. 'To Bella! She will be wonderful, David, my friend. And the theatre is looking magnificent, too – though I don't like to think about the cost!'

David had smiled back. 'I imagine not, if those two evening dresses are anything to go by. But you will certainly have put the Teatro Nacional de São Carlos on the world map.'

They had both finished their drinks, and Manuel had gone in search of Lily, leaving David to his memories of life in Liverpool.

* * *

Lily took Bella's hands as she stood away from the dressing table. Manuel had surpassed himself with regard to the costumes, but she was a little concerned about the very ornate oriental headdress Bella was wearing. She feared it was top-heavy with all those paste jewels adorning the crown, and prayed it wouldn't slip, for she knew that when Bella began to sing she threw herself entirely into her role, heedless of her costume.

'There, you really do look the part of the Princess. Senhora Pereira has your evening dress laid out with the accessories, so you can change when the performance is finished.'

Bella raised her hand to the cumbersome headdress and smiled at the wardrobe mistress. 'I thank you, Elena, but you are sure this is well pinned?'

'If there were a gale onstage it would not move, Bella, I swear it. After the last act and your encores, come straight back here, as we won't have much time for you to change. We cannot keep the President waiting.' Senhora Pereira was filled with pride that such an honour had been given to Bella – and proud, too, that she was the one to dress this new young Portuguese star. With the world in such a state, it was wonderful to have this one night in which to enjoy such a spectacle, and she had always been fond of Bella. She could not say the same about her uncle, though. She knew of no one who either liked or respected him, not since the story of how the family had treated Bella and her mother had leaked out and become public knowledge again.

'Well, Maestro dos Santos will be here to escort you soon, Bella,' Lily announced. 'I had better go and join David so we can take our seats. I must say, they are excellent, and with a good view of the President's box.' As she left Bella in the capable hands of the wardrobe mistress she felt a little nervous, and wondered why. António Salazar was far from royalty – the Portuguese had got rid of King Manuel II in 1910, when they had declared a Republic – but she knew that this night would definitely secure her niece's career as one of the foremost sopranos in the world, and at the unheard-of young age of twenty-one. She had ordered copies of all the following day's newspapers and wished she could send the photos to Olive, but she just wouldn't trust the post. Besides, surely soon the war would be over now and they could all go home for a visit?

Bella's performance had been wonderful and her acting had been superb – she had put her heart and soul into appearing cold and cruel, attributes not in Bella's nature, before allowing the kind princess to shine through at the end. Such a range was no mean feat for someone as young as Bella.

Lily had watched the President closely, from the minute he had seated himself after the playing of the national anthem. He was an austere, ascetic-looking man, someone who did not appear to have much of a sense of humour or compassion, but she'd begun to relax as she realised that he was actually enjoying himself. Perhaps he appreciated the finer things in life, even if he was purported to be a cruel martinet. It was an impressive gathering, she thought, glancing surreptitiously around. Anyone who was anyone was there – and the dresses, furs and jewels of the women had to be seen to be believed, even though many were rather old-fashioned and had obviously been worn on many occasions such as this in the past. Portugal had not entirely escaped the shortages of the war, and the

President was rumoured not entirely to approve of such overt displays of extravagance, although no woman would sniff at the diamonds around his wife's neck.

As the final curtain fell, after no fewer than six encores – four of which had been for Bella and the leading tenor, with the director leading them both out by the hand – the entire audience, including President António de Oliveira Salazar and his wife, were on their feet. Lily knew that somewhere in the crowd – and she hoped in less favourable seats – were Luis Ferreira Silva and his wretched family.

It was only once the applause had eventually subsided that David helped Lily to her feet and they quietly left their seats as Manuel dos Santos was engaged in ushering the Salazar party down the stairs.

It had all been a bit of a rush, Bella thought, her heart racing in the way it always did after a performance, as Elena Pereira fastened the collar of pearls around her neck. It had been Manuel's gift to her for this performance and she realised that it must have been very expensive. Thankfully, her hair had been put up earlier, to be worn under the elaborate headdress, so it only needed a little titivating. Her dress was of a silver satin lamé, with what seemed to her like hundreds of yards of material in the skirt – apparently, this was now becoming the fashion. The bodice was fitted and boasted a deep shawl collar covering her shoulders and embroidered with silver bugle beads which sparkled under the lights. In deference to her age and status as an unmarried girl, her arms were covered by long white satin evening gloves, and she carried a small, pearl-encrusted evening bag, on loan from the wardrobe department

– for in the end, she hadn't been able to find anything she'd liked in the shops and had decided that there had been quite enough money spent on her already.

As Lily and David entered the room, Bella smiled at the expressions on both their faces.

'Oh, Bella! You look like a princess! In fact, you look a lot like Princess Elizabeth!' Lily cried, pride evident in her voice and her eyes. It had been worth all the money, and even though Bella had never wanted this evening to happen at all, now she knew that the girl was glad that it had. She was radiant, Lily thought: if she took after her poor dead mother then Lily could fully understand why Billy Copperfield had fallen for Isabella Ferreira Silva. He had seduced and disgraced her, too, she thought ruefully, but she would make damn sure that nothing like that ever happened to Bella.

'You are ready for this, Bella?' David asked quietly.

Bella nodded. Oh, yes, she was more than ready for this. Her heart was singing, and she knew that not only her mother but her entire English family would be proud of her.

She had achieved her ambition – almost. Her ultimate goal was to sing the role of Tosca – probably the most challenging role in opera – in the most prestigious opera houses in the world. But tonight she was happy with what she had achieved. And now that it was over, her Uncle Luis would no longer be allowed to interfere in her life – of that she was certain.

They were all lined up on the stage to be introduced to the President and his entourage. Lily felt nervous, although she was determined not to show it. She was annoyed that Luis Ferreira Silva had managed to worm his way into the line and into quite a prominent position, too. He must have influence she'd not known about, for she was sure that this was not Manuel's doing. In fact, Manuel was avoiding her glances, so she knew he was not pleased with the situation, either, but was probably hoping it would not be noticed that Luis was on Bella's left side while she and David were on her right.

Bella smiled fixedly, although she was fully aware of her uncle's antics and was seething inside. How dare he! How dare he spoil this evening for her! It was a triumph for herself, her mother and her English family – she despised his family, and always would.

She dipped the obligatory curtsey to the President as Manuel introduced her, and then she smiled up into those cold, grey eyes.

'Senhorita Ferreira Silva, I must congratulate you on your performance, rarely have I heard anyone of your age sing with such passion, intensity and purity. You are a great credit to our nation, a great example to our young women.'

Bella's smile widened, then froze as her Uncle Luis spoke.

'And – I speak also for my family – we are indeed fortunate to have her as one of us – my niece, Your Excellency.'

Bella turned to him, her eyes blazing and her expression disdainful in the extreme. Her unprepared speech to the President was short and to the point, but delivered in a measured, respectful tone.

'I am his *alienada* – estranged – niece, Excellency. This is my Aunt Lillian and my Uncle David Frances. They have loved and cared for me for most of my life. I am what I am today entirely because of them and the family I have in England.'

The President merely nodded, his face expressionless as he shook hands with Lily and David. Then he moved on, while Bella unclenched her fists and turned away from her Uncle Luis, who was standing like a statue, his lips tightly compressed and his eyes smouldering with rage.

'Oh, well done, Bella!' Lily mouthed.

They'd certainly have to go home as soon as possible after tonight. Bella had definitely had the last word, and she doubted Luis Ferreira Silva's credibility with António Salazar would survive for much longer. Bella's performance had been a triumph in more ways than one.

Chapter Thirty

September,
1946

'You are certain that this outfit is suitable?' Joan asked for the second time as she viewed herself in the long mirror on the front of the wardrobe door.

Everyone had assured her that the pale-grey fine wool two-piece, trimmed with bright pink braid, suited her, as did the small matching hat shaped to fit closely to her head, sporting a small cluster of egret feathers to one side. Both Bella and Lily had done wonders with what was previously a plain, old-fashioned day suit – Lily had even stripped the feathers from one of her own hats.

'I just don't want our Lily thinking I don't look up to scratch, not compared to her. I don't want her to have an embarrassment as a travelling companion.'

Monica threw up her hands in despair. 'Oh, for God's sake, Joan! Very few women on that ship will be able to compete with your Lily! For a start, that costume she's travelling in is Dior, I've seen the label in the jacket! And the blouse is pure silk – and none of us has had anything new for years, and certainly nothing in that class or price range. There's enough material in Lily's skirt alone to make at least three dresses! Now the war's finally over, and we don't have to scrimp on material, everyone is going mad – providing they can afford it. You're young and attractive, you look smart and classy, so what are you getting in a state about?'

Joan adjusted the hat slightly – again. 'I suppose it's because I'm going to be totally out of my depth. I'm not used to all this!' She waved a gloved hand in the direction of the two cases that stood by the door. 'I've never travelled in such style before. Let's face it, I've never travelled anywhere outside Liverpool before, either!'

Monica sat down on the bed and pushed back a lock of blonde hair, with signs of irritation. 'And you think your Lily will be completely in the know with everything? She was never used to anything, either, not until she went first to London and then Lisbon, although she always had style.'

Joan sat down beside her friend, looking around the bedroom she shared with her son, Jamie, who was now nearly six years old. 'Well, more so than me, Mon. She just sort of deals with everything instinctively. You know, I still think it should be you that's going over to New York for a month – not me. Mam thinks so, too.'

Monica raised her eyes to the ceiling. 'You're infuriating! We've been through this a hundred times and more, Joan McDonald! I can't afford the time to go to New York, I've three salons to run – and hopefully another in the offing. I have to build them up into something Rick would have been proud of, and that's why I need you to go. We've agreed that you'll go and take as many courses in make-up, skin care, nails, salon design and advertising as you can fit in.' And as many as we can afford, she added mentally, before reminding herself of Claude's adage that you had to speculate to accumulate. And she was very determined to accumulate.

Joan nodded but bit her lip. It still all sounded so very daunting, for she didn't have half the confidence Monica had.

'It's not as if you're going to be on your own, is it? Lily, Bella and David will be there, too,' Monica carried on.

Bella was going to make her debut at the Metropolitan Opera House. To start with, she would sing the lead role of Tosca for just half a dozen performances; for the remaining three months of her contract she would appear in other, but just as prestigious roles. But after that they had few plans. Almost everyone had argued that the role of Tosca was very demanding, and it ideally called for a more mature soprano, but both Bella and Lily had argued long and hard with Manuel dos Santos and the directors of the Opera House, until finally Bella had got her way.

'I don't suppose I'll see much of them – they'll be busy, too – but it will be wonderful for me to see our little Bella take New York by storm. I'm certain that she will, especially after all the rave reviews she got for her final performances in Lisbon. Lily's promised me she'll get me a good seat.' Joan fished in her handbag; it was far from new, but a great deal of polish and elbow grease had restored it to something she was satisfied would complete her outfit. She drew out a handful of documents and laid them individually on the bed beside her.

'Passport, tickets, name and address of the hotels and all the places that run courses for everything we need . . .'

Monica took her friend's hand. 'You'll have a great time, Joan. I do wish I could come with you, but I just can't.'

When the war in Europe had ended last May, and in the Far East in August, Monica had been determined that Joan wasn't going to continue with factory work. Her friend was capable of far more. She herself was putting all her efforts into building up the salons, for it was exactly the right time, she'd told Nelly.

'Women are so fed up, Mam, with having to go without and "make do and mend" for so long – they want a bit of pampering, a bit of luxury, something no one has had for six years,' she'd stressed to her mother.

Nelly had merely sighed and remarked that Monica had always had great ambitions, and it was a pity her sister didn't, too.

So Monica had put the idea to Joan that she act as her interior designer, personal assistant and partner in the salons, for Joan had always been so organised – and she had a very good eye for detail.

Monica wanted a special 'look' for her salons. 'No mishmash of colours and styles, but something distinctive that will define me! Us!' she'd enthused. 'Women want glamour now, and we'll give it to them, Joan. At a cost, of course, but together we'll take the world by storm – well, the hair and beauty side of our bit of it, anyway!'

'What about a collective name, then, Mon? So people will know that if they come to us, they will come out looking glamorous and elegant? Transformed, even!' Joan had suggested, having caught Monica's enthusiasm. 'What about Salon la Belle Monique? You remember how Claude insisted you all use French names? He was right – it did sound classier!'

Monica had grimaced. 'I think that might sound a bit too arrogant. As if I want everyone to think I'm beautiful.'

'Well, just Salon Monique, then. Or what about Les Salons de Eustace?'

They'd discussed names for quite a while until they'd decided to wait until Joan came back from America, when they'd make all the final decisions.

'Put all that stuff back in your bag or you're bound to lose some of it,' Monica instructed. 'And stop worrying, you'll be absolutely fine. You've got nearly five days at sea with your Lily. So when you arrive, some of her confidence should have rubbed off – and you can always ask her advice about what's going on. I . . . we need all the new ideas and styles and products, Joan, that's if we're to be ahead of the game here. That's something Claude always impressed on me, even before Rick was killed.' She smiled, thinking that she found it easier now to talk about him. She still missed him terribly, but the pain was gradually fading.

Joan stood up and smoothed down her skirt. 'I *know* Jamie will be just fine with Mam and Frederick and our Charlie – until he goes away, too – but I just *hate* the thought of leaving him, and for so long.'

'He knows you'll be coming back. Have you told him you'll be able to bring him all kinds of things we can't get here? Toys he's probably never heard of, as well as sweets and chocolate. So much more than you can get on the ration here – that's if you ever lay your hands on them!'

310

'Don't worry, he's given me a list as long as my arm. I know, Mon, that as long as our business succeeds, everything I do will all be for his benefit – I intend to work as hard as you. I want to pay for an education that Jim and I could only dream of for him. He'll stand a better chance in life then.' She wiped away a tear from her eye as she thought of Jim McDonald, and at the prospect of not seeing her son for a month, although he was a placid, easy-going child and she doubted he'd fret.

She and Monica had always been close, but when her friend had suggested this partnership and mapped out the plans she had for the future, she'd been astonished. She was very, very grateful for such an opportunity, although Monica would hear nothing about thanks or gratitude. Monica was putting up the money, with the help of Claude and Nancy, and Joan had a small amount she'd saved, too. She knew Monica had vowed that when the business was a success – there was no room for doubt – she would make sure her parents-in-law had a comfortable and secure old age, as would Nelly and Arthur. Richenda, too, would have a good education and, in time, would have a share of a very successful business, as would her Jamie.

It had been she who had suggested another opportunity for their business, she thought, with satisfaction. 'What about ships, Mon?' she'd ventured. 'You know, all the liners must have some kind of salon – and maybe other facilities, too – for their posh passengers. Some are away for weeks on end. When we sail, I'll take a look at what's on board the *Mauretania*, not that I'll be frequenting their salon. But there's not just Cunard White Star, there's the Union-Castle Line, Canadian Pacific, the Peninsular and Oriental – they go out as far as

India and Australia. There's Alfred Holt, Fred Olsen, oh, I could go on forever. They'll all be sailing again now the oceans are safe.'

Monica had been delighted and amazed at her friend's perceptive suggestion. 'That's a really great idea, Joan! If we could get a contract for our salons on even a couple of them, we'll be made for life. There's nothing to stop us trying, especially if we're right up there with our competitors, offering all the most modern treatments. Who knows? We could even take it in turns to take trips ourselves, to supervise things and make sure everything is being done properly.'

'We could ask our Lily's advice on that, she's good at contracts,' Joan had replied, beginning to feel the excitement rise in her at the new life that was opening up before them both.

Monica now stood up, too. 'Right then, Joan, let's get these cases downstairs before everyone starts fussing and fretting. It's a big ship, so I suppose it will take hours for them to get all the passengers and their luggage on board. But you know what my mam and yours are like, to say nothing of Lily. Although I'm sure she's organised the taxis to be here in plenty of time, and God help them if they're not!'

Olive and Nelly were sitting in Olive's kitchen, waiting for Frederick to get home, for he'd insisted that he make sure the yard was securely locked up before they left. Arthur had gone to make a last check on his new brood of pigeons. Claude had offered to drive him back with Nancy, and to collect Nelly. He was going to run the four of them down to the Landing Stage, to see the ship depart the Mersey for the very last time, as

Cunard had moved the bulk of their ships and business down to Southampton now.

'I just hope he won't be late, Olive, or your Lily will have ten fits,' Nelly confided as she sipped her very welcome cup of tea. They hadn't had an outing like this since long before the war.

'Don't fuss, Nell, he'll be here on time. Leave our Lily to me. Lord, has she got above herself, what with living out in Portugal and all Bella's success. I don't envy those Yanks she's going to have to deal with!'

'You've got to give it to her, Olive, she's certainly stepped up to the mark. I never thought I'd see the day when she'd be mixing and dealing with such people! Imagine, the President of Portugal himself!'

'Neither did I, Nell. But she always had bags of confidence and ambition, did our Lily. They'll all go far, mark my words. That girl will have the world at her feet by the time she's twenty-five. And to think that she landed on my doorstep a half-frozen, half-starved little waif, broken-hearted at the loss of her mam and then . . . *him!*'

Nelly nodded her agreement, thinking of the long-gone Billy Copperfield. Olive had been well rid of him, even though they'd never been married. Her old friend had had a good and happy life with Frederick. 'Aye, that poor Isabella woman would have been so proud of Bella now. Just fancy her standing up to that uncle – and in front of the President, too! That takes guts, Olive.'

'Bella's always had courage, Nelly, even though most of the time you'd never think she'd say boo to a goose.'

Nelly lowered her voice, for she could hear the girls coming down the stairs, and Lily's voice in the hall. 'Do you think there's anything serious between her and that Manuel dos Santos feller?'

Olive shrugged. 'I've asked our Lily that point blank. I'm her stepmother, after all, even though it's Lily and David who have virtually brought her up.'

'And?' Nelly pressed.

'All she'll say is that she is watching the situation – if you please – very carefully.'

'What kind of an answer is that?'

'Obviously the only one we're going to get for now, Nelly. But they know him far better than we do, and I suppose at least he'll look after Bella and her career. It's a brave man who would cross our Lily – you know what she's like about Bella.'

'But surely marriage is more than that, Olive?'

'It is, or at least it should be. But Bella's still very young to even think about marriage, she's only twenty-three.'

'And so should our Eileen have been – instead of letting herself get carried away with all that romantic nonsense. I blame the war. Our Monica says she knew Eileen was too young, and that dreadful woman, Violet Stevens, was so set on having her son wrapped around her little finger, that it was bound to cause problems. And now, of course, she's been proved right, and that doesn't help things between them. I'm sick of the rows – Eileen's only been back two months.'

'Never mind, Nell. She's young enough to find someone else,' Olive sympathised.

At the end of the war, after Harold Stevens had been demobbed from the navy and gone back to Birmingham, things between his mother and Eileen had become so bad that Eileen had finally up and left, telling him he could come to

Liverpool after her, if he really loved her, and more than his mother. So far there had been no sight of him – and no word, either.

'I suppose you're right, Olive, but at least there are no children – thank God! I don't think I could put up with having a baby in the house again, as well as Richenda Jane, even though she's much less trouble now she's nearly five and goes to that fancy kindergarten school. But I just hope that eventually she and Harold can sort out their differences – there's never been the scandal of a divorce in the family. I'd die with the shame of it, especially as Nancy's two girls are both engaged to nice, steady chaps, who definitely aren't Mummy's boys.'

'Let's hope it doesn't come to that, Nell, but the world is a very changed place now. I never thought I'd see the likes of our Joan and your Monica setting up in business with such grand plans, and our Joan going to America – even if it's only for a month. And I never thought I'd see our Charlie emigrating – and to Australia of all places.'

'Well, there's many like him, Olive. They survived the war and are looking for new opportunities, a new life. And with the ten-pound fare offer, well, he'd be daft to pass it up.' She was thinking of Harold Stevens who, like Charlie, had miraculously survived the convoys. She wished he'd be as adventurous as Charlie Copperfield and take her ever-complaining and discontented daughter with him, though she supposed she'd miss her. Monica she didn't worry about – she'd go far – as would Joan and Bella, the other two girls from Mersey View. Olive was right; the world was a changed place.

'I'll wash these cups up, Olive. I think you'd better go into the hall to see what's going on out there and check if there's any sign of Claude and Arthur.'

'And Frederick,' Olive added, before venturing out of the kitchen.

Charlie had volunteered to help with the luggage. But when he caught sight of the amount of it, and heard his Aunt Lily's increasing agitation, he'd gone outside to have a smoke and was surprised to find Bella standing on the pavement. She turned and smiled up at him.

'So, you've had enough of all the fuss and palaver in there, too?' he said. 'Aunt Lily's getting into a state about everyone's luggage and whether it will fit into the taxis she's ordered. I've told her there will be room in Claude's boot, too. Our Joan and Monica have just lugged the cases down, and now Mam's put in an appearance. It's all a bit chaotic!' He took out a cigarette case and offered Bella one.

'Charlie Copperfield, are you mad! Do you not realise what that . . . *thing* will do to my voice?' Her words were softened by her smile as she shook her head in mock dismay.

'Sorry, I didn't think.' He lit his cigarette and took a deep drag before exhaling a cloud of blue-grey smoke. 'Are you happy to be going to New York, Bella? You're not letting Lily push you into it? She can be really bossy.'

Bella laughed. 'You think I do not know that already? Charlie, it is the thing I have wanted most in my life for so many years now. Oh, I know the part calls for someone older, but I can do it! I know I can.'

'You'll be great just the same. Just as long as it's what *you* want.'

She placed a hand on his arm. The war had changed him, she thought. She remembered him as a boy but now he was a man, and a man taking charge of his destiny – just as she was doing. 'We were little more than children when I left for Portugal, Charlie, and you had gone away to sea. Now we are both starting new lives, but I wish you were not going so very far away. It takes weeks to get to Australia, and what will you do when you get there? I worry for you, Charlie.'

'Don't, Bella. I'll be fine. I've got a trade and experience now, remember, and that's what they want. I've a list of firms to contact and a couple of lodging houses in Sydney to see.' He paused and took another drag on the cigarette. 'If you ever get to Australia, Bella, will I see you?'

'Of course, Charlie! I will get the best seats for you, and we will have you to stay in the hotel with us, or on the ship. Only the best will do for my brother.'

Charlie grinned at her, thinking she really had turned into a stunning-looking girl – he'd be proud to show her off to the mates he would surely make in his new adopted country. He was firmly convinced that Australia was the place for him now. This city, this country, was in ruins and it would take years to recover. But Australia, well, it was the future. He wondered if on her travels Bella would get to sing in Brazil, for that's where his father and hers had last been heard of. There was an opera house in a place called Manaus, in the Amazon jungle, or so he'd heard. He hoped Billy Copperfield wouldn't emerge, after all these years, claiming her as his daughter, just like her Uncle Luis had done. But he realised that Bella would be well able to cope with the likes of their faithless, fickle father – and she'd have Lily with her, too. He reached into his pocket again and drew out a little package, holding it out to her. 'This time, will you take it, Bella? It's served me well.'

'Oh, Charlie, the Barcelos rooster! I thought you would have lost it by now, but . . .' She shook her head. 'No, you must keep it for your new life, take a little bit of Portugal with you, it will continue to bring you luck. I have had so much luck and good fortune, Charlie, and everyone tells me that the best is yet to come, so . . .'

There was no time for him to argue as Claude's car drew up outside the house. Charlie tucked the little brass ornament into his pocket and ground out the cigarette. 'You'd better go in and tell them nearly everyone's here now, Bella. There's just Frederick to come, and he'll be along any minute, then we'll have to get all this luggage sorted out, because I think this is the first taxi arriving.' Charlie nodded in the direction of York Terrace where a black hackney was making its way slowly over the rubble-strewn road.

After some shuffling around, the luggage was all finally loaded into the boot of Claude's car and the two taxis. There was an air of excitement hanging over what was left of the street, Monica thought, as she climbed into a taxi with Joan, Bella and Charlie. Lily and David were going in style in the other one, but Bella had insisted she go with Joan.

'Oh, let all the young ones go together, Lily, we'll all meet up on the Landing Stage,' David urged his wife. She was somewhat flustered, he noted, which was quite unlike her.

'But what if they won't let Charlie or Monica anywhere near the ship? They've not got tickets – and neither has anyone else, apart from us three.'

'Lily, they are well used to occasions like this. There will be plenty of officers and crew to help, and probably an army of porters. Just sit back and relax. Think, this evening we'll be having dinner in the grand dining room of one of Cunard's biggest, fastest and best-known ships. Even if she is getting on in years now,' he added, patting her gloved hand.

Lily smiled up at him; he always had the ability to put things into perspective and calm her down. 'I just hope the food will be better than the last time we were on a ship.'

David laughed. 'Coming home from Lisbon? I'll admit it wasn't wonderful.'

Lily smiled at the memory of another trip, taken from Liverpool to Lisbon, in the middle of a world war. 'It's going to be a new and very different life, David, but one I think we are all looking forward to.'

'And even greater success awaits our Bella now,' he added with pride.

'And it will be good for her to have Joan with her on the way out, they can entertain each other.' Lily looked speculatively out of the cab window to where the other taxi was just heading into York Terrace. 'You know, David, I think there is a lot of me in Joan. Oh, I'm not saying that our Olive hasn't brought the girl up well, but Joan's ambitious and she's smart, just as Monica is, and she's very attractive – they both are. They'll do well, and who knows? With the right introductions and clothes, Joan might find herself a new husband. She can't grieve for Jim McDonald forever, just as Monica can't for Rick. They're both still so young.'

'Stop matchmaking, Lily, my dearest wife. We'll deal with whatever lies in the future, as and when it comes.'

She laughed as they turned on to the main road that led to

the Liverpool waterfront. 'Well, it's got to be better than the past.'

Joan, meanwhile, was trying to make sure her skirt wasn't getting creased and that her hat was at the right angle, while Bella and Monica both seemed to be taking this journey in their stride. Charlie seemed bemused by their chatter as Bella tried to remember where the houses, shop and pubs and their occupants had been, before they had all been bombed into rubble.

'I just cannot believe it is so terrible, Monica! It was so bad, even before we left, but . . . this! Everything gone!'

'Oh, it was bad, Bella, very bad, but all that's behind us now. We have so much to look forward to, so many plans and hopes and dreams. It will be a wonderful sight to watch that ship go down the river towards the estuary for the last time. I'm sure there will be a band, and crowds of people with flags and streamers, to see you off. It's something of an occasion – though I bet they don't know that they've got a famous opera diva on board.'

'I wish you were coming too, Monica,' Bella said, with a hint of sadness in her smile.

'So do I,' Joan said quietly.

'Now stop that! You'll have a great time, and I want to see you back here with full notebooks, and boxes and boxes of samples,' Monica said firmly.

Charlie leaned forward in his seat as they finally turned the corner. 'Well, I suppose you can say we're all on our way now, even if it's in different directions. So, full steam ahead for the future, and no looking back!'

All three girls craned their necks to get the last view of the street that had once been their home but which now lay in ruins, except for Olive's house. The weight of everything they had been through settled on them all for a moment. As they each sat silently acknowledging the immense challenges, as well as the moments of light that had crept through the cracks on the darkest of days, they also let it all go. It was as far behind them now as their old street was, now that they'd turned the corner and taken their last glimpses over their shoulders.

'Charlie, you're right. It's full steam ahead to the future. And goodbye, Mersey View.' Monica smiled softly, as she took Joan and Bella's hands in hers.

'And definitely no looking back!' Joan added, while Bella and Charlie exchanged smiles and Charlie patted the pocket with the little brass rooster.

Lyn Andrews

'An outstanding storyteller' *Woman's Weekly*

The House On Lonely Street
Love And A Promise
A Wing And A Prayer
When Daylight Comes
Across A Summer Sea
A Mother's Love
Friends Forever
Every Mother's Son
Far From Home
Days Of Hope
A Daughter's Journey
A Secret In The Family
To Love And To Cherish
Beyond A Misty Shore
Sunlight On The Mersey
Liverpool Angels
From Liverpool With Love
Heart And Home
Liverpool Sisters
The Liverpool Matchgirl
The Girls From Mersey View

Available now

HEADLINE